"Mia— ⟨...⟩ ⟨...⟩ ⟨...⟩ again, gent⟨...⟩ a ⟨...⟩ ⟨...⟩ to face ⟨...⟩.**

Up close, the stormy light coming in from the windows made her eyes seem purplish. Moody. Beautiful.

"Thank you. For thinking of me— Of Cole."

"I...I need to go get my things." Her voice was dusky.

Overpowered by a sudden urge to kiss her mouth, to hold her against his body, Jagger released her arm slowly and stepped back.

She backed toward the door, turned quickly.

"You don't have to do this, Mia."

"It's my job. Either I do it, or I leave and find something else." And she went out, closing the door behind her.

The room seemed drained of energy, as if she'd taken it all with her. He ran his hand through his hair. Christ. What just happened here between her and him?

Did he dare take it anywhere?

The Coltons of Wyoming: Stories of true love, high stakes...and family honor.

THE MISSING COLTON

BY
LORETH ANNE WHITE

First published in Great Britain 2013
by Mills & Boon, an imprint of Harlequin (UK) Limited,
Eton House, 18-24 Paradise Road, Richmond, Surrey TW9 1SR

© Harlequin Books, S.A. 2013

Special thanks and acknowledgement to Loreth Anne White for her contribution to The Coltons of Wyoming miniseries.

ISBN: 978 0 263 90722 3
ebook ISBN: 978 1 472 01581 5

18-0913

Harlequin (UK) policy is to use papers that are natural, renewable and recyclable products and made from wood grown in sustainable forests. The logging and manufacturing processes conform to the legal environmental regulations of the country of origin.

Printed and bound in Spain
by Blackprint CPI, Barcelona

Loreth Anne White was born and raised in southern Africa, but now lives in Whistler, a ski resort in the moody British Columbia Coast Mountain range. It's a place of vast wilderness, larger-than-life characters, epic adventure and romance—the perfect place to escape reality. It's no wonder she was inspired to abandon a sixteen-year career as a journalist to escape into a world of romance fiction filled with dangerous men and adventurous women.

When she's not writing you will find her long-distance running, biking or skiing on the trails and generally trying to avoid the bears—albeit not very successfully. She calls this work, because it's when the best ideas come.

For a peek into her world visit her website, www.lorethannewhite.com. She'd love to hear from you.

For Patience Bloom. And for Marie Ferrarella,
Melissa Cutler, Carla Cassidy, Colleen Thompson
and Beth Cornelison. You guys rock.

Chapter 1

Clouds of dust swirled down Dead River's main street as the small Wyoming town hunkered against the early fall winds sweeping across this vast, drought-ravaged region of cattle-ranch country. A wet front had helped quell the wildfires and brought a dusting of snow to the distant Laramie peaks. But rain had done little to quench the parched ranchlands, and the wind easily cast exposed topsoil adrift.

Jagger McKnight blinked against the blowing grit as he pushed open the door of the Dead River Diner. He was greeted by a blast of warm air and the smell of fried food—yet another greasy spoon, like so many he'd frequented over the past twelve months as he'd drifted aimlessly across the United States. But it was almost 6:00 p.m.—he was cold and famished. He also had questions. A local diner was as good a place as any to start.

Choosing the empty booth closest to the door, Jagger hefted his kit bag onto the red vinyl seat and scooted it toward the grime-streaked window. He removed his jacket, then his cowboy hat. But as his fingers brushed against the ragged scar under his hairline, Jagger stilled, instantly disoriented. A soft panic began to lick through his stomach.

No. Not now...

He concentrated on breathing in slowly and folded his tall frame into the booth beside his gear. Pressing both hands down hard on the table, Jagger focused on the view of the parking lot outside the dirty window. He mentally cataloged what he saw—the gusts of sand piling into soft yellow drifts against a wall. The cracked wall, peeling plaster. *Like the bunker.*

Tongues of panic licked again, a little deeper, faster. And for a white-hot instant he could no longer see the parking lot. He was back. Trapped. Golangal Valley. A desert windstorm, the sound of blowing Afghan sand like screaming banshees as it funneled through rocks. They were surrounded by heavily armed insurgents in the hills. An invisible enemy. Dark was coming.

A pot banged suddenly in the diner kitchen and Jagger jumped, his pulse spiking as his brain scrambled to translate the noise into mortar fire, explosions.

Enough! You can stop this...

He turned his concentration back to the present, to the two Harleys parked out front of the diner. Across the parking lot, two eighteen-wheeler semis were angled for an easy exit. On the opposite side of the street, a young woman pushed a covered stroller as she bent into the wind, a scarf protecting her face. Civilian. Semis. Harleys.

No grenades hidden in scarves, or the folds of a burka or clutched in the small brown hands of a liquid-eyed child. No tanks. No guerillas around the side of the wall. If Jagger wanted, he could simply stand up, step out the diner door, hit the road. He was free. Free to go.

A tumbleweed bounced past the semis, driven by the vagaries of wind, en route to nowhere in particular. Just like he'd been—drifting. Seeking to numb his nightmares with too many beers, too many late nights, too many one-night stands with women whose names he couldn't even begin to remember. A shrink would have a field day with him, but Jagger had walked away from all that medical crap. He *had* to do this himself.

And now, at least, he had a small hook on which to hang a future, however tenuous.

It had come to him Tuesday night, almost nine weeks ago—something to grab on to, something he could use to claw back a semblance of his life, and he'd grabbed it like a lifeline.

Maybe the timing had just been right. Maybe it was destiny. Maybe blind folly or sheer desperation. Hell knew. But on that Tuesday night, Jagger had been nursing a warm beer in a dive bar on the outskirts of Casper in east-central Wyoming when a breaking CNN news story on the TV behind the counter had riveted him to his stool.

It was a piece about a kidnapping—a three-month-old baby girl named Cheyenne Colton had been snatched right out of her crib in her family's mansion on Dead River Ranch about forty miles northwest of Cheyenne. The child's governess had been shot dead in the process. The CNN reporter had noted similarities between this kidnapping and another thirty years earlier, when a baby boy, Cole Colton, had been abducted from the very same mansion at around the same age.

A few weeks later, the TV news reported that baby Cheyenne had been located unharmed. Baby Cole, however, had never been found. The infant was presumed dead, all leads in that case long gone stone cold.

The story had rattled Jagger. Thirty years ago, also at

three months old, he himself had been abducted in a car-jacking gone terribly wrong. He'd been raised by one of the kidnappers under a false identity until his real family had finally found him shortly after his ninth birthday.

Was it possible that Cole Colton could still be alive, raised under a false name, never knowing where he'd come from?

Jagger's family had never stopped searching for him, had never once allowed themselves to presume their son had died. Why had Cole's family given up? Cole's father, according to the news, was Jethro Colton, a billionaire rancher from Wyoming. He certainly had the financial means for a protracted search. And why had there never been a ransom note?

The reporter in Jagger had latched on to these questions with a desperation he didn't like to acknowledge in himself, but deep down he knew that in the unsolved mystery of Cole Colton he'd finally seen a glimmer of something that he could focus on. If he could get to the bottom of that thirty-year-old mystery, and find out what happened to that baby boy, it could be his absolution, his way back into mainstream society, back into a journalistic career he'd all but forsaken.

Jagger had bought a small laptop in Casper, and a cell phone, and he'd begun to research the Colton family, focusing first on the billionaire patriarch himself, Jethro Colton. It didn't take Jagger long to discover Jethro had once been a petty criminal who'd done time for robbery. This had piqued Jagger's news instincts further. He'd begun to slow down on the beer, started getting better sleep and sworn off sex with nameless women.

Jagger learned that after being released from Wyoming Medium Correctional Institution just over thirty years ago, Jethro Colton had mysteriously come into some big money. He'd used it to buy Dead River Ranch—almost two thousand acres of cattle country in the Laramie foothills—where he'd fashioned himself into one of the most notorious, ruthless and prosperous cattlemen in Wyoming. *Forbes* magazine had not long ago run a feature on him, dubbing him Wyoming's Billionaire Rancher.

However, there was a dark cloud over Jethro Colton. After Cole was born to Jethro and his first wife, Brittany, she was killed in a drunk-driving accident. Then just after Brittany's funeral, Cole was abducted from the mansion in what appeared to be a robbery gone wrong. The Dead River P.D. and the FBI mounted an extensive search. No ransom note ever came. And all leads eventually died.

This information just raised further questions for Jagger. Ranching did not ordinarily billionaires make. And where had Jethro's sudden cash injection come from? How had the petty ex-con gotten so stinking rich overnight—proceeds of an earlier crime? Organized criminal links forged in prison? Was his first wife's death really an accident? And why had Cole been abducted, if not for ransom?

Could it have been revenge? Payback?

Had the child been murdered?

Or was there a faint possibility that Cole Colton was still alive, living somewhere under another name, oblivious to his own past, just as Jagger had been for the first nine years of his life?

Then, near the end of July, after Cheyenne Colton had been found and one of Jethro's ranch hands had been arrested in connection with the crime, Cheyenne's mother, Amanda Colton, along with her two sisters, Gabriella and Catherine, appeared on national television offering a reward of $500,000 for any tips that might lead to finding their long lost half brother, Cole.

The move surprised Jagger. All of a sudden the family was looking again? Why?

With his news instincts now on fire again for the first time in over a year, something else had awakened deep inside Jagger—a desire to find justice for a baby boy who could so easily have been him. A tiny victim without a voice.

With a renewed sense of purpose, and yes, Jagger knew this newfound passion might just be another way to beat back the nightmares—but it was a better path than the one he'd been on—he pitched his story idea to a major television network on the premise that he, a kidnap victim himself, would go undercover at Dead River Ranch in an effort to solve a thirty-year-old mystery tied to a billionaire ex-con. And in some way, he would bring justice to Cole Colton, alive or dead.

The television producers jumped on the idea. With the TV deal came an agent, then a book contract. Jagger McKnight was back! *This* story would be his route back into a semblance of life as he'd once known it, before Afghanistan. Before the ambush. Before he'd been forced up against a journalistic line he'd been unable to cross, and because of it, everything he thought he'd known about himself had been shattered. Dead River Ranch and a thirty-year-old cold case had become Jagger McKnight's personal Rubicon.

"What'll you have, handsome?"

Jagger jumped and glanced up sharply.

A brown-haired waitress was leaning on one hip, chewing gum, her pen poised over her order pad. She had a coffee stain on her apron and a weary look around her eyes. Her name tag said "Grace."

"Ranch burger is on special," she said with a jerk of her

chin toward the menu that she'd managed to place on the table without Jagger noticing.

He cleared his throat and quickly scanned the menu.

"Special looks great," he said with a forced smile. "Extra fries. And a Budweiser. Thanks."

Grace scribbled the order onto her pad then lifted her eyes, holding Jagger's gaze a fraction longer than necessary. He recognized the look—it was one he'd seen in the faces of the nameless women he'd taken into his bed. The waitress found him interesting—attractive, even. And suddenly, like a sharp, blinding flash of light through his body, Jagger yearned for something clean and sunshiny fresh. For bright mornings without hangovers, for pure smiles. For the scent of shampoo with a name like Spring Breeze. The aroma of freshly baked muffins, laundered sheets that smelled like flowers and pine. A real and good woman in his arms. Hell, he couldn't even articulate to himself what he was feeling right now—where these intense feelings came from. But they startled him in both their suddenness and ferocity, and inside he felt himself beginning to shake again.

One day at a time, McKnight. Just focus on the story...

"So, you just passing through, hon?" The waitress said as she took the menu from him.

"Looking for work." He forced another smile and the waitress flushed slightly as she tucked the menu under her arm.

"My name is Grace. I'll be right back with your beer."

She sashayed pointedly behind the counter, and while she yelled his order through a hatch into the kitchen, Jagger took stock of the diner and its patrons.

In the booth across from him, two gray-whiskered men in plaid shirts nursed coffees, their large bellies propped up by faded denim and suspenders. Probably the semi drivers on a pit stop before they hit the road for the long, lonely night haul. Jagger had caught plenty of rides with men like them over the past year, sat beside them in truck cabs, allies through the solitary night.

Behind an old-style cash register on the diner counter near the door was a woman who looked to be in her early sixties with dull, dyed-black hair. She was writing something in a notebook. Diner manager, or owner, figured Jagger. Farther down the counter, three men were perched on padded stools, their backs to Jagger, cowboy hats at their sides. Their bodies were honed, their skin tanned. Men who labored physically for a living—ranch hands most likely.

A few more cowboys gathered around a table at the back of the diner where the lights were dimmer and music played from a jukebox—the ubiquitous Wyoming sound of country and western. Overhead, a fan slowly paddled the warm, greasy air.

Grace returned with his beer and plunked it on the table along with a glass.

"So, where are you looking for work, then?" she asked as she placed a caddy containing ketchup, salt and pepper in front of him.

Jagger reached for the beer and took a fast, hard draft straight from the bottle. He swallowed, relishing the sensation of calm spreading through his chest. "I heard Jethro Colton at the Dead River Ranch is hiring." He dug into his jacket pocket and produced the job ad that he'd cut from the newspaper.

He slid the piece of paper across the table so Grace could see it, and he tapped it with his fingers. "Says here Dead River Ranch is seeking general ranch and maintenance hands—fencing, haying, minor mechanics, working cattle, four-wheeler operation." He took another swig of beer and grinned. "Right up my street. Pay includes beef."

The three men at the counter suddenly stopped talking.

One turned and eyed him. Jagger gave him a nod. With a subtle tip of his head, the cowboy returned Jagger's acknowledgment before returning his attention to his meal on the counter. But Jagger could *feel* the men listening now. The black-haired diner boss had stopped writing in her book and was now studying him intently from her post at the counter. Slowly she reached for the phone at her side, dialed.

A soft prickle of unease ran up Jagger's neck.

"That would be Gray Stark, the ranch foreman, who's looking for hands," Grace said with a nod to the piece of paper. "Jethro Colton's dying—he's not doing any hiring anymore, that's for sure."

"Dying?"

The chef placed a plate of food in the hatch and yelled out a number.

"That'll be your order—I'll be right back." Grace hustled to fetch it and placed the plate in front of him.

"So you know about folk out on Dead River Ranch, then?" Jagger said.

"Some," Grace said. Her gaze flicked to the diner owner talking on the phone, and she lowered her voice. "Dead is a small town. Talk gets around."

"What's wrong with Mr. Colton?" Jagger asked as he bit into his burger.

"Leukemia. He's been given maybe six more months to live, max. He's refused all treatment and is basically waiting to die. His family is real choked about it, trying to rally his spirits and get him to see a specialist. And they've been trying to find his long-lost son, Cole Colton, who could possibly be a bone marrow donor."

Bone marrow—so that's why the renewed search and big reward.

"Long-lost son?" he asked, chewing his burger, feigning ignorance.

"Yeah—baby Cole was kidnapped thirty years ago, right out of his nursery, just like the recent kidnapping on the ranch.

Jagger swallowed his mouthful then said, "Must be rough on the old guy, being sick at the same time his niece was kidnapped. It must've brought back old memories." He reached for his beer. "I heard about the recent abduction on the news up in Casper."

Behind him the diner door opened, a gust of wind blowing in and bells chinking. A cop, burly, balding, swaggered up to the counter as the door swung slowly shut behind him.

"Evening, Maggie," the cop said to the woman up front, his voice loud, resonant. "What's the pie today?"

Jagger watched in his peripheral vision as Maggie poured a cup of coffee for the officer and dished up a slice of warm pie from under a dome. She squirted a good helping of cream atop the pie and slid the plate in front of the cop. She leaned over the counter to talk quietly to him. The officer forked a mouthful of pie into his mouth, chewed slowly as he listened then slid his gaze toward Jagger.

For an instant the officer's eyes met Jagger's and Jagger wondered if Maggie had called the cop on the phone. That sense of foreboding burrowed deeper.

"Yeah," Grace was saying. "That recent kidnapping stuff has opened old wounds like it was yesterday. It's all the talk of town. Pie in the sky if you ask me—the sisters looking for Cole Colton now. That baby boy is long dead, I figure."

Something in Jagger tightened.

Grace shot another glance over her shoulder before saying, "So it was really on the news in Casper, our little town of Dead River?"

"On CNN," Jagger said, taking another bite of his burger. "Serious!"

"A wealthy Wyoming ranching family like that? A kidnapping case echoing a cold case three decades old." He swallowed. "Yeah, it's got the makings of national news. People love that stuff." He stabbed some fries with his fork, delivered them to his mouth.

The waitress bent forward and lowered her voice further, her eyes bright. "*And* there's been a murder on the ranch," she said conspiratorially "Did you know about that?"

"No," he lied. "What happened?"

"First baby Cheyenne's nanny, Faye Frick, was shot dead during the kidnapping. And then, last month, when wildfires were cutting the ranch off from town, one of the maids, Jenny Burke, was murdered in the pantry. The head cook, Agnes Barlow, was also attacked in the barn *and* someone tried to abduct Kate McCord, the pastry chef."

Jagger whistled softly—he'd known about Faye Frick, but not about the maid or the other attacks. "And no arrests have been made?"

"*No,*" Grace whispered earnestly, her eyes darting back to the counter where her boss was still talking softly to the cop. Jagger wondered who was making her more nervous—the police presence or her watchful employer.

"The only arrest was Duke Johnson, the ranch hand who admitted to kidnapping Cheyenne, but the police still don't know who asked him to do it—he said he got an anonymous note." Grace huffed. "Sounds weird, if you ask me."

Jagger dabbed a fry in ketchup. "You think the kidnappings are linked, Grace?" he asked softly, still watching the cop and Maggie from the corner of his eye. "Is that what people in town are saying?

"They figure it's an inside job," she whispered. "And I—"

"Grace!" Maggie barked suddenly from the counter

Grace jerked up, spun around.

"Folks at the far end are waiting to order! Ain't got all night, babe. And I got a dozen more applicants who'd line up for your job tomorrow. *Younger* applicants."

"Bitch," Grace whispered under her breath. "I gotta go." But she hesitated as she swiped back the wayward tendrils escaping her braid. "If you want to talk more later, hon, I'll be at Joe Bear's bar down the road after my shift. It's next to the Roundup Motel."

"Maybe later, then," Jagger said with a nod and another forced smile.

She smiled, a little shyly now, and bustled off.

As Jagger sucked back the last of his beer he saw the cop pushing back off the counter. The man headed toward Jagger's booth, fingers hooked into his weapons belt.

The officer stopped at the table, his gray eyes unblinking. Jagger's gaze lowered to the name tag on the man's uniform—Chief Hank Drucker, Dead River P.D. Jagger knew men like him. Big ego. Small town. Crime his game. Jagger became conscious of the pistol in the concealed holster under his shirt—a gun he'd never felt he needed stateside, until Afghanistan changed everything.

"Chief Drucker," Jagger said quietly with a nod toward his name tag.

"I heard you asking about the Coltons."

"I'm looking for work," Jagger said simply, scooping up the last of his fries and delivering them to his mouth.

"Colton's isn't the only ranch in town."

"Biggest game in town, though," Jagger said around his

mouthful. "And they're advertising for help." He jerked his chin toward the advert still on the table.

The chief's gaze lowered to the clipping, then shifted to the tattoo partially exposed on Jagger's forearm—the talons of an eagle poking out beneath his rolled-up sleeve.

The cop's eyes lifted to meet Jagger's. "Where you from, stranger?"

Slowly, he swallowed his mouthful. "Is there a problem, Chief?

The diner seemed to go dead quiet. The jukebox segued to a new tune. One of the ranch hands got off his stool and leaned his elbow back against the counter, facing Jagger. Warning bells began to clang softly at the back of Jagger's mind. He thought of possible exits. Escape. His blood pressure was rising fast—not good. He didn't want to have a flashback now, in the middle of it all.

"How about you put some ID on the table, son. There's been trouble on Dead River Ranch, and it's my business to make sure there's no more where it came from."

The cowboy pushed off the counter, came closer. "Everything okay, Chief?"

"Just fine, Tanner. As soon as our stranger here gives me some identification."

The cowboy remained to the side of the chief, his eyes fixed on Jagger. The others at the counter watched, bodies tense. The diner walls seemed to come closer, air going thicker, hotter. A buzz began in Jagger's head.

Raising his palms in mock surrender, Jagger reached with his right hand for his pocket. He removed his wallet, but as he opened it to show his false Montana driver's license, a creased photo of a woman cradling an infant fluttered down to table. It landed faceup.

The chief went stock-still.

The mouth of the cowboy next to the chief opened.

Grace, who was passing by the table with empty plates in hand, stopped, her face paling as she stared at the photo, then she flicked her gaze back to Jagger. Behind the counter, Maggie was watching intently.

Time seemed to stretch, warp. The ceiling fan whined softly in the silence.

Jagger scooped up the photo and shoved it back into his pocket.

"Where'd you get that?" asked the chief. Something had changed in his voice.

Jagger slid his fake license over to the chief. "Here's my ID."

"I said, where'd you get that photograph?"

"It's mine. Had it for years."

Slowly the chief picked up Jagger's ID, examined it, then lifted his gaze to study Jagger's face. "You from Montana, then, Ray Cartwright?"

"Been working ranches there for years," Jagger lied. "I was laid off during the summer drought."

"You ever been in trouble with the law, Cartwright, ever done time?

Jagger surged suddenly to his feet and slapped a wad of cash onto the table. "Will there be anything else, Chief Drucker?"

Silence.

Jagger shrugged into his jacket and reached for his hat. He tilted it low over his brow. Gathering up his kit bag, he said, "Then, if you'll excuse me…"

The chief stepped back, but barely.

Jagger exited the diner, his pulse thrumming. The door behind him swung shut, silencing the country music and cutting off warmth. Outside, the wind whistled through buildings as the sun disappeared in a red-orange haze behind the mountains. Shadows were already crawling out from crevices, fingering across the valley, dragging cold in behind them.

As Jagger narrowed his eyes against the blowing grit and traversed the cracked parking lot, he was watched from the diner windows. Before turning down the main road, he cast one last look back. The neon light above the building had flickered on, a lurid pink. The word *Dead*... blinked against the sky. The other words, *River* and *Diner,* were not displaying. A dark thrill sank through Jagger as he aimed for the highway out of town—he was onto something. Felt it in his gut. And it was enough to keep his mind out of the past. For now.

His plan was to hitch a ride and hopefully reach Dead River Ranch before full dark. Jagger had little doubt that in the interim, Chief Drucker would be running "Ray Cartwright's" Montana license through the system. If Jagger's ex-CIA pal, Miles Smith, had done a decent enough job, the fraudulent ID might hold. But the clock on his cover had started ticking. A little sooner than Jagger had hoped.

"We have a problem," the voice said into the phone. "A stranger in town asking too many pointed questions about Jethro and what happened thirty years ago."

A beat of silence. "You sure he's trouble?"

"He's got a photo of Brittany Beal Colton before she died, holding her newborn son, Cole, wrapped in the same blue blanket he went missing in."

"*What?* Where did he get it?"

"Don't know. The man has the same coloring as Cole Colton...dark-brown hair, blue eyes. Spitting image of Jethro in his younger days."

Silence shimmered. Tense. Then the person on the other end of the line spoke you the words, "What are you saying, that you think he could *be* Cole?"

"I don't know what to think. But he's on his way to the ranch tonight and my gut tells me if he gets there, there's going to be trouble. Big trouble. Too many questions." A pause. "You need to make sure he never reaches the farm or we could both be exposed."

"Make sure?"

"Eliminate him."

The call was ended.

Dust swirled yellow as the last rays of sun winked out and a frigid cold began to descend from the mountains.

About fifteen miles into his walk not one vehicle had passed Jagger. The night was cold and the darkness was almost complete, save for a faint glimmer of stars above. Exhaustion, mental and physical, was beginning to creep up on him, the shadows playing tricks with his mind, making him edgy. Then, as he crested a ridge in the road, he finally saw the lights of the ranch twinkling in the distance. Relief washed softly through him.

He took a small flashlight from his duffel bag and left the road, cutting across the burned back fields of the ranch—going along the road would take an hour longer, he figured.

His flashlight cast a small halo of yellow into the blackness as his boots crunched over stalks of burned grass, releasing the scent of ash. Everything around him was dry, cold, whispery. He aimed for what appeared to be a narrow dirt track bisecting the fields.

But as he neared the track, something scuttled into the dead stalks beside him.

Jagger stilled, heart hammering. With his free hand he reached for the 9 mm pistol in the holster at the back of his jeans.

Aiming his weapon alongside the flashlight beam, he

panned the darkness, his finger ready near the trigger. Perspiration beaded on his forehead under his hat as the old and too-familiar tongues of panic began to lick again at his gut. In the back of his mind he could hear gunfire, screams. He could smell blood and death.

A sharp flash of light sliced suddenly through his vision. Jagger dropped fast and flat to the ground. Mouth dry. Heart racing.

Was it real? Another flashback? Jagger inhaled slow and deep, trying to grasp hold of his sanity and stay present. His past was playing tricks with his head again. Probably just a big rat out there in the field. He got to his feet and shakily slid the pistol back into his holster. Thank God there'd been no one around to see him.

He resumed walking, but froze again when he thought he heard hooves galloping on hard-packed ground. Another trick? He spun around, peering into the blackness beyond the range of his small beam.

Then suddenly, out of the darkness, over a ridge, came a bright, bobbing light—moving in time with the sound of thundering hooves. It looked like a one-eyed mounted cyclops coming straight at him. As the apparition drew closer Jagger realized the rider was wearing some kind of headlamp. The horse was black as pitch. The rider's clothes were also all black as night.

Jagger raised his weak flashlight and waved it so that the rider would be sure to see—and avoid—him.

But the rider veered straight for the beam of light, kicking his horse into a higher-speed gallop. He was barreling straight at Jagger.

Jesus.

Confusion whirled through his head. "Hey!" he screamed. "Watch out!"

But the rider thundered forward—purposefully trying to hit him!

Jagger dropped his duffel bag and went for his gun again. He aimed at the one-eyed apparition.

"Stop or I'll shoot!" he yelled, squinting into the glare of oncoming light, white and bright as a hunting spot.

But the thundering silhouette didn't stop. The horse snorted, a pitch-black dragon breathing fire, white clouds of steam caught in the beam of Jagger's flashlight. As the horse reared Jagger glimpsed a lighting bolt of white across the animal's chest. He yelled again, "Stay back! I'm armed!" Then he squeezed the trigger, aiming to the left of the one-eyed horseman, trying to spook the thing. He fired.

It didn't work. The horse dropped back onto all fours and came at him.

Jagger lunged to the side, but it was too late—the horse's chest rammed into his shoulder like a mallet, spinning him like a fairground top into the darkness. His gun went flying and he smashed into the ground, striking the back of his skull hard against something sharp.

Jagger staggered to a kneeling position, then got up onto his feet, his vision blurring. He could hear mortar fire again. Automatic weapons. Smell flames. He could see the boy coming, hands held out from his robe. Empty hands...

Focus. This is now...focus or you could die!

The rider had swung the horse round. The hunting spotlight pointed at him. Jagger blinked. Defenseless, disoriented between past and present, he staggered forward, raising both hands, palms out.

With a loud whinny, the horse reared up and pawed the air again. Then, as its hooves hit the ground, the rider barreled at Jagger again. This time Jagger dived for the safety of a ditch, but as he went down, a shod hoof thwacked across his temple and sliced a white streak of pain through his brain. He lay there on his back, in the ditch, unable to move, barely able to breathe, fading in and out of consciousness. He could feel blood, hot, wet, down the side of his face. His blood. And the world went black.

The first rays of morning sun shimmered gold over the mountains as Mia Sanders raced her horse—a bay mare that ranch wrangler Dylan Frick had chosen especially for her—over fields crisp with frost.

The mare, Sunny, was Mia's to ride for the duration of her employment at Dead River Ranch, where she'd worked as staff nurse for the past twenty-eight months. Early mornings, when the sun was just cracking over the distant peaks, was Mia's most cherished time to ride.

Today was her first day off after working 24/7 through the trauma of the wildfires. The fires, combined with the kidnappings and the murders on the ranch, plus the stress of Jethro Colton's illness, had taken a toll, not only on Mia. Everyone on the ranch was exhausted and on edge.

Mia was also still adjusting to the arrival of Dr. Levi Colton last month. Jethro's estranged son had given up his first year residency in Salt Lake City to move onto the ranch to help care for his father. In the process, Levi had taken over command of the infirmary. That made him Mia's new boss, this after she'd run the place on her own for over two years. While she liked Levi well enough, change by its nature disrupted, and it was making her rethink her time here on Dead River Ranch. Perhaps she was ready to move on now.

But on this golden morning, before the world really awoke, fishing was all that was on Mia's mind. The Laramie trout streams would provide her some rest and respite, and refill her soul. She kicked Sunny into a faster gallop as she traversed the burned back fields. Cold wind tore at her hair and her father's old wicker creel bounced against Sunny's flank. Her fly rods were in their cases, tied securely to her saddle. As depressing as these burned fields were, Mia looked beyond them, toward the untouched foothills where aspen and alders gleamed with fall colors in the mountains' décolletage. Where she knew the rivers would be cold and chuckling and full of flashing rainbow trout.

But as she crossed a track that bisected the field, something caught her eye—something that didn't fit. A lump—a glimpse of blue and dark brown among the blackened stalks.

Mia reined in her horse, breathing hard. *It looked like a person.* Her blood quickened.

She urged her mare forward and with shock saw that the lump was a man, lying in the ditch, his hat discarded nearby. Quickly she dismounted, dropping to her knees in front of him. He appeared unconscious, face turned to the side. Blood pooled under his head.

Mia switched instantly into nurse mode and reached for his pulse. He was alive, and he was breathing. But his pulse was weak and his skin ice cold. Quickly she took in details—the man was tall, about six feet. Lean. Dark hair. Possibly in his thirties with a shadowed jaw, gaunt cheeks. His cowboy hat lay several feet away. He was dressed like a ranch hand—jacket lined with shearling, scuffed cowboy boots. Blood had dripped down the side of his face, leaking into his ear. She moved his head slightly. There was a gaping wound on his temple.

Mia ran back to her horse and fumbled to unhitch the first-aid kit she always carried. Returning to the victim's side she opened the kit and quickly snapped on latex gloves. She pressed a wad of gauze to the man's wound. With her free hand she reached for the radio on her belt. As staff first responder, she carried it always.

She keyed the radio. "Dr. Colton, calling Dr, Colton!" Mia released the key and cleared her throat.

Silence crackled.

It was early. Maybe Levi Colton was still cuddled up in bed with Kate—the pastry chef he'd already fallen in love with since his arrival on the ranch. A pang of unbidden jealousy sparked through Mia, but urgency pressed back.

"Mia for Dr. Colton—come in please, Dr. Colton, this is an emergency!"

As she spoke she noticed the deeply-scuffed and flattened earth around the victim. Hoof marks everywhere. And the burned grass around the man had been trampled to ash. Had he been thrown from a horse? Then she caught sight of an empty hip holster beneath his open jacket.

Where was his pistol?

She glanced up. There was no gear lying near him, either. Had he been attacked, robbed? Her pulse began to race—please, not another tragedy on this farm. What on earth was going on?

The radio crackled to life. "Mia, it's Levi—what is it?"

Relief washed through her. She keyed the radio. "There's a man unconscious on the back field beyond the employee gate. He's bleeding from a head wound. Breathing is steady but his pulse is weak and hypothermia is probable—I don't know how long he's been out here but he's wet from frost." She took in the length of his obviously toned body. "No other injuries immediately apparent—we need to get him to the infirmary stat, Levi."

Any other emergency help was at least fifteen miles away in the tiny rural town of Dead River and rudimentary at best. The infirmary, right now, was this man's best bet.

"Stand by—I'm on my way." She heard the sudden seriousness in Levi's tone.

"Bring a spine board. I don't want to risk moving him without it. He might have been thrown from a horse."

Sheathing her radio on her belt, she tore open a pouch from the kit and quickly unfolded a silver emergency blanket. She tucked it around the stranger before shrugging out of her own down jacket and draping that over him, too. Cold air struck her body immediately.

Mia cleaned blood and dirt away from his wound to get a better sense of the damage. Then, using butterfly sutures from her emergency kit, she pulled the edges of the gash together as a temporary measure. She placed a soft gauze bandage over the top. As she worked, Mia saw a cloud of dirt rising in the distance, catching the low angled rays of the early sun—transport was coming.

"Hey, there," she said softly, cupping the victim's face. "Can you hear me? What's your name? Is there someone we can call?"

He gave a soft moan and stirred. Relief washed through her— He was responsive.

"Help is on its way. Try not to move, okay? We're going to get you warm. Safe."

She heard the engine now, purring in the distance as it bumped over the farm track.

"Hang in there, big guy," she whispered, taking his hand in hers. His skin was cold, roughened. No ring. Mia swore softly to herself for even noticing.

But she had. And it gave her a niggling little feeling that maybe she wasn't quite over being abandoned at the altar. Yet.

"My name is Mia," she said softly. "Dr. Levi Colton is on his way."

He moaned again, in pain.

Keep talking. Keep him with you....

"You got any ID on you? Can we call someone?"

He groaned, moving his head. And his eyes flickered open. He stared at her. His eyes were a startling smoky blue, his pupils wide, dark. Fear crossed his features.

"Shhh, it's okay. Don't move. Can you tell me your name?"

Confusion creased his brow, then he winced as the muscles pulled at his wound. Blood seeped afresh into the gauze.

He closed his eyes, sifting out of consciousness again.

Mia felt inside his jacket pockets, searching for a wallet, a phone, anything that could help ID him. Her fingers came into contact with what felt like stiff paper. She pulled out a photo and sucked in a sharp breath of surprise. It was the same photograph that Jethro Colton had framed in his sitting room—the image of a woman cradling a tiny infant swaddled in a blue blanket.

Cole Colton and his mother, Brittany.

Mia turned the photo over. On the back was written simply the name, *"Cole."*

Her gaze shot to the stranger's face. No. That was ridiculous. It couldn't be him.

But he was the right age and build and coloring.

Mia felt inside the left-hand pocket of his jacket and touched something soft. Pulling it out, she found herself staring at a strip of baby-blue flannel. On it was embroidered with the name "Cole." It looked as if it had come from the same blanket swaddling the baby in the photograph—the blanket little Cole Colton had been kidnapped in.

Her chest tightened.

"Cole?" she said quietly.

He moaned, his eyes moving behind his lids.

Could it be possible? Had the Colton sisters' televised

appeal brought this man here, their missing half brother, Jethro's first-born son?

The farm truck pulled up behind her, doors opening.

"Over here!" Mia called out as one of the ranch hands came running with a spine board, Levi right behind.

"I've stopped the bleeding," she told Levi. "He came round for a few minutes, but he's lapsed into unconsciousness again." She moved aside as Levi dropped to his knees.

"He's not one of the farm hands, is he?" Levi said.

Mia was silent.

Levi glanced up, met her eyes.

"I think he might be Cole," she said quietly. "Cole Colton."

Chapter 2

Back in the infirmary, heat turned on high, Mia and Levi carefully maneuvered their patient onto an adjustable hospital-style cot. He was heavy, his clothes wet, and Mia was already breaking a sweat.

Levi had ascertained there was no spinal injury. He examined the stranger's pupils, using a small flashlight as he held back each eyelid in turn.

"Pupillary response normal," he said quietly. "Reflexes normal. Pulse within acceptable range. He's breathing fine on his own...."

But the man was still unconscious. Although the gash on his temple looked nasty and had bled profusely, it was superficial. The concern was the possibility of a brain hematoma.

Levi carefully felt his patient's skull, searching for signs of further injury to his head. Mia watched the doc's gloved hands moving through the man's dark brown hair. It was thick, glossy. Her mind slipped back.

She knew what it was like to run her fingers through a man's thick, dark hair. Soft and sensual. She shook herself, startled at the sudden and unwanted memory, at the empty hole in her stomach that came with it.

Her gaze went to the stranger's face. His skin was sun browned, his lashes dense above the flare of well-defined cheekbones. He had a strong jaw, shadowed with stubble. Hawkish brows. His mouth was beautiful, wide, the lips etched as if with an ancient Roman sculptor's precision.

It had been a while since he'd had a haircut. And even in repose there was something edgy and hungry about him, a little dangerous. Mia liked the look of him, found it sexy. The hole in her stomach gnawed a little bigger and wariness whispered through her. This stranger had the kind of looks that had done her in more than once before.

It wasn't that he looked particularly like her ex, but something about the sheer, smoldering physicality of this man brought Brad to mind. That, in turn, reminded Mia of her own failures, mistakes. Of her feelings of inadequacy as a woman—of her newfound fears of intimacy. Of all the pain and longing she'd come here to Dead River Ranch to escape and bury.

And she *had* buried it. Hadn't she?

Over these past twenty-eight months Mia had started to believe she'd finally conquered something inside herself. But here it was again, raw, scratching at her mind from just under the surface.

The doc's hands paused suddenly in the man's hair.

"What is it?" she said, leaning a little closer.

"Bring that light over this way."

Mia angled the examining light over their patient's head as Levi parted his hair.

"A scar," Levi said, running his gloved finger gently along the length of it. "A nasty one and fairly recent, too.

I'd guess about a year ago this guy sustained a pretty serious head injury."

Mia knew what Levi had to be thinking, that a fresh concussion on top of an older one could have a compounded effect. It could pose a whole other set of complications.

"Help me get him out of his wet gear, Mia, we need to get him dry and under a heated blanket. I'll suture that wound properly once we've given the rest of him a thorough once-over."

Mia helped roll the stranger onto his side as they proceeded to wrestle him carefully out of his wet denim jacket. Beneath the jacket he wore a button-down chambray shirt in pale blue. His sleeves were pushed up, partly exposing a tattoo on his right forearm.

Mia thought of the stranger's eyes as she unbuttoned his shirt. Baby Cole had had blue eyes.

Peeling back his shirt, Mia exposed another tattoo across the man's left pec—an image of a dog tag being carried aloft by wings. Underneath, in an unfurling scroll, were the words *Death before Dishonor.*

The smaller tattoo on his forearm was an eagle in flight with hooked talons, as if coming in for prey.

Mia wondered if he was ex-military. The dog tag with wings emblazoned symbolically across his heart might signify the death of a solider, perhaps. Someone about whom he'd cared deeply.

Death before Dishonor.

Had he received his earlier head injury in combat?

There was not an ounce of excess fat on this man. His chest was honed to perfection, his abs like a washboard—an anatomist's dream, each muscle defined as if for individual study. Mia lowered her hands to unbuckle his belt, suddenly overly conscious of the dark whorl of hair that snaked down his stomach and disappeared seductively into his low-slung jeans.

Feeling hotter than she should, she realized his boots would have to be removed before the jeans could. She tugged off worn Western boots that had clearly seen the business end of a ranch. She tucked them out of the way under a chair against the wall. On the back of the chair she hung his shirt and wet jacket.

The cold dampness of his jeans made them difficult to maneuver. Mia was perspiring with the effort now, her cheeks flushing as she tugged the denim down over powerfully developed thighs, strong calves, beautifully curved muscle. As a nursing student she'd always had a keen appreciation of a human body in its prime. This body was no exception.

Mia paused. "Another scar," she said quietly. "Along his inner thigh. Also fairly recent." And it was a nasty-looking one.

Levi grunted. He was focused on removing the dressing and temporary adhesive sutures Mia had applied to their patient's temple.

She returned her attention to the scar. It ran up the length of his inner thigh, disappearing into the hem of pure white boxer briefs—the way she liked men's underwear. Sexy in its simplicity.

This errant thought disturbed her, a nurse. She should remain detached, a professional. Hell, who was she kidding? Professionals had private thoughts about patients all the time, both good and bad, of a sexual nature and otherwise.

Mia wondered if this ragged scar up the inside of his leg had been incurred at the same time as the scar under his hairline. Whatever had happened to him, he'd taken a beating, and not that long ago.

She removed his briefs, her heart quickening at the sight of the dark, dense flare of coarse hair between his substantial thighs. She swallowed, unable to look away immediately.

He'd been blessed where men obsessed about being blessed. Size mattered—mostly to males, she thought. Another memory mushroomed hotly inside her. Making love two days before her wedding day. Straddling Brad, moving naked over him, the room hot. She hadn't had sex since—not once in over two years.

Mia suddenly felt molten hot and desperate deep inside. She shot a glance at Levi, worried for a moment that he'd somehow be able to read her mind, or that he'd sense her sudden tension. Because something about this dark stranger now naked on the examining table was unraveling everything she'd knitted so tightly together over the past two years. And it unsettled her big-time.

Mia covered him quickly with a soft electric blanket, adjusting the thermostat to high, and she began to rub his feet and hands softly to warm them. As she worked, her thoughts strayed back to her wedding day. Or, rather, the wedding day that wasn't. Brad failing to show at the chapel, leaving her waiting outside with her three bridesmaids and her uncle who'd come from England to give her away. A soft Pacific Northwest rain had begun to fall that day, but as the hours had ticked by, getting her hair wet was the last thing on Mia's mind. She thought about the gown, wasted. The hairdressers, flowers, caterers, champagne, the venue…the money her mother had spent, money she hadn't really been able to afford. A ball of emotion swelled, low and painful, in her throat.

She hated Brad. He was a coward for failing to call it off before the actual day dawned, for publicly humiliating her like that. Even more, Mia hated herself for allowing his actions to have utterly devastated her self-confidence, her sense of self-worth as a sexually attractive woman. She hated the shame that came with being an abandoned bride. A shame she'd been unable to shed, that had become almost pathological.

Her big, hotshot smokejumper, her macho alpha-dude, the man she'd once loved with all her heart despite his often-rough manner—had proven a yellow-bellied coward at heart. While she'd waited outside the chapel, and his best man had tried calling his cell phone, Brad had been boarding a plane bound for Nigeria where he'd already accepted a job with a private security firm to protect foreign mining interests. He'd gone to hide in a place where he wouldn't have to face her, apologize or explain his actions. Where he could hide among other macho die-hards who carried guns with enough bullets to equal their egos.

Where he'd never have to be trapped in suburbia, with a suburban wife.

Anger flushed hot up Mia's neck and her mouth went dry, all the old rage and embarrassment coming back.

"How's his temperature now?"

Mia jumped. Levi was talking to her. She hadn't heard a thing. Clearing her throat quickly, she said, "Excuse me?"

He threw her a glance, frowning slightly. "What is our patient's temperature?"

"Uh…" She checked quickly. "It's back within normal range now," she said, her voice hoarse.

"You okay, Mia?" the doc said, suddenly watching her closely.

"Fine," she said crisply.

He paused, still studying her. Heat reddened her cheeks. "I said I'm fine, Levi."

He gave a nod. "We're good to suture."

Mia brought the equipment.

As Levi stitched the wound he said, "I'll arrange for a CT scan at Cheyenne Memorial Hospital as soon as possible. In the meantime, we'll keep a close watch on his vitals. If anything changes we'll need to medevac him."

"You think he's military, given the tattoos?" she said, watching Levi work.

The doc grunted, pulling the surgical thread through skin. "Hopefully he'll come around soon and tell us himself."

As Levi spoke, the stranger's hands suddenly fisted at his sides, his neck muscles going iron tight. He jerked his head sharply away from the doc and let out a scream—like a battle cry, unearthly, primal. The sound echoed around the room, shocking both Mia and Levi stone cold.

"He's regaining consciousness," she whispered. "And he's highly agitated."

"Agitation is normal," Levi said brusquely, reaching for the suture needle hanging from a thread on his patient's brow. "The longer a person has been in an unconscious state the more violently stimulated and confused they can become."

But as Levi grasped for the suture needle, the man jerked his head away and flung his fist at Levi again, his legs thrashing violently, throwing off the blanket. The doc jerked back, but not in time to avoid a punch to his mouth.

Levi cursed, blood welling on his lip.

"Hold him down!" he snapped at Mia as he reached for the needle again. The wound was bleeding profusely again.

She leaned her body across the man's naked torso, attempting to press down on both his arms. This time he swung his fist at her. She jumped back, adrenaline pumping though her system.

"It's like he's fighting for his life," she said.

"We can't sedate him now!" barked Levi. "Not until

we know what's going on with his head injury. Go get some muscle in here, Mia, to help steady him before he hurts himself—I need to stop that fresh bleeding and finish these sutures!"

The man's eyes suddenly flared open wide and wild.

Levi and Mia froze for an instant. He looked terrifying.

The stranger lay there, exposed, his naked and powerful body stock still. He stared at Mia, then Levi, then swung his gaze across the room with an unfocused and feral intensity that unnerved Mia.

But instead of going for help, Mia leaned quickly forward and cupped the side of the stranger's jaw gently with her palm.

"Hey," she whispered softly, looking right into his frantic eyes. "It's okay, you're safe here—you're in the infirmary on Dead River Ranch. My name is Mia Sanders and I'm a nurse. Dr. Levi Colton here needs to finish stitching the wound on your temple, okay? Can you hold still while he does that? Dr. Colton has given you a local anesthetic, but you still need to relax, hold still. Can you do that for me?"

He stared at her, muscles wire-tight. Then slowly his pupils began to contract as he tried to draw her into some kind of focus.

"Cole?" she said, looking into his blue eyes. "Is that your name, Cole Colton?"

A frown furrowed into his brow.

Levi shot her a questioning glance.

"I'm going to call you Cole, for now, anyway, okay?" Mia said, slipping her hand into his. His palm was rough and she laced her fingers through his.

She felt his muscles relax, and his eyelids fluttered closed as he drifted out of consciousness again.

"Squeeze my hand, Cole. Give me a sign that you can still hear me."

He squeezed his fingers so tightly around hers it almost hurt. And he didn't relax his grip. A tear escaped from beneath his dark lashes and ran down the side of his rugged face.

Something sharp caught in Mia's throat. She shot a worried glance at Levi—leaking from the eyes could be a sign of brain trauma.

"I think it's tears," she whispered. She could feel need in his grip—he needed her touch and that made emotion burn behind her own eyes.

Levi quickly resumed stitching. After a while the stranger's grasp on Mia's fingers relaxed and his breathing turned soft, calm and rhythmic. "I think he's sleeping," she whispered.

"You've got some kind of magic, Nurse Sanders," Levi murmured.

Yeah, and it always works on the wrong kind of men.

Mia freed her hand carefully, unnerved by the strange intimacy she'd felt with this mysterious man's hand in hers. She stepped away from the cot and gathered up the blanket. Re-covering him, she turned her back on both him and Levi and began to aggressively fold the man's damp clothes, setting them into a pile on the chair that she'd later take down to Mrs. Black for laundering. But the main reason she'd turned her back was to hide the emotion burning in her eyes from Levi. She'd been blindsided by something, and it was so unexpected. Why now?

Why this man?

But Mia knew why. It was because he reminded her of Brad, had the same dark and kinetic intensity that did her in sexually. And she sensed that, like Brad, this man was damaged inside—he'd been through something close to hell. She'd heard it in his scream, and his pain called to the healer in her.

She could virtually hear her mother's voice as she folded the damp jeans.

Men like him are not cut out to be husbands, Mia, or fathers who stay home and mow lawns. You can't fix, or tame, men like Brad. Don't take on another project that's going to hurt you....

A project. That's what her mother had called Brad.

She hadn't bought it. Until it was too late. Until she'd been driven into therapy where she'd been asked about prior relationships and then told she had a subliminal and destructive attraction to this type of adrenaline-hungry and flawed alpha male. She was drawn like a moth to the white-hot alpha flame. She repeatedly bashed her stupid heart against the jagged rocks of men who'd ultimately crush her.

The therapist went so far as to suggest her father was the reason, and further, that she was trying to subconsciously emulate the relationship that had nearly destroyed her mother.

That's when she'd quit therapy and moved to Wyoming to heal herself. To the Laramie Mountains with their ice-cold trout streams full of rainbow-flanked fish. To the wide open prairies, big sky country, where things didn't hide in drippy shadows. Mia had wanted escape the dense, lushness of the Pacific Northwest, the cloying reminders of everything that had gone wrong.

So she'd cut everyone out of her life who knew of her humiliation, who reminded her of her shame. And she'd liked it here, where people didn't know. Where she could start fresh.

But it also had left her walled up, unable to trust, with a sense of time and life passing her by.

Levi finished suturing and covered his neat line of dark stitches with a light gauze bandage. He went over to the sink where he removed his gloves and washed his hands. Grabbing a tissue, he held it against his split lip.

"I'll call the hospital in Cheyenne, arrange for a CAT scan and an appointment with a neurological specialist as soon as they can get him in," he said, dabbing the tissue. "I know it's your weekend, Mia—but I need you to watch him 24/7, rouse him at regular intervals, check his memory."

"No problem."

"You sure?"

She gave a light laugh. "It's my job—the emergency calls never come when you want them."

He tossed the bloody tissue in the trash, grabbed a fresh one. "I'll get Trevor Garth, ranch security, to notify the Dead P.D. about our stranger." From the counter, he scooped up the strip of blanket and the photo Mia had found in the man's pockets. "I'll take these up to show Jethro and let him know what's happened."

"You think it could really be him—Cole Colton?"

Levi glanced at the stranger, lying peacefully now. He fingered the piece of baby blanket, thoughtful. Then he looked up, met her eyes.

"Wouldn't that be something."

She gave him a smile. "Your half brother."

An odd look flitted across Levi's face, and Mia wondered suddenly what Cole Colton's arrival might mean to the young doc. Levi, the illegitimate son, had given up a lot to come to Dead River and finally reconcile with his father. And now, to suddenly find a long-lost half brother. A first-born heir.

And what would it mean to the Colton sisters?

"Maybe I should keep his clothes for the cops," she said. "Instead of sending them down to Mrs. Black. They might need them for evidence or something. Especially if he was mugged."

"Right, yes, good idea. I'll let Trevor know everything's here." He hesitated. "And Mia, call me, stat, if there's any change in him. Any change at all."

She nodded.

The door swung slowly shut behind him and Mia was left alone with their John Doe. Trevor Garth, the ranch's head of security, had had his hands full of late. Not only that, he was now engaged to marry Gabby, the youngest Colton sister. A Christmas wedding had been planned.

Mia moved the blanket higher up over her patient and readjusted the thermostat, thinking that she didn't really want to be around come Christmas. She wasn't sure she could face someone else's wedding yet. She didn't want to go home for Christmas, either. She lowered the hospital-style bed so that it was at normal bed height and she set the alarm on her watch to wake her patient.

Taking a chair under the window, Mia leaned her head back, suddenly drained. She closed her eyes, listening to the mounting wind outside. A bare branch ticked against the infirmary window. The storm front that had been forecast was blowing in earlier than anticipated—she could have been caught out there, alone in the mountains, had it not been for her John Doe. Mia drifted into a light sleep. She dreamed of her wedding, standing alone outside the church.…

A sharp knocking startled Mia awake. Her eyes flared open and panic rushed momentarily through her—but it was just a branch rapping harder against the pane as the wind increased. Outside the sky was turning purple with clouds. She must have drifted off.

As she stared out the window, Mia felt a prickling

awareness down the back of her neck. She spun round. He was watching her from the bed, eyes intense. Unblinking.

She got up, went to his bedside, sat carefully on the side of his bed.

"Hey," she said softly, touching his arm. "I'm Mia Sanders. I found you in the back fields of Dead River Ranch this morning. You're in the infirmary in the Colton household. I'm the nurse on the ranch. You received a gash on your head and were unconscious for a while."

His gaze moved slowly left, then right, settling back on her. The darkness in his eyes was disconcerting, the same hue as the brewing storm outside.

With his eyes open he had even more presence. He seemed more…everything. More male, untamed. More sexually dangerous to her. Mia felt an odd little clutch in her stomach as the infirmary walls seemed to press in on her. The space felt suddenly too small, too hot. Too closed.

He watched her face, eyes unmoving.

The wind outside tossed a sudden clatter of dead leaves against the window and his body tensed. Fear raced across his features.

"It's okay," she said, watching his pupils carefully. "Just a storm brewing. Can you tell me your name?"

Confusion washed through his eyes. He glanced slowly around the infirmary as if something in the decor might yield an answer. His hand went to the bandage on his head and that whisper of fear ran through his features again.

"I don't know," he said, very quietly. His voice was a low baritone, gravel cloaked in velvet. Wind gusted outside again, clacking the leafless branch hard against infirmary window.

"Do you know what day it is?"

His gaze dropped to his wrist, as if in search for a

watch that wasn't there. Mia wondered if that, too, had been stolen.

"No," he said.

"Wednesday morning, September eighth. Now remember that," she said with a smile, "because I'm going to ask you again soon what day it is—to check your short-term memory." She hesitated, then said, "Could your name be Cole Colton?"

His eyes narrowed sharply and a deep V furrowed his brow as he struggled to remember. Then he looked away in defeat.

She leaned forward. "You had a photograph in your pocket of a woman named Brittany Beal Colton who died thirty years ago. Brittany was Jethro Colton's first wife. In the photo she's holding their infant son, Cole, who was kidnapped not long after his mother's funeral." Mia paused. "You also had a piece of baby blanket with the name Cole embroidered on it—just like the blanket he was wrapped in when he was abducted."

"Blanket?"

Mia nodded.

His eyes darted frantically around the infirmary again and he swallowed, fisting and unfisting his hands. Mia's gaze was drawn to his eagle tattoo, the way his muscle motion made the talons flex on his skin, as if the claws were reaching out. She thought about his tears, the way his fingers had clutched hers so tightly, so desperately.

"You're in Jethro Colton's house now," she said softly. "The closest town is Dead River, fifteen miles away. We're about forty miles northwest of Cheyenne, Wyoming's capital. Does any of this ring any bells?"

He stared up at the blonde. Mia Sanders, she'd said. A nurse. For a moment, when he'd first opened his eyes, he'd seen another face peering down at him—the face of a blonde woman holding a door open, her features crumpling at the sight of him as her hand went to her heavily pregnant belly. Nausea washed through his stomach as he struggled to pull the memory into better focus, to identify the pregnant woman. But it scuttled into the recesses of his mind even as he grasped for it.

His head began to buzz. He felt dizzy.

He focused on Mia instead. Her buttery-colored hair was shiny and it was caught back in a braid. Soft wisps had come loose around her heart-shaped face. Her cheeks were flushed, and her lips bow shaped. Pretty. Real pretty.

She reminded him of sunshine. Apples. Health. Her skin was flawless, her eyes soft blue. The light in her eyes made him think of summer days when the sun was high and warm. Of lemonade, watermelon wedges and water spouting from red fire hydrants. Sparkling drops like jewels against the sky.

Chase, come out the water now and get your watermelon before Jimmy eats it all!

God, where was that voice coming from—Chase? Jimmy?

His heart began to thump.

Another woman's voice, different, called from somewhere deep in his memory. *Jagger! Jagger, get down from the tree—you'll kill yourself!*

The voice morphed into another woman's…. *Cole, can you hear me…are you Cole Colton?*

Names, words, scenes, voices…circling…dizzy. He put his hand to his throbbing head.

Who in hell *was* he?

Anxiety crackled and sparked through him. His head hurt like hell. Pain—it was familiar to him, a constant. He knew pain. Why? He reached up and carefully fingered the bandage on his temple again. Mia reached for his hand, stopping him. "Don't. You shouldn't touch," she said softly, eyes strong, unwavering. "At least, not yet. Give it time to heal a bit."

The skin of her hand was soft and warm against his. He could detect a scent of…Spring Breeze—was that the name of a shampoo? Panic, confusion, tightened in his chest. His heart thumped faster.

What was he doing here? How had he gotten here?

Roads—many roads had led here. Clouds of sand whipped suddenly up in his mind, swirling, violent dust dervishes. He could feel the sting of driving grains, like glass, sandpapering his skin. A turban was wrapped over his face. The desert mountains were dry. Cold. The grit of sand was getting between his teeth, up his nostrils, caking between his eyelashes. The sound of an explosion *whumped* through the air.

He winced, closing his eyes tight and clenching his fists.

A boy—it was just a boy coming over the sand, the wind flapping his dun robe against skinny legs. Brain matter spattered suddenly across his face and over the backs of his hands. He could feel it, the warm wetness of a boy's brain on his hands. *What was happening? Why in hell did he not know who he was?*

He sucked in his breath, his heart slamming, gaze flashing around the room as he tried to sit up, get moving. Get out.

"Hey, hey, don't try and rush things," she said, holding his shoulder down. He looked into her face. Her features were calm. She smiled and it lit her eyes. "It's okay," she said. "Anxiety, agitation—even fear—are normal when someone comes around after being unconscious. The longer the coma, the worse it can all feel. It'll come back, just give it time."

The pressure of her hand against his shoulder was reassuring, and real, and he willed himself to calm. He told himself he wasn't trapped—he was just in some doctor's rooms. With increased focus, he re-assessed his surroundings. A drip stood near his bed. A blood-pressure machine was affixed to the wall. He was on some kind of cot, naked under the blanket that covered him. He caught sight of a pile of clothes folded on a chair, cowboy boots underneath. A gun holster was draped over the back of the chair. His stuff?

"What happened to me?" he said, throat sore. "Where did you find me?"

"We don't know what happened yet," she said calmly. "All I can tell you is that on my ride this morning I came across you lying injured and unconscious in a ditch out in the back fields. You had a nasty gash on your head and you were mildly hypothermic. You must have been out there for some time during the night judging by the moisture in your clothes."

Night...why was that so sharply familiar? No, Knight... McKnight.

"You had no ID on you, just the photo and the piece of baby blanket." She hesitated, her gaze shifting to the chair with the clothes. "You had a holster but your gun was gone.

Shots...he could remember shots. Had he fired them?

She moistened her lips, which drew his attention to her mouth. Full lips, pink, kissable lips. His gaze lowered farther, taking in her Western shirt, the fine gold chain that slipped down into her cleavage

He raised his eyes back up to meet her gaze. "I had no ID? But I did have a piece of blanket and a photo?"

"I think you were mugged, that someone took everything of value. The police should be here soon to take a statement."

"Can I see it, the photo and baby blanket?" he said.

"Dr. Colton has taken them up to show Jethro, his father. I'll go up and get them for you in a little while."

"And the name on the scrap of blanket was Cole?"

She nodded.

He frowned. Cole. The name felt so familiar. Important somehow.

Kidnapped—she'd said that Cole had been kidnapped, in a blue baby blanket after his mother's funeral.

The thought made his heart gallop and his skin go hot. Memories, names, spiraled suddenly through his brain, different threads twisting upon each other like double helix DNA strands winding tighter and tighter upon themselves.

"And you said that Cole was abducted thirty years ago, while wrapped in a blue blanket?"

She smiled again. "Clearly nothing wrong with your short-term memory, then. That's a good sign."

His mouth went dry as the strands of memory suddenly began unraveling themselves, and his confusion clarified into two hard lines.

He'd come here looking for answers. For justice for Cole and to find a way back into journalism that didn't involve war.

He was Jagger.

Jagger McKnight.

Ex-foreign correspondent. Most recently embedded with the United States military in Afghanistan…he stopped himself right there, not willing to go back any deeper.

"You're remembering?" she said, watching him intensely.

He was a storyteller. He got the kinds of news stories that others could not, or would not, because they were afraid to take the kinds of risks he took. But Jagger would take those risks, not only because he fed off the adrenaline, but because he believed passionately in providing a voice for the underdog, the silenced, the abused, the disenfranchised. The starving and the persecuted. He'd go into totally foreign countries, all alone. And once on the ground he'd run with whatever the story handed him. He'd learned to improvise, to go under cover when needed.

It's how he'd found acclaim.

And now, this particular assignment had just handed him a tool he'd never have dreamed up—amnesia. These people thought he might be Cole Colton. He had to run with this, for as long as he conceivably could.

"You *do* remember, don't you?" she whispered, her eyes lightening. "You *are* Cole Colton?"

He shook his head. "I can't remember a damn thing," he whispered. "I have no idea who I am."

And as he lied to this beautiful nurse who had probably saved his life, a chilling thought struck Jagger. Someone had tried to kill him out there—someone wearing a mask and a hunting spot, and riding a black horse.

He'd quite possibly been left for dead.

But why had his assailant taken his ID, yet left that photo? Why plant a piece of baby blanket on him?

Did his attacker want people to think he was Cole—a dead Cole?

Why?

An icy chill washed over his skin. There was more to this story than he'd thought, and now he was even more determined to expose it. But Jagger could not trust a soul on this ranch—not even this nurse—because his attacker was still out there.

And might try to finish the job of killing him.

Chapter 3

Mia knocked. When no one answered, she quietly opened the door to the sitting room off Jethro Colton's bedroom. It was empty, the fireplace cold. Dark wood shelves lined the walls, hosting framed pictures of the Colton family along with a collection of books. But it was a large photographic study positioned above the fireplace that always immediately drew Mia's eye—a portrait of Jethro as a young rancher in his prime, watching over the room.

In the image, Jethro was standing in front of a fence—tall, dark, honed, his cowboy hat in hand, his stallion beside him. The photographer had managed to catch an intensity of light and purpose in the rancher's eyes and a command in his posture.

Mia stilled in the middle of the sitting room as a sudden feeling of recognition rippled through her. The John Doe she'd left sleeping quietly in the infirmary looked startlingly like Jethro in his younger days.

Again she wondered if the stranger was Jethro's first-born son. If so, where had he been all these years? And of all ironic fates to befall him right now, to have his memory dashed from him right on the doorstep of his biological father's home.

The door leading from the sitting room into Jethro's bedroom was slightly ajar, and voices came from inside—Levi's and Jethro's, a tone of quiet urgency. It made a change from all the yelling that had emanated from that bedroom a mere few weeks ago when Jethro was refusing any treatment at all after he'd suffered his first major health setback from the leukemia.

Mia went up to the door, knocked gently.

"Come in!" It was Levi, taking charge. This meant Jethro had taken a turn for the worse. The old codger rarely ceded an opportunity to lord it over both family and estate staff.

Mia entered. The room felt hot and close and smelled of a sick person. Jethro was propped against pillows, a moss-green duvet up to his neck. He looked like a pale and sunken Scrooge being swallowed by his linens, as if the large four-poster bed was actually growing in stature as the man inside it shrank physically away, bit by bit each day. As if the bed might yet consume Jethro Colton wholly in the weeks to come. It was a bit of a shock to see him so suddenly frail.

Levi stood at his father's bedside, silhouetted against the stormy light coming in from the window behind him. Next to the bed was an oxygen machine and a drip that contained morphine. Because of Levi's coaxing, Jethro had finally allowed Mia to administer pain meds and oxygen, and to monitor his vitals. Beyond that, she'd been told hands off.

Jethro's attention was riveted on the piece of baby blanket and photo clutched in his hands. The old man's eyes shone with emotion and were rimmed with red.

Mia went round to Levi and drew him quietly aside. "Everything all right?" she whispered.

Levi nodded. "I told him about the stranger, showed him what the man had in his pockets—it's upset him."

"He's come around fully," Mia said of their patient. "But he has no memory of who he is or why he's here."

Jethro's head snapped up as he was jerked out of his memories. "Nurse Sanders, go to my sitting room—fetch me that framed photograph on the middle bookshelf." His voice was thin and wheezy, but no less commanding. His arrogance had not yet been fully sucked out of him.

Mia went into the sitting room as ordered. She knew exactly which frame Jethro was talking about—it held the same image she'd found on their John Doe this morning. She brought the frame to Jethro's bedside and he took it from her hands without glancing up at her face.

"It's the same," he said hoarsely, the fingers of his left hand absently working the soft scrap of blue blanket, his eyes going distant again.

Jethro sat like that, silent, his eyes haunted, as if he'd been sucked down some dark and tormented memory hole.

Finally he looked up at his son. "Brittany was already unhappy by the time Cole was born, you know." Another beat of silence passed as Jethro appeared to gather up more memories. "Her sister, Desiree, embroidered this baby blanket. She gave it to Brittany the day Cole was born. The embroidery is distinctive."

Jethro closed his eyes. Outside, in the distance trees were bowing as the increasing storm winds tore yellow leaves from their branches and scattered them free across the fields.

"So, you do recognize the piece of blanket, then?" Levi prompted.

Jethro nodded, his eyes still closed. "Cole was swaddled in it when he was taken, shortly after Brittany's funeral. That's what I told the police—that Cole was abducted with this blanket, right out of his crib."

Mia glanced at Levi to see if he'd picked up on Jethro's curious phrasing.

That's what I told the police....

She'd overhead Levi asking his father last month about a rumor that Desiree had been spotted in Jackson with an infant almost three decades ago. But shortly after the rumor surfaced, Desiree had been found murdered. No baby in sight, if there ever was one. Jethro had gone into apparent medical distress when Levi had broached this matter, but after Levi had left the room Jethro seemed fine again.

It had fed Mia's suspicions about how much Jethro Colton might actually know about the abduction of his son and what he might be hiding. Levi's half sisters, however, had quickly shut down this line of thinking. They loved their father too much even to consider that he might be hiding something about his own child's kidnapping.

But whatever secrets Jethro Colton might harbor, they seemed to have him in their grip now, as he clutched the scrap of blanket so tightly that his knuckles were going white.

"Brittany started drinking because of her depression," he said. "It cost her her life—driving drunk." He opened his eyes and glanced up, a shadow of remorse twisting his features, emotion glazing his eyes. "Before the depression she was different. I did love her, you know."

Mia swallowed.

Jethro refocused abruptly, as if he'd made up his mind

about something. "Go fetch him, Mia," he ordered. "Bring my son up here, now. I want to see him. Now."

"Jethro," Levi said, stepping forward. "The man has no identification, no memory. We don't know that he *is* Cole—neither does he."

"Even if he did have identification, it wouldn't say 'Cole Colton,' now would it?" snapped Jethro. "Of course not! He'd have been living under some other name. But he did have *these*—" Jethro held up the piece of blue flannel and crumpled photo, his breath starting to wheeze as his stress level rose.

"And you said yourself that he has the right coloring, Levi. You said he's the right age…" He faltered as he struggled for another breath. "It's him." He coughed. "It's Cole. My son—my first-born son. He's come home. Everything's going to be alright."

Levi reached quickly for the oxygen machine and turned it on. A loud beep emanated from the machine as Levi brought the tubing and nasal cannula up to his father's face. Jethro shoved Levi's hands away. "Just bring me my son. I want to see my Cole."

And it hit Mia right there—Jethro Colton *needed* this stranger to be his missing child, and that psychological need was rising inside him like a desperate tide. He *needed* things to be right again at this dying phase of his life.

"Jethro," Levi countered firmly as he brought the oxygen tubing up to Jethro's face once more. "You need the oxygen."

Jethro pushed his son's hands away again. "First I want to see Cole. And I won't have him see me attached to some goddamn breathing machine."

"He has *amnesia,* Mr. Colton," Mia said, stepping forward. "I must caution you, even if we bring him up here, he won't know who you are."

Jethro swung his head round as if noticing Mia for the first time. His eyes were still piercing despite his frailty. Or perhaps because of it.

"You're saying Cole will never know where he's been all these years—that his memory won't come back?"

"It could be short-term amnesia, Jethro," Levi interrupted. "I've organized a CAT scan for him tomorrow morning at Cheyenne Memorial, and a consult with Dr. Rajit Singh, a neurologist. We'll know more after that."

"How did he reach my ranch? *Someone* must have seen him. Did he come through Dead River? Did anyone in town see him, talk to him…?" Another fit of coughing and wheezing forced Jethro to double over and his face went red with pain as he clutched his chest, struggling to breathe.

"We'll find out," Levi said. "Trevor has put in a call to the Dead River P.D. The police are on their way." The doc glanced at Mia in frustration. "Mia, how is our John Doe? Is he capable of a short trip upstairs? Because as soon as Jethro has seen him we can connect up this oxygen and the drip."

"I'll go check—he was looking okay, otherwise I wouldn't have left him alone. He wanted to see the blanket and photo we found on him, thought it might jog his memory."

But Jethro gathered the blanket tightly to his chest. "It better be Chief Drucker who's coming—" he wheezed between coughs "—and not one of his imbecilic officers. I've got no time for those two…" Another spasm of coughs wracked the sick man's body.

Levi's jaw tightened as he once again tried to coax Jethro to take the cannula. Mia left quickly to fetch their patient.

But the dying patriarch still managed to yell after her.

"Nurse Sanders! Fetch my daughters, too! They need to know he's come home!"

As Mia exited the sitting room she almost collided with Mathilda Perkins carrying a tray with orange juice. The head housekeeper gave a startled exclamation of shock.

Mia caught her breath, equally surprised. "I'm so sorry, Mathilda," Mia said with a laugh that released the tension that had been building in her since her discovery this morning. "I didn't see you coming."

Mathilda straightened her spine and tilted her chin up. "I have Mr. Colton's orange juice. I...I like to bring it to him myself."

"Yes, of course. I—" But before Mia could finish Mathilda swept past her with an efficiency honed by decades of service to this family.

Mia hurried down the wide passage, making for the curved dark-wood staircase that would take her down to the employee wing where the infirmary was located. Persian rugs swallowed the sound of her footfalls. And it struck her suddenly—how long had Mathilda been standing outside that bedroom door? She could have heard everything. News of "Cole's" return and Jethro's reaction would ripple through the ranch employee grapevine like wildfire now.

It would be nothing new for the staff to eavesdrop on family dramas. In fact, it was hard to avoid. Servants were constantly required to be underfoot and because of it, the mansion was continually alive with some gossip or other. Mathilda, in particular, liked to be in the know so she could nip any nefarious whisperings about the family in the bud. She was fiercely protective of her long-time employer.

Mia started down the wide staircase thinking Jethro's daughters had been right—the mere thought that Cole was alive, and back, was arousing a fierce passion in their father. It might give him a will to live, to accept more aggressive treatment and fight this cancer.

As Mia reached the second floor landing she saw Misty Mayhew, the new maid, coming up the stairs, arms clutched around a wide vase of flowers, her dark hair fighting against a tight bun at the nape of her pale neck.

Her bright blue eyes flashed.

"Mia—hi!" Misty stopped on the landing and peered at Mia through the yellow blooms destined for Jethro's room. "I heard about the stranger," she said excitedly. "Is it really *Cole?*"

Misty had only recently been hired to replace Clara who'd been dating the ranch hand arrested for the murder of Faye Frick and the kidnapping, yet Misty was clearly already deeply immersed in the scandals of the household and guileless in her questions.

"Who said it was Cole?" Mia remained guarded, as always. She had never quite fit in with the rest of the downstairs employees, yet she was not one of the upstairs bunch, either.

"Everyone is talking about it!" Misty said, cheeks flushed. "Jake Masters, one of the wranglers who went with Dr. Colton this morning to fetch the victim, said you found a piece of Cole's baby blanket and a photo of his mother on him."

So it was already out.

A quiet defensiveness went up inside Mia. It wasn't a secret what she'd found, or what had happened. But her patient also deserved some respect.

"Misty," she said quietly, deflecting the question, "I need you to do a favor for me. Mr. Colton wants Miss Gabby, Amanda and Catherine by his bedside. Could you please go find them once you've taken care of those flowers? I think Miss Amanda is out at the stables. She was attending to one of the geldings when I returned Sunny to her stall this morning. I don't know where Miss Gabby and Cath are."

A shadow of defiance—so slight it might have been Mia's imagination—flickered through Misty's eyes.

"Thank you, Misty," Mia said, brusquely moving past the maid and starting down the stairs. "I need to get back to my patient."

Before heading to the infirmary, Mia quickly made her way down into the basement laundry in search of some clothes for "Cole." He couldn't very well go up to see Jethro wrapped in a blanket, and the Colton laundress, Bernice Black, had a constantly-growing selection of garments that she collected from both family and staff for the Goodwill store in Dead River. She'd been doing this for years.

The air in the basement laundry was humid, warm, laden with the scents of fabric softener and detergent. Dryers and washing machines rumbled.

"Mrs. Black?" Mia called above the sound.

No reply—both Bernice and her husband, Horace, were in their sixties and somewhat hard of hearing.

Mia called louder but still no response.

She walked past the machines, going deeper into the laundry. Around the corner she saw the back of Bernice. Her steel-gray hair hung in a straight ponytail down her spine as she worked an iron over a pair of heavy-duty jeans.

The woman stilled suddenly, as if sensing Mia's presence. Turning slowly, Bernice's milky-white eye settled on Mia. Her good eye was hidden by shadow.

Mia swallowed, always oddly unnerved by this woman who'd been a part of the ranch since before Jethro bought the land all those years ago. The Blacks still lived in their original log cabin on the property, well apart from the other outbuildings. Bernice was rumored to be of Native American blood and some of the staff claimed she could see things not visible to others. Many of them avoided coming down into her basement domain for that reason.

"Mia," Bernice said, her voice papery, husky. "Is it clothes for the stranger that you want?"

A chill washed over Mia in spite of the damp heat from the dryers. "I...actually, yes. I was wondering if you have anything in your Goodwill stash that he might use temporarily. He's about six foot two, broad shoulders—"

"I know." Bernice Black went to her special cupboard and extracted a shirt. She shook it out and held it up. "Dylan Frick just brought me a whole bag of his clothes the other day, some barely even worn. He's suffering since his dear mother's murder, you know. I think he needed to clean out his closets, erase the ghosts." Her gaze went distant, as if seeing things behind Mia's shoulder.

"There's no good that will come of all this," she murmured. "No good at all. Faye's spirit will not rest until the past is exposed."

Mia rubbed her arms. "What do you mean?"

"There is no present that is not rooted in the past, Mia. The past is always the answer to the present. And to the future."

"How did you know what size our John Doe is?"

"Jake Masters, one of the wranglers, described him."

"Yes, of course." It was just the gossip, nothing supernatural. Mia shook the silly thoughts and reached out for the shirt. "Thanks, Mrs. Black, that shirt will be great. Any pants?"

Bernice rummaged on the shelves, gathering several pairs of jeans, more shirts, underwear, socks. She offered Mia the pile.

"Thank you," she said with a forced smile. "I'll replace these for Goodwill once we get him some new stuff."

"Of course," Bernice said, shuffling back to her ironing. But she hesitated.

"Be careful, Nurse Sanders." She kept her back to Mia and her voice suddenly sounded strange. "Things—people here—are not what they seem. Veils and mirrors and tricks of smoke."

"Ah, yes, thanks again, Mrs. Black."

Mia hurried back past the dryers and upstairs faster than she intended to. Once up in the bright, warm lights of the kitchen, she felt ridiculous. Of course Bernice Black was right. Of course things were not what they damned well seemed. There was a killer among them, dark secrets being harbored. Nothing was going to be "as it seemed" until this was over, and justice was done.

The kitchen staff all looked up and stared as Mia entered clutching her pile of men's clothes.

"What?" she said.

"How is he—how is *Cole!*" Liz Dane, the cook's assistant, said coming forward, wiping her hands on her apron, her green eyes bright with interest under her red curls.

"Liz!" Agnes snapped at her young assistant. "Get back to stirring that pot or the bottom of the custard will catch! Make sure you keep the movement clockwise." But the older cook's eyes told Mia she was just as hungry for news.

And as Mia took in their expectant faces, it struck her for a second time how much this extended family *wanted* the stranger to be Cole. It would be like a big happy ending to a nightmarish fairy tale—the stolen baby returned to the Colton castle as a grown prince, the handsome firstborn son and primary heir to the ranching empire. Mia understood the psychology of it—good news was *needed* in the face of death and fear.

And death had come very close to everyone in this kitchen. Jenny Burke who had worked alongside them had been shot dead in the pantry just around the corner. It was still sealed off, her murder still unsolved.

"We don't know yet that he is Cole," Mia cautioned them. "But he does need something warm and nourishing to eat." She smiled. "Is there any soup, Agnes? And maybe some bread and fresh fruit?"

Fiona Cudge, one of the upstairs maids who was in the kitchen collecting a tray with tea stepped forward and said, "Jake Masters said the stranger has the right coloring to be Cole, and he looks to be the right age."

"Jake Masters has clearly been busy," said Mia.

"Well, it's not just Jake. Tanner Doake saw the man in the Dead River Diner last night when he stopped there for dinner."

Mia's pulse quickened. "He was at the *diner?*"

All looked at Fiona.

"Well, yes, he was. Around six, according to Tanner."

"Did he speak to anyone?" Mia said. "Did he give anyone his name?"

"He spoke to Grace, the waitress," Fiona said, suddenly forgetting the tea growing cold on the tray. "He told Grace he'd come looking for work on Dead River Ranch. He showed her the advertisement he'd cut out of the newspaper."

"Advertisement?"

"It was in his pocket."

Not when I found him it wasn't.

"*And* Chief Drucker asked the man for his ID," Liz interrupted, forgetting about stirring her pot again. "I heard Tanner telling the others."

"Liz!" Agnes grabbed the wooden spoon from the girl's hand and started stirring the pot herself. "Go warm up some of that leftover soup from last night for our guest. And heat up some of the fresh artisan loaf from this morning."

Liz set her mouth in a grumpy pout and went over to the large stainless steel fridge.

Mia stared at Liz's back. "You said Chief Drucker actually *saw* the stranger's ID?"

"Well, that's what Tanner told the other ranch hands," Liz said, coming out of the fridge with a container of soup. She began to ladle it into a bowl. "Tanner was eating in the diner with two of his buddies yesterday. He said the stranger looked like he was trouble from the get-go, like he was going to give Chief Drucker all manner of hell— Tanner and his pals were ready to jump in and help if he did."

"Liz—the fruit?" snapped Agnes, setting the lid back on the steaming pot, her cheeks pink from warmth and irritation.

Liz rolled her eyes behind Agnes's back. "I'll get to it." She opened the microwave, put the bowl inside, slapped the door closed and adjusted the timer. She wiped her hands on her apron.

"The stranger had gear, too," Tanner said. "A big duffel bag. Heavy looking."

So his bag, ID, the employment ad, gun—it all must've been stolen. An odd mixture of protectiveness, compassion and curiosity surged through Mia.

"Did Chief Drucker happen to mention what name was on the ID?" she asked Liz.

"Not to Tanner he didn't. But Tanner did see the chief looking at it." She paused, and the rest of the kitchen staff seemed to stop moving.

"That's when the photo fell out of his wallet," Liz said.

Silence. Just the sound of the pot boiling, the microwave humming and a kitchen timer ticking.

"The photo?" said Mia.

"Yes, the one with Mr. Colton's first wife, Brittany, holding baby Cole wrapped in the blue blanket. Tanner saw it himself, on the diner table. They all saw it—Grace, Maggie, the diner owner, Chief Drucker, the other ranch hands, the old men at the booth across from him."

Mia's mind raced. Someone had gone to the trouble of rendering the stranger unconscious, stealing his wallet, ID, duffel bag, pistol, job advertisement, *anything* that might identify him, yet they'd left him with a piece of baby blanket and that one photo? Could he have been followed from the diner by someone who'd seen that photo? But why?

"Well, now he has no memory of who he is," Mia said.

"Conveniently so!" All spun toward the sound of the strident female voice.

Mathilda had entered the doorway unnoticed, and she stood there now, shoulders squared, chin held high, her silver hair gleaming under the light above. The staff straightened their spines almost imperceptibly. Liz went immediately to fetch the fruit basket into which she put an apple, oranges and a banana. She placed the basket on a tray next to the bowl of steaming soup.

"What do you mean by 'conveniently'?" Mia asked Mathilda.

She felt the others listening intensely as they worked.

Mathilda came into the kitchen, still handsome in her sixties with strong features and thick hair.

"It's common knowledge that as soon as any of the Colton children turn thirty, they receive a portion of their inheritance. And suddenly this stranger appears—precisely when Cole would have turned thirty? It sounds fishy to me." Mathilda picked up a ledger near the kitchen phone. "There's also the big reward that the Colton sisters offered on national television. I don't trust that man and neither should any of you." She waved the ledger at them. "This stranger could be pretending to be Cole, and right now Mr. Colton is in a weak state. He's vulnerable to just such a con artist. He could be pretending to have amnesia."

"And what good would that do him?" Agnes said, spoon in hand. "If he's a con artist why not just pretend to be Cole? And if he's after the reward, I can't see what good amnesia is going to do him, either."

"I don't know," said Mathilda. "All I'm saying is that this family is vulnerable right now and desperate to believe. That's a bad mix in my humble opinion."

"Well," Mia said, gathering the pile of clothes tighter in her arms. "A DNA test will prove definitively either way. Meanwhile our patient needs food, and I need to get back to check on him. Liz—could you bring the tray?"

Agnes jerked her chin at Liz, ordering her to do as asked. The young redhead grabbed the tray and scurried behind Mia toward the infirmary, more than happy to oblige and perhaps sneak a peek at the mysterious stranger.

As they neared the infirmary, Mia heard a distant chorus of chimes echoing through the mansion halls. Someone was at the front door.

Jagger was back in hell, trapped in the gutted building. An acrid scent filled his nostrils—fire smoke, the sick smell of blood and guts, burned human meat. Bile rose in his throat as he felt the stickiness on his hands.

A hand clamped onto his shoulder, shaking, rousing. He tried to scream, to fight the grip, but it was as if he was trapped in molasses.

"Cole?"

He stilled. A woman's voice. Gentle.

"Cole...are you sleeping? Can you hear me...?"

It was *her* voice—a golden gossamer thread reaching down into his darkness, drawing him up, up. To the lightness of day. Life.

Jagger's eyes flickered open. Soft blue eyes, full of compassion and warmth, were watching his face intently. Her hand was gentle against his bare shoulder.

His mouth and throat were dry, sore. His head pounded. *Where was he?*

Now he could smell food, and his stomach clenched sharply with hunger. Slowly the room took focus behind her. He was in the infirmary. The nurse—Mia Sanders—she'd rescued him. He'd been attacked by someone on horseback, and he'd been left to die out in the fields. Someone had planted a piece of baby blanket on him.

Could *she* have stuffed the blanket scrap into his pocket before calling for help? he wondered as he looked into her eyes. He had only her word for it that it was already on him when she arrived.

He swallowed, pulling her pretty features into clearer focus, trying to read her expression. Hell, she had the kind of face he liked.

"Mia," he said, voice coming out in a hoarse whisper. "Hey."

Her mouth curved into a smile, lighting her eyes. "You remember," she said.

Jagger's gaze went to the window. It was still day outside. Windy. Leaves blowing from the cottonwood outside danced past the windowpane. The sky was low with cloud. He shifted his gaze back to her.

"I brought you some soup," she said. "And some clothes." She helped him sit up. The blanket fell away from his chest, and her gaze dropped instantly to his bare torso. She flushed slightly, and with surprise Jagger realized he found this modesty attractive.

"That's an interesting tattoo," she said, as if trying to explain her interest. She cleared her throat and reached for a pile of clothes, handing him a plaid flannel shirt. "Do you remember anything about where you got the ink?"

He shrugged into the shirt, wincing in pain as every muscle in his body protested. His head was pounding with each beat of his heart. "I wish I did."

"You've got one on your arm, too."

"I saw—an eagle."

"The one on your chest looks like something military," she said as she watched him buttoning up the shirt. "Something to possibly commemorate a passing soldier?"

Jagger's hands froze as Cpl. Lance Russell's face filled his mind. *Careful, Jagger. She's testing you. Or simply curious. But you can't trust anyone out here, not yet. Any one of them on this ranch could have ridden that black horse into you....*

Quickly, he resumed buttoning, trying not to think of the look on Russell's pregnant wife's face when she'd seen Jagger standing at her door. He'd gone to tell her how her husband had died. She knew already, from military authorities, but he'd needed to go to her himself. She would rather it had been her husband on her doorstep, instead of Jagger. Guilt gushed cold into his chest. There was nothing he could do to outrun this. He could only move forward.

Mia moved a small table closer to the bed and set the tray of food on top.

"Want to put the jeans and fresh underwear on, too?"

He angled his head slightly. "You going to help me?"

Again she smiled, but this time she gave a soft laugh, too. "I think you can manage."

He liked that she wasn't offended, that she was open to him.

She turned her back, busying herself with something on the counter against the wall as he worked himself into the clothes. He noticed that his old, damp and bloody clothes were still on the chair.

He swung his legs over the bed, stood shakily and zipped up and belted the jeans. He held his hands out to his sides. "Ta da—it all fits. How do I look?"

She turned and slowly ran her gaze over him, approval quiet in her eyes. "They were Dylan Frick's clothes," she said. "He's the head wrangler here—a renowned horse whisperer in these parts." She paused. "It was his mother, Faye, the nanny, who was killed during the kidnapping."

Jagger stilled. "Kidnapping?" He feigned a frown. "You don't mean…the Cole kidnapping you were telling me about?"

She sighed heavily. "No. A recent one."

"What?"

"You should eat."

"I can eat and listen."

Mia seated herself in the wingback chair under the window, looking suddenly drained. Compassion slid through Jagger. She'd been through a lot this morning, too.

"See?" He said lowering himself to the edge of the bed and picking up the spoon. "Eating. Listening."

She gave a soft snort, but he could detect a smile teasing her lips.

"Is that my stuff?" He jerked his chin to the pile of clothes on the chair as he scooped up a spoonful of soup.

She nodded. "I kept them in case the police want to take a look, for evidence or something."

Great. He hoped it wasn't going to be Hank Drucker from the diner.

"Tell me about the recent kidnapping," Jagger said, taking a mouthful of soup. If he was going to keep up this amnesia ruse, he needed someone to present him with information he'd otherwise have no way of knowing.

"About nine weeks ago, someone anonymously offered one of the ranch hands—Duke Johnson—cash to kidnap Jethro Colton's granddaughter for ransom. Duke broke into the nursery when most of the family and staff were away at the annual rodeo. But Faye was in the nursery, surprising him. Duke shot her dead in a panic before taking the baby in the crib."

Jagger swallowed his soup, staring at her. "So they did arrest him?"

Mia nodded. "But he claims he doesn't know who sent him the note offering him money for the kidnapping."

"Seriously?"

"Well, that's his story and he appears to be sticking to it. And that's all the cops have to date, as far as we know. The irony is that Duke took the wrong baby. Jethro Colton's youngest daughter, Gabby, had offered to babysit Avery, the infant daughter of Trevor Garth—he's the head of security here. Avery is the same age as Cheyenne and Gabby had put her to sleep in Cheyenne's crib. When Duke broke in, he assumed Avery was Cheyenne, and took her instead. This fact was kept from the media to keep Avery safe."

Jagger whistled softly. This was good. Already he had something he could use. He spooned up some more soup, careful not to rush Mia, to rouse suspicion.

She leaned forward, resting her arms on her knees. Her braid swung forward over her shoulder. "You know what's weird? Cole Colton was kidnapped from this very same house, also right out of the crib in his nursery."

He swallowed another mouthful, his mind racing. "So

you think there's a connection between the two kidnappings, then?"

"I have no idea—it's what some people think, although I can't imagine what the connection would be. In Cheyenne's case, the motive appears to have been ransom. In Cole's case, there was no ransom note at all."

"Could someone have been trying to hurt Jethro personally by taking his son, then?"

Mia studied him in silence as she entertained this possibility. "Could be," she said very quietly. "Levi seems to think Jethro knows more than he's letting on about what happened thirty years ago."

Jagger's pulse quickened. "How so?"

But Mia clammed up suddenly. She got to her feet. "They're my employers, Cole. And you could be his son. Or… I really shouldn't be speaking about them at all." She went to the closet and took out a small flashlight.

"You're talking to me as if I am Cole."

She shrugged, her back to him. "Better than calling you John Doe, no?'

"Mia?"

She turned to face him.

"I guess I need to thank you for saving my life," he said. She looked momentarily ruffled. "That's my job, Cole."

"Not necessarily—"

"It is," she said, coming up to him with the flashlight. "I worked as an E.R. nurse before coming here. And I volunteered for Search and Rescue. I went into nursing precisely because I *wanted* to save lives. I felt I could make a real difference there. Patients come into emergency broken, dying, desperate, and sometimes you can put them back together. You go home at the end of each day feeling you did something meaningful."

Jagger stared at her. She was beautiful to him, in more ways than one.

She sat on the bed beside him. "I need to check your pupillary response again, do you mind"?

He turned to face her. He could smell her shampoo again, and it hit Jagger—he'd been imagining someone just like Mia back in the diner when he'd thought of sunshine and shampoo. Happy mornings. The thought sent a weird chill down his spine.

"What is it?" she said. "You look like you just saw a ghost—did you remember something?"

"I…I don't know. It was just a feeling."

"What kind of feeling?"

"Nothing, it was nothing."

She eyed him, then nodded. "Look up to your right."

He did and she shone the light into his eyes. "Follow the light."

He blinked against the brightness and followed the small beam as she moved across his field of vision. Her lips were close. Her chest was rising and falling softly as she breathed. Jagger felt a warmth stir deep in his groin. He might have been hit on the head, but he was still all male, and he was responding to this woman so close to him. He wondered what it would be like to kiss that mouth, part her soft lips.

She paused suddenly, and Jagger knew she'd seen his sexual interest in the widening of his pupils. Her breathing quickened, and she stood up, clearing her throat.

"Looks good," she said crisply. But Jagger noticed her cheeks had gone pink. She was physically attracted to him, too.

"Do you think you're up to visiting Jethro Colton now?" she said. "He's asked to see you—he says he recognizes the baby blanket."

"He *does?*"

"That's what he says."

"You don't believe him?"

She hesitated. "That's a long time ago to recognize a blanket."

"It is," he replied, wondering who in hell had planted it on him, and where it had been all these years. If Cole Colton was abducted while swaddled in that same blanket, and his attacker had been in possession of it, he probably also knew what had happened to the baby all those years ago.

Or he could be the kidnapper himself.

"And the photo?" Jagger asked. "Did Jethro recognize that, too?"

She snorted. "We all did. It's identical to one he has framed in his sitting room."

That meant any number of people in the diner could have recognized that photo, too, especially if they were connected to the ranch, or had been here.

Perhaps they remembered the photo from old newspaper reports about the Cole Colton kidnapping. Jagger had, after all, copied the photo from one of those old news files that had been digitized, and he'd had it printed onto photographic paper.

"Why do you think Jethro stopped looking for his son?"

Her gaze shot to him and a slight frown furrowed into her brow. "I don't know that he did—I don't know all the details. It was a long time ago."

Jagger was quiet awhile. "If it was my son, I'd never give up."

She studied him, as if seeing him anew. "You know this about yourself?"

"I know this about myself," he said quietly. "I don't know how, but I just do."

Mia was silent, something shifting through her eyes and features. And Jagger could tell she liked this about him.

"You ready to go up now?"

He got to his feet. "As ready as I'll ever be."

"Take my arm if you feel wobbly, okay?" She paused, looking him intently in his eyes. "And Cole, please, you have *got* to tell me if you feel nauseous. You took a bad knock to the skull. Bleeding on the brain is silent, it can happen fast and it can kill you. Got that?"

He inhaled deeply. "Yeah," he said. "I got that."

But as they were about to move, a knock sounded on the door and it swung open wide.

Police Chief Hank Drucker filled the doorway with his burly frame.

"Chief Drucker?" Mia said, startled.

The chief ignored her, his narrow-set eyes locked solely on Jagger.

"Trevor Garth said we'd find you in here." The chief stepped into the room and it seemed to shrink around him. The man was not tall, but he was wide and he had a way of sucking up space.

Jagger remained silent as he met the chief's stare.

A slender male officer with blond hair entered behind Drucker

"Officer Deluca," Mia said. "Good to see you again." She sounded facetious, but her tone was lost on the blond cop who shot her a happy grin before quickly returning his attention to his boss.

"So," Drucker said, standing in the center of the infirmary, thumbs hooked into the belt. "We meet again."

"You said he was *dead*," the voice on the phone said.

"I thought he *was*—I couldn't feel a pulse!"

"What kind of person can't feel a pulse on a live man?"

"It was cold, my fingers were numb."

The person on the other end of the line swore. "It was supposed to look like Cole had returned, but was mugged and killed in the field, dammit. Then all these questions, this interest in what happened thirty years ago would have stopped. For good."

"What about forensics? A pathologist would have discovered the body wasn't Cole's."

"I had a way of dealing with that."

"How? Getting rid of the body? After everyone had seen it? I don't see how th—"

"That's not your concern! I'm not paying you think, understand?"

Silence.

"You screwed up. And you're just damn lucky he lost his memory in the process. Now you need to finish the job and kill him *before* his memory can return, and *before* they figure out he's not Cole. If not, we're screwed. Got it?"

Silence.

"Did you hear me?"

"Are you sure he's not the real Cole Colton? I mean—"

"He's not."

"How do you know?"

But the phone went dead.

Chapter 4

"What do you mean, 'we meet again'?" Jagger said, his gaze going to the portable fingerprint case in the blond cop's hand. His mouth went dry.

The last time he'd had prints taken was prior to shipping out to Afghanistan where he was to be embedded with a military unit. He wondered if Drucker would have access to the military record of his prints. His juvie record was sealed, but Jagger had also been fingerprinted while he was a journalism student. He'd been outside the United Nations in New York, protesting the Iranian government's imprisonment of a female journalist. When police tried to move him, he'd resisted and was arrested.

It was a just a matter of time until Hank Drucker learned from his prints that he was Jagger McKnight, that the Montana license was fake and his cover as amnesiac Cole Colton would be blown.

Ticktock. The clock had started.

Outwardly, Jagger remained calm, a blank look on his face.

"We met at the Dead River Diner," Chief Drucker said, his eyes dissecting Jagger. "You were in around six, having a burger and beer. You claimed you'd come looking for work at Dead River Ranch."

Claimed. The chief obviously hadn't bought that story. Jagger gave no reaction.

The chief took a step closer to Jagger. Mistake, because it forced the man to look up at him, which gave Jagger a psychological advantage.

"You were asking a lot of pointed questions about the Coltons and the kidnappings," the chief said.

Mia's eyes flashed to Jagger and she frowned.

But Jagger continued his blank stare. "I'm sorry, I don't remember."

Mia stepped forward. "Look, Chief Drucker, my patient has no memory of who he is. The injury to his head has caused amnesia."

My patient.

She was taking this personally, aligning herself with him in a subtle way, standing up for him against this cop. Jagger warmed further to her. He could use Mia on his side. She was not part of the Colton clan, and as both the family and ranch nurse she was in a unique position. She could be a good intermediary for him *if* he could keep her trust.

"Levi Colton has informed me what happened, *Miss* Sanders," the chief said coolly, not bothering to glance Mia's way. In his peripheral vision Jagger saw Mia bristle visibly at the chief's pointed use of the word "Miss." He also noticed Mia immediately raising her left hand to waist level where she began to worry an empty ring finger with her thumb. A nervous tick? Or something more?

Jagger was an acute observer—it was part of the reason he'd become one of the top foreign correspondents and investigative journalists out there. Until last year.

Until he'd been unable to break professional rules he'd once lived by.

"You don't recall anything about the diner?"

Jagger cleared his throat, pulling his mind out of the past. "No, I don't remember anything prior to waking up in this infirmary."

"Chief Drucker," Mia said, her voice strident and tight now, her thumb still urgently worrying her empty ring finger. "I don't know how to be more clear—my patient has suffered a serious blow to the head that left him in a coma for several hours. He does *not* recall his name or where he comes from. This is not entirely unusual. His amnesia could be short term, or it could take longer for his memory to return. There's a remote chance it might even be permanent—he has evidence of a prior head injury, which could have complicated things. We'll know more after tests tomorrow."

Still ignoring Mia the chief said, "And you had no ID on your person?"

"Obviously you've already been briefed by the Coltons," Mia said crisply. "In that case you already know about this man's lack of ID. Besides, *I* was the one who found him, not Levi Colton. *I* was the one who searched his pockets. And there was nothing in them apart from a strip of blue baby blanket and an old photograph. I presume Levi and Jethro have told you this already?"

Chief Drucker turned to Mia now, his thick neck flushing with the redness of irritation.

"We'll take your statement separately, Miss Sanders. Outside."

She inhaled and her mouth flattened as if to bite back

a retort. Her eyes glittered and her cheeks turned pink. Jagger liked her fire—this woman might appear soft and gentle on the outside, but inside she had spine and a temper. He found this heat in her sexy. He imagined she'd be good in bed, and the errant thought shocked him. But it was there now, lodged in his brain, coloring everything when he looked at her. And as he stared at her, his vision swirled. The room started to spin… Jagger's knees buckled slightly under him and he staggered sideways, reaching out to balance himself on the back of a chair.

He bent over. His heart was racing, his skin hot. A thread of fear stabbed through him. He might be feigning amnesia, but his head was spinning like a fairground top.

Mia rushed forward, taking his arm. She hooked it over her shoulders and using her body to take the brunt of his weight, she eased him toward the bed and helped him lower into a sitting position.

Jagger put his head between his knees, defeat washing through his body—his injury was real. He was weak. How much damage had that horse and rider actually done to him?

Bleeding on the brain is silent, it can happen fast and it can kill you, got that…

Mia spun to face the police. "You need to leave. Now."

The cops remained unmoving, watching. She ignored them, bending toward Jagger, her fingers feeling for his pulse. "Tell me what's happening," she said softly, near his ear, her ponytail falling forward over her shoulder. He could smell pine, lemons. He could hear ocean surf, feel sunshine. He could see his old home in the Florida trailer park, then the face his biological mother in California. Confusion spiraled through him as time and memories twisted in on themselves again.

"Just…dizzy," he said. "Confused."

"Nausea?"

He shook his head. She looked worried.

"You shouldn't stand for too long or move too fast yet—you lost a fair bit of blood, Cole." She checked her watch as she counted the beats of his heart. Her fingers were soft, cool. He could see the small charm affixed to the gold chain around her neck. The charm nestled between her breasts, pulsing slightly with the beat of her own heart. Jagger fought a desire to just lean into her breasts, her scent, let her envelop him, yield his months of fatigue and mental pain into her care. His eyes burned with the thought. The need. And he hated himself for it.

Jagger had not allowed anyone to care for him—truly comfort and hold him—since he was nine years old. He had not allowed himself to open his heart to love after the P.I. found him in the Florida trailer park he'd once called home. The cops had brought a social worker with them to tell him that he was not Chase Smithers, as he'd always believed. And that the woman who'd raised him was not his biological mother, but a wanted criminal. She'd been part of a carjacking ring that had taken his real parents' sedan before the thieves had realized he was inside, strapped into a baby seat in back.

His little life had been ripped apart that day the cops came, and he'd never really figured how to put certain pieces together again. And this sudden, raw need overpowering Jagger now tilted his world dangerously off-kilter. It was as if he'd arrived at some kind of tipping point, and he'd exhausted all mental and physical resources. He hadn't lost his memory, but he might as well have—because right now he did not know himself at all. He felt suddenly, oddly, lost.

Vulnerable.

And damn, he hated vulnerable.

"Look at me, Cole."

He raised his eyes.

"You need to be honest with me. You need tell me if you feel any nausea at all. None of that male I-can-handle-it crap, understand?" She said, holding his gaze.

He broke her gaze. It was too intimate. She was seeing too much of his vulnerability. This woman had a way of getting under his skin, into his head. He focused instead on the carpet pattern around the cops' boots. Wrong move. Because all he saw now was Cpl. Lance Russell's dusty, bloodied boots—legs without a body attached.

Yeah, he felt as if he was going to throw up, all right. He'd felt like this for months, sick to his stomach every time the wretched images stole into his brain. *This* was why he'd kept moving. Drifting like a tumbleweed. Trying to escape the memories and flashbacks he was now convinced would never leave him.

Jagger curled his hands tightly around the edge of the cot, fighting the urge to launch to his feet right now, and just go. Hit the road. Never look back.

But he forced himself to hang on to the cot.

One step at a time. Get this story—focus on that. And you might find justice for Cole, a small boy abandoned, stolen.

"Cole." Her voice was soft. "Look at me, Cole."

Jagger lifted his eyes again, slowly. "I got it, Nurse." He forced a wry smile.

"Good," she said quietly, her features serious. She released his pulse, then stood erect and faced Drucker. "Let's start again, shall we, Chief? Clearly our patient doesn't remember meeting you." She turned to Jagger. "This man with the wonderful manners here is Dead River P.D. Chief Hank Drucker. And this is Officer Pierce Deluca." She turned back to face the cops. "I found our patient lying unconscious in a ditch in the burned-out field beyond the employee gate at around eight this morning."

Deluca got out his notebook, flipped a page and started scribbling down notes.

"I was going for a ride, going fishing. It was my day off. When I saw him lying in the field I dismounted immediately and found he was bleeding from a head wound." She cleared her throat. "I called Dr. Colton on the radio for help and continued to administer first aid while waiting. I noticed lots of fresh hoof marks around his body, scuffed-up dirt and flattened grass. It looked to me as though he might've been thrown from a horse, and that a hoof had sliced across his temple. But then I noticed no belongings nearby—just his hat. I searched his pockets for ID, a phone, anything that might tell me who to call."

"And you found a piece of blanket?" There was accusation in the chief's tone. Deluca looked up from his notebook expectantly.

"Yes," she said, voice cool. "I found a scrap of blue flannel embroidered with the name 'Cole.' Along with a photo of Brittany Colton holding her baby wrapped in a blue blanket with similar embroidery."

Deluca flipped a page, continued scribbling.

"And you didn't put the blanket in his pocket?"

"What?"

"It's my job to entertain all possibilities, and to keep all avenues of investigation open. You do understand."

Her mouth closed in a tight line.

"And you didn't remove anything from his pockets?"

"I didn't steal anything, if that's what you're suggesting." She was angry now.

"Well, he wasn't thrown from a horse," Drucker said. "I personally witnessed our John Doe here leaving Dead

River on foot around 7:30 p.m. yesterday, carrying a duffel bag."

Deluca was frantically scribbling down notes, flipping pages.

"But there were fresh hoof marks all around him," Mia countered. "If it wasn't his horse, it was someone else's."

"What happened to your kit bag, sir?" Drucker said, directing the question to Jagger.

"I didn't know I had one," Jagger said, wondering why the chief had failed to mention his fake Montana driver's license with the name Ray Cartwright on it. What game was Drucker playing here—keeping his possible identity from him?

"Those are his clothes on the chair." Mia pointed. "And his holster—his weapon is missing."

Another hot hard look from the chief. "You were carrying concealed?"

"That's within his rights," Mia snapped. "This is Wyoming. Half of the ranchers out here carry concealed."

Jagger felt a smile teasing his lips now. Mia Sanders was this close to punching Chief Drucker in his squat face, and he loved her for it. For the distraction.

"Would you like to step outside while we finish this, Miss Sanders?"

"No," she said quietly, folding her arms across her stomach. "And it's *Mizz*."

Jagger was liking *Ms.* Sanders more with each passing second. And it suddenly mattered to him that she was single, no ring. Which unsettled him. His ex, after all, had left him because he was unable to commit to marriage. He cursed inwardly. Everything about this woman was messing with his head. He wondered, also, why Drucker was underscoring Mia's relationship status, and why it so visibly rattled her.

"You can't recall any of this, sir?" The question was again directed at Jagger.

"No, I don't."

"And you don't know your name?"

"I told you, I don't remember *anything* prior to waking up on this cot in this infirmary."

"You have zero recollection of coming into the Dead River Diner yesterday evening?"

Jagger closed his eyes and inhaled deeply. "None."

"You don't remember talking to a waitress named Grace, or to me?"

"No! Like I said, I don't recall anything."

Silence.

Jagger waited for the cop to say that he'd seen the Montana driver's license, the name Ray Cartwright. He waited for the cop to say he'd seen the photo of Brittany and Cole Colton fluttering to the diner table.

But he didn't.

Slowly Jagger opened his eyes. The cop was still watching him. Intently.

"We've taken the blanket and photo into evidence," Drucker said.

"You can't do that. It's all he has," said Mia. "Showing him that blanket again, letting him feel it, might help jog his memory."

"If it is a piece of Cole Colton's baby blanket," Drucker said coolly, "it's evidence in a thirty-year-old kidnapping case. Mr. Colton has already confirmed that he recognizes the unique embroidery on the flannel. And how this man came to be in possession of that blanket is now also under investigation."

Mia glowered at Drucker. "He might be in possession of it because it's *his*."

"A DNA test will be done in due course. Now, if you

don't mind, sir, we'll take your prints." Drucker motioned to Officer Deluca who quickly folded his notebook and reached for the fingerprint case he'd placed on the counter.

"Prints?" Mia said, watching as Deluca brought forward the bag and set it on the small table near the bed.

"We'll check them against missing persons reports," Drucker said. "And we'll do a criminal records check."

Mia's gaze swung to Jagger's, a frown suddenly creasing her brow. Drucker had succeeded in sowing doubt in her mind. Score one to the chief.

"We'll take photos of your tattoos, too, if you don't mind, sir." This time Officer Deluca spoke. "Dr. Colton mentioned that you had distinctive ink on your chest as well as on your arm."

"And if he *does* mind?" Mia said, looking uncertain now.

"You do want to find out who you are, don't you, sir? Because this will help," Deluca said.

"It's fine, go ahead," Jagger said. Fighting it would raise suspicions. But nevertheless, tension twisted through him.

Deluca opened his kit, removing an ink pad and print cards.

"What about the DNA test?" Jagger said, watching him.

"We'll use a technician from our police lab to conduct the DNA test," Drucker interjected. "Mr. Colton has agreed to leave any DNA testing in the hands of law enforcement technicians and the police lab in order to maintain a clear and clean chain of evidence in the event this goes to trial. It could make the difference in securing a conviction. The fewer holes we leave for defense lawyers to poke into, the better."

"Sir, your right hand please?" Office Deluca held out the ink pad and looked a little embarrassed.

"And when will your tech come and do the test, then?" Mia asked.

"He's away testifying at a trial in Cheyenne. It could be a week, or more, then we'll need to wait on results."

"But what if Cole wants separate DNA results sooner—through a private lab? I mean, his priority is finding out who he is—"

Drucker turned sharply to face Mia. "The D.A.'s office has advised us to keep a clean chain of evidence. Mr. Colton has agreed to comply. I expect you will, too."

"Clean chain of evidence?" Mia glowered at the cop. "You make it sound like he's guilty or something."

"No one on this ranch is beyond suspicion after the recent spate of crimes, Miss Sanders. There's still a killer out there, and I'm just doing my job."

Whatever the reasons for delaying a DNA test, it suited Jagger just fine. He allowed Deluca to take his hand and press his thumb into the damp inked padding, rolling it left to right before transferring it to a white print card.

While Deluca finished up with the prints the chief bagged the pile of clothes on the chair, along with the empty holster.

"Did you fire your weapon, sir?" Drucker said

"I didn't know I had a weapon."

"We found two spent 9 mm casings."

So they'd been out there already—before even talking to him or Mia. Jagger shrugged. "Means nothing to me, I'm sorry."

"Jenny Burke was shot and killed in the pantry with a 9 mm caliber bullet."

"You can't think that *he* had anything to do with Jenny's murder, surely?"

"Who's Jenny?" said Jagger.

"Look, I want you to leave now, Chief Drucker. My patient needs rest."

"I'm sure he does," said the chief, looking at Jagger. "We're done. For now."

Deluca handed Jagger a towelette to wipe the ink from his fingers. "Would you be so kind to remove your shirt, sir, so I can quickly grab a shot of those tattoos?"

Jagger removed his shirt, wincing again in pain. The cop took several photographs. He had kind, hazel eyes and Jagger wondered how many years would it take for Drucker to rub the compassion out of his young rookie.

As the cops finally made for the door, Mia called after them, "How long will it take before you get results on the prints?"

Drucker gave a soft snort as he opened the door. "If we find anything, you can rest assured, Miss Sanders, we'll be back."

The door closed behind them. Mia stared at the door then swore bitterly under her breath before spinning around. "It's like he's purposely delaying a DNA test—why would he do that?"

"Who knows what the D.A. told him, or how my amnesia might impact a trial? He's just being a cop, Mia. They're trained to keep their distance."

"I suppose. He… I just don't like him."

Jagger studied her for a moment, then lowered his gaze to her ring finger. She saw where he was looking and her eyes narrowed defensively.

Jagger stood and went up to her. He took her hand and gently thumbed her ring finger where she'd been worrying it.

"You okay, Mia?"

She swallowed and her lids flickered, a sexual energy suddenly surging thick between them.

"I'm fine," she said, her voice husky.

"He got to you, didn't he, when he called you Miss? Why does that even worry you?"

A coolness entered her eyes. She extracted her hand from his. "It's none of your business." She'd put walls up. Cold and concrete. Just like that. "You ready to go up and see Jethro?"

"Yeah, let's get this over with."

She made for the door. "I'll show you the way."

"Mia?"

She stopped, her hand resting on the doorknob. "What?" She didn't look at him.

"Thank you—for having my back, for standing up for me."

"I don't know that I should have."

"Why not?"

She turned slowly. "Because Drucker might be right. Because you could be a felon, a con artist on the make. You could have gotten those tattoos in a prison for all I know. I have no reason to trust you—"

"But you do."

She swallowed.

"Why, Mia—why do you trust me?" Jagger wanted her fully on his side before any of Drucker's accusations hit the fan, and to do this he needed to understand exactly what made Mia Sanders tick. Such as why she bothered her ring finger, why her unmarried status was such a sore point.

He'd be lying if he said he wasn't interested in Mia for other reasons, too, which conflicted him. Because as Jagger looked into her soft blue eyes he felt the first stirrings of guilt, and he knew he was heading straight into a double bind. The more Mia opened to him, the more she helped him, the more difficult it would be to keep up the lies.

"It's just a gut feeling," she said quietly, holding his

gaze. "But don't let that get to your head, John Doe. My mother always said I had wretched judgment when it came to men."

"As in when you tried to marry one?"

She yanked open the door. "Come. Jethro Colton is waiting," she said, sidestepping his question. "He won't take his oxygen until he's seen you."

But already she'd told Jagger a lot.

Chief Drucker and Officer Deluca strode down the gravel driveway that led to the stables. Clouds, fat and puce with rain, lowered the sky, and the wind scattered autumn leaves at their boots. Drucker could scent snow in the air. He had little doubt the surrounding mountains would be white by the time these clouds finally lifted.

He checked his watch. It had been almost a full twenty-four hours since he'd first spotted "Ray Cartwright" in the diner. He'd known right off the bat the guy was trouble— gut instinct after being in law enforcement for over thirty years. Bad winds had blown him into Dead River Ranch, like buzzards to a kill.

"You didn't tell him you'd seen his Montana license," Deluca said, matching Drucker's strides as they neared the stables where Officer Karen Locke was still questioning ranch hands. "You didn't let on that you knew his name was Ray Cartwright, not Cole Colton."

"Just because his license says he's Ray Cartwright doesn't mean he's not Cole Colton," Drucker said gruffly. "Or that he's Ray Cartwright.

"What do you mean?"

Drucker swore to himself. The guy was a numbskull. This was the tradeoff for budget cuts. He had to scrape the bottom of the employment barrel and surround himself with cheap idiots like Pierce Deluca and Karen Locke.

"Here's the thing, Deluca—if Cole Colton was kidnapped and raised by his abductor, do you think they're going to call him Cole Colton?"

"Uh, no. I guess not—they'd secure the kid a false ID—a name like Ray Cartwright."

Drucker grunted.

"So he really *could* be Cole Colton."

"It's possible."

"Imagine," said Deluca. "We could be solving a thirty-year-old cold case that even the feds couldn't crack years ago."

Yeah, and the last thing Drucker wanted was feds nosing around his turf again. Which was exactly why he was being careful in dotting all his 'i's', crossing his 't's', ensuring his own lab ran the DNA analysis. This was *his* gig to control now.

"Too bad he can't remember who attacked him," Deluca said as they approached the stables.

Dylan Frick was in the paddock to the left of the stable buildings, working a stallion. He wore a black hat, black jeans. Wind whipped the horse's tail and ruffled its mane as it trotted in a frisky circle around Frick, spurred by the storm electricity in the air. The image of man and horse was striking against the thunderous clouds mushrooming over the mountains. Drucker wondered how long Frick would push that animal before thunder cracked.

"Maybe he *can* remember, Deluca," Drucker said, slowing his pace to watch Frick and the horse.

"Why would he lie about it, then?"

"Because he could be a fake, that's why." *Bonehead.* "If he's not Cole, he could be after Colton's fortune."

Officer Karen Locke exited the barn, gave a wave and jogged toward them, wind blowing her short brown hair. Drucker felt Officer Deluca straightening his shoulders beside him like a goddamn cockerel. He wondered whether Deluca and Karen were already sleeping together. Or if it was just a matter of time.

"I still have a few more interviews," she said as she neared, pink-cheeked and breathless. A few raindrops bombed to the earth, and Drucker motioned that they should talk while heading to the cruisers parked in the circular driveway.

"Trevor Garth gave me a list of who was working the evening shift and night shifts yesterday, so I started with them. Then I—"

"Keep Garth at arm's length," Drucker interjected.

Locke glanced up. "You don't trust him?"

"He was a good cop in his time from what I hear. But he's too close to the family now—he has vested interest. I don't want him to be controlling our investigation or interview process in any way, even on a subliminal level."

Locke moistened her lips, glanced at Deluca. "Yes, sir." She cleared her throat. "I also asked the early morning shift if they'd come across any of the victim's belongings, or if anyone heard anything during the night. So far, nothing."

"Keep talking to them. Deluca, you go back to the diner, speak to Grace again. Find out from Maggie who the rest of the patrons were yesterday, round them up and see if you can get any more information from them. And locate those two truck drivers, find out if they saw our victim on the road that night. Or anything suspicions. Anything at all. And while you're at it, look for possible links to Duke Johnson, our kidnapper in custody."

"Do you want me to run these prints when I get back, sir?" Deluca said, holding up the kit.

"I'll do that," Drucker said, taking the kit from Deluca's hand.

Surprise rippled across Deluca's face.

"You've got your plate full, Deluca. We're a small P.D. up against a big ranch, large staff—many of them drifters who are not inclined to be open with law enforcement. This is a major case and I need you out there. I'll handle the prints."

"Are we going to bring in outside help?"

"No reason to at this point. I'll see you both back at the detachment." Drucker headed back to his cruiser, fingerprint case in hand. He could feel Deluca's and Locke's eyes on him.

But there was no way in hell he was calling in reinforcements. And if there was a hit with these prints—he wanted to be the one to find it.

Chapter 5

Mia walked a little too fast, hands clenched tightly at her sides as she led their John Doe to the elevator that would take them up to Jethro's room on the third floor of the family wing. She hated that he'd noticed her fiddling with her ring finger. She hadn't even realized she'd been doing it. She also detested Drucker for managing to get a rise out of her, for exposing her deep and personal sense of failure, shame, inadequacy.

Reaching the landing, she pressed a button in a brass plate set into the paneled wall.

Dark, wooden doors slid open quietly, exposing a mirrored gilt interior. Hesitancy rippled suddenly through Mia, her fears of intimacy rearing up at the prospect of stepping into the confined space with this particular man, as if this elevator represented a threshold and once she crossed it with "Cole," there'd be no turning back. It was an irrational thought, but it curled through her mind nevertheless.

"Are you sure you're up to doing this now?" she asked. "You could rest first, then—"

"I'd like to get it over with, Mia. Meeting Jethro Colton might shake something loose in my memory."

Mia inhaled deeply, nodded and stepped inside. Cole followed her.

As she pressed the button for the third floor she caught sight of her own reflection. She looked drained. Her thoughts went to her fishing gear that was still in the stables from this morning. Her first day off in weeks had been snatched away by yet another turn of weird happenings on this cursed ranch. The events of the past few weeks had exhausted her.

It was no wonder that the emotional wall she'd so carefully built up around her heart had been fractured. It was fatigue, she told herself as the elevator doors slid shut. Nothing a good night's sleep and a few proper days off wouldn't solve.

But as the elevator began to rise, the surrounding mirrors confronted them both. He was watching her with his dark, smoky-blue eyes, as if dissecting, weighing her up, seeing right into her heart and mind. Mia swallowed. She felt hot. The space felt tight, and a feral tension radiated from him. He was tense, she thought, possibly afraid of his memory loss. Compassion sliced through her tension.

And that was exactly what had gotten Mia into trouble in the past—that kind of feral intensity in a man, the way he looked at her, and knowing he was hurting inside, damaged. It spoke to her on every level, powerful. Consuming.

It's how it had unfolded with Brad, from the first instant she'd laid eyes on him. The desire in her gut had been jagged and white-hot. Knowing he was grieving the loss of two good men from a recent fire just fed her desire to touch, hold, comfort. Mia couldn't explain why these

things coupled inside her the way they did. All she knew
for certain was that she was wired this way.

And that she needed to stay away from men like that.
Broken heroes who could break her, too—or so her therapist had said.

Mia looked at her feet. Her hands felt clammy, a soft
panic rose in her stomach.

And she knew, suddenly, with certainty, that while she'd
thought she'd gotten over it—Brad, her rejection, being left
at the altar with her stupid dreams of home and children
shattered—she hadn't.

She still wasn't healed. Maybe she'd never be.

And for all those reasons she was angry with the man
in front of her.

*Good grief, Mia—he's a John Doe with a head injury.
Get over yourself.*

"Who's Jenny Burke?" he said, his gaze still intense on
her. "What happened to her in the pantry?"

Mia exhaled, relieved for the distraction. "She was one
of the maids. Pretty, long brown hair, brown eyes, in her
midtwenties. She was briefly engaged to Trip Colton—
Jethro's former stepson who lives in one wing of the house
with his mother and sister."

Cole raised a dark brow. "Interesting."

Mia gave a half shrug. "Yeah—the lives of the rich and
famous. Jenny was found shot dead in the pantry shortly
after Trip broke off their engagement and took his ring
back. When the ring was found in Trip's room people
thought maybe he'd done it."

"Did he?"

"God knows—right now nothing would surprise me
about this place."

He studied her in silence. She could feel him thinking,
weighing it all up.

"And she was killed with 9 mm pistol?"

"I can't believe Drucker even suggested you could have done it."

"Why not? You said you'd believe anything right now."

She looked at him anew, a tiny thread of doubt curling through her mind. "You…weren't even here."

He smiled darkly. It put a dimple in his cheek and fanned lines out from his blue eyes. Mia wanted to look away, stop the increasing rate of her pulse, the attraction she knew she must be showing in her face.

"Who knows," he said quietly, his eyes holding hers. "I could be a nefarious felon, tattoos and all. Could have been hiding out in the woods—sneaking into the house—at least, that's what Drucker might like to think."

A smile teased her mouth in spite of herself. Yet that whisper of caution ribboned a little deeper through her.

The doors opened. With relief she stepped out, but Cole caught her arm, hooking it through his. Mia glanced up at him in surprise.

"I might collapse, feel dizzy again." He smiled that devilish smile of his.

"Yeah. Right," Mia said. "This way."

But as they walked, Mia couldn't deny that the solid, warm sensation of him moving beside her, the energy from his touch, felt damn good. It made her realize how much was missing from her life. She'd spent the past twenty-eight months rebuffing any of the ranch hands' attempts to get to know her better—she'd truly isolated herself.

"You're toying with me, Cole," she said softly.

"What makes you say that?"

"I suppose it would make sense that it runs in the family—Jethro is an incorrigible womanizer."

"Is that what you think I'm doing? Flirting?"

She looked up and met his eyes. Mistake. Her chest clutched and heat fanned down through her stomach.

"It's the door near the end," she said, quickly looking away as they rounded a corner.

Cole gave a soft whistle as he took in the opulence down this section of the passageway—the oil paintings, the plush Persian rugs underfoot, carved statues on pedestals spaced at intervals along the walls. "Fancy."

"Yup."

"Do you have an opinion on why anyone would murder Jenny Burke?"

Mia sucked in a deep breath of air, calming herself. "Jenny had been snooping around in people's rooms while cleaning, and one of the rumors is that she found something."

"Something that someone wanted kept secret."

"Well, that's what they're intimating."

"The staff are intimating this?"

She nodded. "And from Drucker's questions, that was also the angle of his investigation."

"And Drucker has made no headway in her murder case?"

"No arrests, if that's what you mean. Jenny was shot in the face, on the evening just before the wildfire cut the ranch completely off from town, so it made initial investigation difficult, and it compromised the scene."

"Good timing on the part of the bad guy, huh—using the fire as a smokescreen. How long did it take before the cops could actually get in?"

She stopped in her tracks and shot another glance up at him. Again, those smoky blues were fixed on her. She cleared her throat, but her voice came out thick. "You're asking an awful lot of questions specific to Jenny Burke."

As she spoke Drucker's similar words sifted into her

mind… *You were asking a lot of pointed questions about the Coltons and the kidnappings…*

A dark look crossed his face and Mia could suddenly hear Mrs. Black's voice in her head.

Be careful, Nurse Sanders…things—people here—are not what they seem. Veils and mirrors and tricks of smoke.

Mia repressed a shiver.

"I think you would ask pointed questions, too, Mia," he replied quietly, "if a police chief was asking where your missing pistol was, and whether it took the same caliber bullets that killed a staff member here. And if you knew that this chief was also going to run your prints for a possible criminal history, and meanwhile you have no idea who you are or what you might have done."

She swallowed. "Touché," she said quietly and resumed walking. "I'm sorry."

"You said Jenny was snooping. What for?"

"I don't know." She stopped in front of a door. "This is Jethro's suite."

Mia rapped on the door. Again there was no answer. She quietly opened it and led Cole inside.

Jagger followed Mia into the sitting room. It was decorated in tones of green offset with dark wood. A door leading off the room was ajar. Jagger stalled as he caught sight of the portrait hanging over the fireplace.

"That's Jethro Colton," Mia said, watching him closely. "You look like he did when he was younger."

"God, yes, I can see that," Jagger said quietly, a strange feeling in his chest. "I can see why everyone thinks I'm Cole—it's not just the blanket or the photo found on me."

He could also see why someone might have thought to frame him as Cole. The resemblance was uncanny.

Voices—both female and male—rose suddenly in strident argument from inside Jethro's bedroom.

"I *know* you recognize the blanket, Dad," a woman was saying. "But Chief Drucker said he could be a con artist! He could be on the make—this could all be a ruse!"

"Just let Drucker do his investigation, shall we?" another woman's voice countered. "He said he's got some leads. A DNA test will tell in the end."

A baby cried.

Mia pulled a face. "You ready?"

Jagger sucked in a deep breath of air and squared his shoulders. "As I'll ever be. Let's do it."

Mia rapped sharply on the bedroom door.

All went dead quiet inside. Then footsteps could be heard hurrying across the wooden floor. The door opened wide, exposing a young woman with long red hair and big green eyes. Shock rippled visibly through her body as she laid eyes on Jagger. Her mouth dropped open and she stared.

It was Gabriella, the youngest Colton daughter—Jagger recognized her from the extensive research he'd done on the family.

Her hand went slowly to her mouth. *"Cole,"* she whispered. Then she appeared to gather herself. " I… You look just like my father did when he was young."

She came forward as if to hug him, then stopped, uncertain. Then she hugged him, anyway. Fast. She stepped back just as quickly. "I…I don't know what to say in a situation like this." The gleam of emotion filled her eyes. Her hands, Jagger noticed, trembled slightly, her paleness replaced by a soft flush of excitement.

"I'm Gabriella Colton. Everyone calls me Gabby. Please, come in," she said, reaching for his hand. "He's waiting."

Jagger stepped into the bedroom but Mia held back, uncertain. Jagger turned to her. "Please, Mia, come with," he said quietly. "I might need my nurse."

She hesitated, looked at Gabby.

"He's right, Mia—you're his nurse," Gabby said. "And Lord knows, father should be allowing you to nurse him properly, too. You'd better come in."

Mia entered at Jagger's side and he felt quietly bolstered by this intriguing woman's presence, her quiet strength coupled with a rare warmth and gentleness. He sensed her separateness from all that was going on, and he felt, subtly, that they had beginnings of an alliance. He'd be lying if he said he didn't want to get to know her on a more personal level, too.

But his mission was this family. The secrets of the past. And he needed to learn them fast. That police chief had started the clock ticking.

Gathered around a dark, looming antique four-poster bed were Jethro's other two daughters. Jagger recognized them as Catherine and Amanda.

Amanda was holding her baby on her hip, obscuring Jagger's view of Jethro Colton himself.

Dr. Levi Colton stood at the far side of the bed.

They all stared in quiet awe as Jagger approached.

"This is Amanda and Catherine," Gabby was saying. "And Cheyenne, Amanda's daughter. And you've met Levi."

Amanda reached forward to shake his hand, exposing a clear line of sight to the man in the giant bed, propped up by pillows. Jethro Colton. He had tubes in his nostrils leading into an oxygen machine next to his bed. A drip fed into a tube taped to his hand.

Even in his pale, weakened state, the man had presence. Intrigued, Jagger came forward.

Jethro stared at him, his complexion draining to sheet white—as if he'd seen a ghost of the past, a ghost of himself.

He raised his hand, trembling as he sucked a wheezy breath through the tubing.

"Cole?" he whispered, extending his veined hand slowly toward Jagger. "My son—is that you?"

Everything seemed to shift in the room as daughters and son stared first at Jagger, then their father. The weight of the moment—the love in this family, the bond—was tangible, however it had been forged.

Jagger swallowed, caught by the throat.

He'd always wished for that feeling, that family bond. But by the time his real family had found him it had been too late. He'd become someone else already. He'd bonded with a lie, a mother who was a kidnapper, a criminal—a woman who'd known all along that his biological parents had been seeking him. This revelation had shattered his young heart. Quite irreparably, it seemed. Because Jagger was left empty after that, incapable of bonding again with his blood brother and sisters, his real mom and dad.

The old man's eyes glazed over with emotion. "Please, come closer. Let me get a good look at you."

Jagger went up to the bed. He reminded himself this man was a petty ex-con who suspiciously turned himself into a notorious billionaire. He was a man with possible organized crime connections. A man who long ago seemed to have given up searching for his kidnapped son.

A man whom Jagger felt in his gut knew something about what had happened that dark day thirty years ago and was hiding the fact.

Jethro took Jagger's hand in his. The sick man's skin felt thin and cold.

"By the love of God," Jethro whispered. He drew in another machine-aided breath, closing his mouth as he inhaled deeply through the tubes in his nostrils. "It's how I imagined...you would be, if—" he sucked in another breath through his nose "—you ever came back."

Came back. Jethro didn't seem shocked by the fact "Cole" was alive, but that he'd come back.

Jagger noticed the framed photograph beside Jethro's bed—the same image he'd printed out and carried in his wallet. The copy of which Chief Drucker now had in evidence.

Would Drucker be astute enough to notice Jagger's image had been re-printed from digital newspaper archives on recently-purchased photographic paper?

Ticktock.

The Colton daughters glanced at each other, an unspoken exchange and fresh hope gleaming in their eyes.

"All these years I've wondered where you might be..." Another pause as Jethro closed his mouth to draw in another breath through the cannula. "Where have you *been?* How did you come to—" He was besieged by a sudden coughing fit.

Levi quickly brought a glass of water to his father, but Jethro waved him away.

"Mr. Colton," Jagger said carefully, "I received a bad blow to the head. I don't remember anything about my past, not even my name."

Levi set the glass of water on the bedside table, "I told Jethro about the amnesia. I explained that your memory loss could be short term—that it could return once swelling goes down. Or it could be long term, compounded by an earlier head injury. It could also have been induced by the shock of the attack." He hesitated. "Or possibly even from something that happened before. We'll know more once you've seen a specialist."

Yeah, Jagger knew all about specialists and psychologi-

cal trauma versus physical brain damage—he knew how to pull that one off because he'd been there.

Jagger saw Amanda's eyes go the bandage on his head. Her baby wriggled and protested, and she soothed her by stroking her head. "And we'll do a DNA test, Daddy," Amanda said, watching Jagger with her serious brown eyes. "When Chief Drucker can get his technician here. Then we'll know for certain."

"But the blanket—he was wrapped in that same blanket when he was taken. I'd...recognize the embroidery anywhere..." His voice faded into a papery wheeze, his eyes going distant, dark, haunted.

"We looked," he whispered into space. "We all did—the police. Everyone." He closed his mouth and drew in another strained breath through the nasal cannula. "And we waited for the ransom note. It...never...came... I blame... self..." He went silent for a while. The only sound in the room was the loud hum of the oxygen machine and Jethro's ghostly breaths. His eyes fluttered closed. His lids were translucent and veined.

Levi caught the attention of his sisters and made a motion with his head for them to go into the sitting room.

"It's the morphine starting to do its work," he whispered. "I'll catch up to you after he's fallen asleep."

They quietly filed out and Amanda closed the door to the bedroom, leaving Levi and Jethro alone inside.

"Is it okay if we call you Cole?" Gabby said once they were in the sitting room.

"It's better than John Doe," Jagger said. "What did your father mean when he said he blames himself?"

"My father just needs rest," Amanda interjected, still jiggling an increasingly restless Cheyenne on her hip. "He's at serious risk for infection, pneumonia—this is all obviously very emotionally trying for him. He's not thinking straight."

Jagger studied the child and mother. This was the infant who was the target of a kidnapping attempt gone wrong two months ago. Her little baby face went red as she squirmed.

Jagger met Amanda's eyes. They were a luminous pale brown, a direct and assessing quality in her gaze. She had long brown hair, no makeup. He knew from media reports that she was a large-animal veterinarian. He liked her vibe on the spot, the directness in her gaze, the quiet intelligence and confidence about her.

"I'm just relieved he's using the oxygen machine in our presence," Catherine said. "Until you arrived, Cole, he'd never have agreed to that." Her pretty blue eyes glittered with fierce emotion. "He might even concede to more aggressive treatment now. Dad might actually begin to fight for his life. And if you *are* a bone marrow match, Cole—"

Gabby reached out and touched her sister's arm, tempering her. "One step at a time, Cath. First the DNA test."

From his research Jagger knew that Catherine was the middle Colton daughter. She had long blond hair, looked more like her mother, Mandy. Jethro was truly blessed with beautiful women but they didn't quite match something he saw in Mia. He cast a quick glance in her direction.

She had an impatience in her eyes as she watched them all.

"I'm sorry, I didn't mean to rush anything," Cath said to Jagger. "It's just been such a difficult period. The diagnosis was so sudden, and he's been given so little time to live. If he doesn't accept more aggressive medical treatment he's…" Her voice hitched. She cleared her throat. "But your being here has given him hope. It's given us all hope."

"I might not be Cole," Jagger cautioned, quietly.

"That doesn't matter," Gabby interrupted. "Right now, it's just the possibility that you are Cole that's given him new energy."

And it struck Jagger square in the face. This family needed him to be Cole. They needed to believe he was their long-lost half brother returned, and they were prepared to hold on to this hope in the face of logic until the bitter end, until they were ultimately proven wrong.

No wonder they'd agreed to Drucker's delayed DNA testing.

Jagger wondered about the psychology of it—why a stubborn man like Jethro Colton might not fight his illness until faced with the possibility his son had returned. Could it be subterranean guilt, a sense this illness was his due? And "Cole's" presence had somehow absolved him of that guilt, giving him back the perceived right to fight for his life?

"Gabby's correct," Amanda said. "If Dad believes you're Cole, even for a while, I feel he'll agree to see the specialists. We must use the time we have now to convince him to fight back and fight hard."

"Yes," Cath said. "The truth doesn't really matter right now. All that counts is—" her eyes filled as she turned to Jagger "—is that you could be Cole. And of course," Cath added, "once the DNA tests have been done, you might yet prove to be a potential bone marrow donor. That's why we went on national TV, pleading for information on you in the first place. Perhaps you saw us on television, and that's why you came?"

"I…don't know," Jagger said as a sudden wave of very real dizziness swamped him. "I don't remember." He braced his hand on the back of a wingback chair for support as the room seemed to sway.

Mia cleared her throat and stepped forward quickly. "I think our patient needs some rest now."

The women in the room all turned to look at her as if she'd suddenly materialized out of the paneling—clearly a family used to servants standing silently in background as they lived out their lives.

"Of course," said Amanda. She turned to Jagger. "We're all just getting our heads around this. It's a big shock. And we're so sorry for the incident on our ranch—for your injuries. Whoever did this, the police *will* find him, and they will bring him to justice. In the meantime we'll do whatever we can to help. Anything you need, please, let us know."

Mia took his arm and Jagger was grateful since the dizziness unnerved him.

"Where are you taking him to rest?" Gabby said as the nuts and bolts of the situation began sorting themselves out in everyone's minds.

"To the infirmary. The cot—"

"Don't be ridiculous," said Gabby. "We'll get a suite ready, of course. The Blue Suite on the third floor, in the family wing. It has two bedrooms and a kitchenette. You can take one of the rooms, Mia. You can monitor him from there."

"I…ah…I think I'd prefer to—"

"That way you won't have to come all the way up from the employee wing to check on him. Levi said that you needed to monitor him 24/7 until you're sure there's no hematoma or anything." She pressed the intercom on the phone.

"Mathilda, are you there? It's Gabby."

"Miss Gabby, yes, I'm here." Mathilda's voice came through as clearly as if she was in the room with them.

"Can you please have one of the maids prepare the Blue

Suite for Cole," she said looking at him. "Mia will be staying with him."

Behind Gabby the door to the bedroom opened and Levi came out.

"The morphine has kicked in," he said. "He's relaxed, sleeping now." Levi hesitated. "He also wants someone to call for Max Finch, his estate lawyer. He'd like to see Finch over here first thing in the morning."

"Why?" Amanda said, the worry instant in her eyes. "Does he want to do something to his will? Is he...okay?"

Levi raised his hands, calming them. "Jethro's doing better than expected." He glanced at Jagger. "You've given him a new desire to fight this, you know. He's finally agreed to meet with a specialist."

Cath's hand flew to her mouth. Gabby's eyes went bright with a sudden surge of emotion.

"And no, he didn't say exactly why he wanted Finch," Levi said.

They all turned to look at "Cole" and the atmosphere in the room shifted as the thought hung unspoken between them—Jethro might be changing his will to include his first-born son. Yet no one was certain that this man in front of them was even him.

"Are you still there, Gabriella? Do you need anything else?" Gabby jumped as Mathilda's voice came through the speaker.

"Ah, no, thank you, I didn't realize I still had the speaker on," she said softly, switching it off.

While the relief was tangible that a corner might have been turned with their father's health, uncertainty and an edginess remained.

"Come," Mia whispered, taking Jagger's arm. "Let's get you some rest."

"Oh, Mia, before you go—" It was Levi. "I've arranged

a 10:30 a.m. CAT scan and a consult with Dr. Rajit Singh, a top neurologist at Cheyenne Memorial. Can you take him?"

"I… Of course."

"Jethro said you can use the ranch Escalade. It'll be ready for you in the garage. Keep up with the 24/7 checks in the meantime. Page me if you run into anything."

"Yes, of course." But Jagger heard a sudden strain in Mia's voice.

"Will you be up to dining with us tonight, Cole?" said Catherine.

"No," Mia interjected. "I…I mean—"

"Mia's right," Levi said. "Our patient needs rest, and they have an early start for Cheyenne in the morning."

Gabby came forward and took Jagger's hands in hers. She looked deep into his eyes. "Anything you need, please don't hesitate to ask. We'll see that the kitchenette is stocked, that you have clothes, toiletries, incidentals— whatever you need. There's a list of household extensions next to the phone in the suite, just call. And thank you, for coming. This is so good for everyone, especially after what we've all been thought these last few weeks."

Jagger could almost read the subtext in her clear, green eyes… *Please be our brother, Cole. Please let this wish have come true.*

"The Blue Suite is this way, down at the other end of the hall," Mia said coolly as she led him out. She walked briskly, just ahead of him, as if she was trying to escape him even as she'd been lumped with him—a proximity or intimacy she hadn't asked for.

"The room has a nice view of the ranch," she said over her shoulder.

"You're trying to make conversation, Mia."

She gave a dismissive shrug.

"Look, I'm not interested in a view of the ranch," Jagger said, preferring the view of her tight butt in slim-fitting jeans. He liked the way she walked—long legs, Western boots. He liked the way her braid moved across her back.

She opened the door for him. "Blue Room. All yours."

He hesitated in front of her. "You okay, Mia?"

"I wish you'd stop asking me that. It's my job to monitor *your* well-being, not vice versa."

He met her gaze with a measured look. He could read anxiety, frustration in her eyes. Anger, even— She was a simmering stew of energy right now. Clearly she didn't want to be thrust into his aura like this.

"You can take the big bedroom off that end of the sitting room," she said crisply, leading the way in. "I'll take the small one on the right."

He stepped inside. The suite had a kitchenette, a living room area with a television and a small fireplace. Each bedroom also had an en suite bathroom.

She flung open drapes. "Mathilda will have this sorted out shortly."

"How long did you say you've worked here, Mia?"

"Why?"

"I guess I'm wondering why you stay."

Her eyes widened briefly and a look of guilt flashed through her features.

"You think I'm unhappy here—is that what you're saying?"

He gave a wry smile. "I think you'd rather be somewhere else right now."

She flushed.

"Is it the job, or me?"

"I...I'm sorry, Cole. It's...there's been a lot of weird stuff going on. It's wearing me down. All of us, not just me."

"Yet you continue to stay."

She caught her bottom lip in her teeth.

"They frustrate you, don't they?"

She inhaled deeply. "Yeah, they do. I've been running the infirmary myself for over two years, until now. Jethro put Levi in charge last month. I think it was to ensure he stayed at the ranch, felt needed."

"Must be quite the adjustment," he said. "Suddenly taking orders from someone after being boss for so long."

She gave a half shrug. "He's the doctor. I'm the nurse. That's the way it goes."

"How old is Levi?"

"Twenty-seven. A year younger than I am."

"And he's practicing already?"

"He was doing his first year internship in Salt Lake City when Gabby went to ask him to come—they begged him."

"Because Jethro was ill?"

She nodded. "They're desperate to do whatever it takes to help their father. He's a cantankerous old b—" She stopped herself. "Jethro Colton can be difficult, but they all love him in their own way."

"Codependency," Jagger said. "Makes the world go round.

She went suddenly quiet, and her thumb began to worry her finger again. He followed the movement with his eyes, and she stopped, suddenly aware of what she was doing.

"Levi had to quit his residency to do this. It was a huge sacrifice."

"And possibly a big inheritance payoff in it for him."

"I don't think that's what Levi is about, Cole. And as tough as Jethro can be, he does care for them all deeply in his own way. I've been here long enough to see that. He'd kill for them."

"Would he, really?" Jagger met her eyes.

She frowned. "You're serious."

"Just trying to get my bearings."

"I meant it as a figure of speech," she said. Yet her eyes told Jagger something different.

"What are you not saying, Mia?"

"Look, he's a hard man, there's no doubt about that. There's been talk about him, about how he came by his wealth."

"You mean, as in it's not all legal?"

Her mouth flattened and her eyes darkened again with suspicion.

Be careful, Jagger, you need her trust.

"He's my boss, Cole. And I'm speaking out of line." She made for the door. "I need to go get my medical bag and some clothes. You should lie down, watch TV or something."

"Mia." He caught her arm.

She spun round, startled. He looked down into her eyes.

"What's really eating you? Because something is."

"You don't know me, Cole."

"I might have no memory, but I'm not blind."

She moistened her lips, swallowed. "You better let go of me."

He did, instantly.

She marched to the door and Jagger thought he'd blown it already.

But she spun around suddenly and glared at him. "Okay, you really want to know what's getting up my nose? It's always about them!" She waved her hand in the direction of Jethro's room. "But you're the victim here—*you* need to know your identity as soon as possible, and a DNA test would help. Yet the family is content to drag this out Chief Drucker's way, because it *suits* them. Finding their long-lost half brother might help their father fight his illness, but what about Cole? You? What about justice and finding the kidnappers who took you? Finding out where you've been?" She heaved out a breath.

"It's mercenary. Sometimes it just gets to me—the wealth. The way people are used." She flushed, then ran her hand over her hair. "I...I shouldn't have said that—any of that."

He stared at her.

And right there, Jagger McKnight got Mia. Wholly. He understood her compassion and her fire, her need to stand up for the underdog—because it was the same motivation that defined *him*. His need to be a voice for the disenfranchised was the driving principle behind his journalism. It's what pushed him into extreme and dangerous situations in foreign countries.

It's what had taken him into Afghanistan.

It's also what had cost him.

"This should really be about Cole," she said quietly. "If you're not Cole, it should still remain about Cole, baby Cole, even if he's no longer alive, because the crime was never solved. There was no justice done. And justice needs to be done."

Jagger's heartbeat quickened. He had an ally in Mia Sanders. Even though she might resent being thrust into close proximity with him like this, they had a common goal—justice for baby Cole who'd been snatched from the safety of his crib.

Like Jagger had been snatched away from his own parents.

Mia's comments also told Jagger that she thought there might be more to the kidnapping than was being spoken about in this family.

She made for the door again.

"Mia—" He took her arm again, gently, and turned her to face him. Up close, the stormy light coming in from the windows made her eyes seem purplish. Moody. Beautiful. Her chest was rising and falling and he could see her pulse in the creamy column of her neck.

"Thank you. For thinking of me—of Cole."

"I…I need to go get my things." Her voice was husky.

Overpowered by a sudden urge to kiss her, to hold her against his body, Jagger released her arm slowly and stepped back

She didn't move. She seemed trapped by the dark hunger he knew she could see burning in his eyes. Her breathing grew lighter. And it just fueled the heat building inside Jagger.

Wind lashed against the house suddenly, and rain began to tick against the windowpanes. It seemed to jerk her back to reality.

She backed toward the door, turned quickly.

"You don't have to do this, Mia."

"It's my job. Either I do it, or I leave and find something else." And she went out, closing the door.

Jagger stared at the door.

The room seemed drained of energy, as if she'd taken it all with her. He ran his hand through his hair. Christ. What just happened here between her and him?

Did he dare take it anywhere?

He went to the window. A sharp crack of lighting made him tense. Thunder rumbled shortly after. And rain hammered, slanting in wind.

Guilt stirred deeper into Jagger. She wasn't like any of the other women he'd been with after Melinda.

He didn't like deceiving her. She deserved honesty.

And Jagger's instincts told him that she'd been hurt. In

a relationship. A serious one, given the way she fiddled with that wedding-ring finger.

He had no intention of hurting her further. He snorted softly to himself. This was a double bind he'd not expected.

Chapter 6

"They're putting him in the family wing, in his own suite. Security will be more complicated now. And that nurse is going to be like a damn bodyguard stuck permanently to his side."

"If she's in the way, we'll have to get rid of her, too."

"She's taking him to Cheyenne tomorrow for a 10:30 a.m. appointment at the hospital. That's your best opportunity. And make it look like an accident this time or you're just going to bring the heat down tenfold."

Several beats of silence.

"What if it *is* him. I mean, it could be th—?"

"It's not Cole. Understand this—that man is *not* Cole Colton."

Another stretch of silence. "And you know this for sure?"

"Yes, dammit, I know it."

"How?"

"I told you, that's not for you to worry about. Just finish the job, and you'll get your share."

"If you know that he's not Cole, do you know where the real Cole is? Is he still alive?"

The phone went dead.

Thunder rumbled and he cursed under his breath as he pocketed the phone.

Mia made her way quickly down the passage, her footfalls quiet. Once around the corner, she sucked air in deep and leaned back against the wall, gathering herself. What had just happened back there? Her stomach was trembling inside. Her skin felt hot. His aura was like a dark sexual magnet that re-arranged every molecule in her body and sucked her insidiously toward him.

She'd almost kissed him. If he hadn't pulled back when he did…

Mia scrubbed her hands over her face.

She couldn't afford to make a mistake like Brad again. And this man was an unknown, a total mystery. If he wasn't Cole, he could be dangerous. He could be anybody. He might even have loved ones waiting for him, worrying about him.

And if he did turn out to be Cole…Mia didn't want anything personal to do with the Colton family. This ranch was a job, that was all. And even that she was re-thinking.

Dammit, why was she taking her mind down this road? She pushed off the wall and hurried down the stairs. But even as she rushed down to the employee wing where the infirmary was housed, Mia felt trapped. She'd been instructed to sleep in his suite tonight, to take him on a road trip tomorrow. A soft panic rose inside her. She was scared of her own feelings reawakening like this, and what it might mean. Mia couldn't do sex with no strings. Once involved in a physical relationship her heart got entangled as much as her body did.

She blew out a breath of air. Get tonight over with, take him to Cheyenne tomorrow. Then, once the neurologist told them what they were dealing with, Levi could take it from there. After tomorrow "Cole" wasn't going to need her help 24/7.

She'd be clear.

As Mia made her way along the passage of the employee wing, thunder cracked outside and rumbled away into the foothills. Lights flickered down the hallway.

Another bolt of thunder exploded right overheard. The lights went out.

Mia stilled—the pitch blackness was sudden and complete. She groped for the wall and began feeling her way along the passage, wondering when—or if—the backup generator might kick in. She had an emergency flashlight in her room, and that's what she aimed for.

Outside thunder rumbled again. The lights flickered on then off again. Mia froze. In that brief moment of light she thought she'd seen someone. A man. Tall. Like a freeze frame, then gone.

Her heart banged against her rib cage as memories of Jenny Burke's murder in the pantry flashed through her mind, of Agnes being attacked in the barn, of Faye being shot upstairs.

Suddenly the lights went on. A man's shadow loomed to her side. Mia swung round and screamed as a hand clamped down over her mouth from behind, stifling the sound in her throat. She choked, trying to cough. She could taste salt, sweat on his skin. His body was hard. Male. Big.

Fear rose thick and instant in her throat.

"Shhh," he whispered into her ear. "Don't be afraid. Just no noise, please, and I'll let you go. Got it?"

Mia nodded, eyes burning.

Slowly the man released his hand from her mouth. She spun round and gasped.

"Trip? What…what the *hell!*"

He raised his finger to his lips. "No noise, remember?"

She lowered her voice to an angry whisper. "What the hell are you doing down here in the female staff wing!"

He was holding a duffel bag in one hand. He used the other to quickly tuck his shirttail back into his jeans.

"Oh," Mia said. "Dumb question, right?"

"I came from upstairs—thought I heard banging down here."

She pulled a face. "Yeah, right."

"And you didn't see me." He gave her a seductive wink and chucked her under the chin.

Mia gritted her teeth as he left, wondering what maid's door he'd really come out of this time, and who on earth was stupid enough to sleep with Trip Colton, Jethro's womanizing stepson who still, oddly, lived in part of the house with his mother and sister.

After gathering her medical bag, some toiletries, a nightgown, a change of clothing and her laptop, Mia went back upstairs to attend to her patient.

When she entered the sitting room the lights were out, everything quiet. But the warm glow of a small lamp emanated from the door of Cole's bedroom, which was ajar.

"Cole?" she called gently.

No reply. One of the maids had been here and put fresh flowers and a bowl of fruit on the kitchen counter.

Mia went into her own bedroom and set her gear on the bed. Taking the medical bag, she went quietly to his room. She edged the door open. "Cole?" she whispered.

He was fast asleep, his bare chest partially covered by

a white sheet that set off his tan. He'd showered—his hair was damp and the room filled with the scents of soap and shampoo that had been provided in the bathroom en suite.

Mia saw that he'd removed the bandage on his temple, presumably because it had gotten wet. The stitches were dark. Bruising had started.

She stilled, just watching for a moment. He was gorgeous in the rugged, man's-man kind of way she liked. Her gaze went to the tattoo on his chest. Again she wondered about his history, the nightmares that seemed to haunt him—things he couldn't remember when conscious.

She could just let him sleep. Or wake him to put another dressing on. But airing the sutures was good, too. She set her bag down and went to his bedside, sitting softly on the edge of the bed, reaching for his pulse.

He moved, murmured as her skin touched his, but his breathing soon became deep and regular again, which was a good sign.

His pulse was also fine.

She pulled the sheet up over him, clicked off the light and tiptoed out to her own room thinking about a soothing soak in the tub and sleep.

After she'd eaten and bathed, Mia laid her clothes neatly out on a chair, ready for an early start on the road tomorrow. She set her alarm to wake her in two hours when she'd check that her patient hadn't lapsed into a coma again.

Outside, rain lashed against the windows and wind whistled through the mansion eaves. In the distance thunder rumbled softly as the storm moved down the valley. Snow would be thick on the distant peaks tomorrow, she thought, as she clicked off her bedside lamp and tried to get comfortable in the foreign bed.

She drifted into a fitful sleep and then into a hot dream where she was twisting and tangling in sheets with Cole,

naked. Then he suddenly became Brad, and she was straddling him, her thighs opening wide as she sank down onto
the hot, hard length of him. Mia threw her head back in
ecstasy as she rocked her pelvis against his, her arousal
almost painful, her muscles screaming for release.... Then
suddenly, a scream cut the night. Raw, as if from her own
throat.

She woke. Shocked. Confused. Heart hammering.

The scream came again.

Him!

She lurched from her bed, stumbling through the dark
as she found her way into his room. She clicked on his
lamp.

He was writhing in his sheets, wet with perspiration,
his face twisted in unspeakable agony, fists clenched. Suddenly he stilled, and another moan came from deep in his
throat, unearthly, as he balled the sheet in his fists and
arched his spine. The sound, the sight of him like this,
chilled her to the bone and the hairs down the nape of her
neck rose.

"Cole!" she said, grasping his shoulders, trying to shake
him awake.

He hit at her, and Mia lurched back then grabbed his
arm. "Cole! Wake up! It's me—Mia!"

His body stilled. Behind his closed lids his eyes were
moving rapidly, as if in a dream. He had tears down his
face, leaking out his lids. Emotion ripped through Mia's
chest. In a secret place, in his dreams, this mystery man
was haunted by something terrible and unspeakably painful. She thought of the scar under his hairline, the vicious
and twisted scar up the inside of his thigh. What had happened to him?

"Cole—" she whispered, placing her hand on his forehead, smoothing the damp hair back from his brow. "It's all right. You're safe with me."

His eyes fluttered open. Horror—she saw sheer horror in his eyes.

Mia cupped the side of his jaw, forcing him to focus on her. "Cole, it's me, Mia."

Slowly his dilated pupils shrank.

"Mia?" He sounded confused. He glanced around the room, swallowing. He pulled himself up into a sitting position, breathing hard, the sheet falling down to his waist. His skin was slick with perspiration. He caught her gaze, and embarrassment flashed through his features.

She sat beside him. "It's okay. What's going on Cole? Tell me what you were dreaming."

His smoky eyes turned dark and tormented again. "I don't know. I...must have had a nightmare."

For a fleeting moment Mia had the odd sense he was lying.

She took his temperature and checked his pulse again. Then she put a clean dressing on his brow.

"You can't remember your dream?" she said quietly.

"No."

"Was it about the attack last night or something from before?"

"I don't know, Mia."

She still felt he was lying, although she couldn't pinpoint why. "If you tell me, it might give us a clue about your past, about who you are."

He looked away, something raw in his profile.

Mia felt shaken herself. Right to the core. She'd heard people scream in that way—once, it was a woman trapped in a car in a highway accident. Another time it was a man who'd lost his wife and son in a house fire. He'd dropped to his knees as the firefighters held him back, and he screamed as he watched the flames devouring his house, his home, his family. It was not a sound easily cataloged in the human brain. It was something primal. Whoever this guy was, Mia felt in her heart that he was not here to scam Jethro Colton out of some inheritance. Her instinct told her that he'd come to Dead River for something more basic.

But she didn't feel he was being completely open, either—and as that whispering suspicion unfurled inside her, she wondered what he could be hiding. Or what was trapped in his lost memory.

"Do you want something to eat, Cole?" she asked quietly. "Or some tea, maybe?"

He shook his head.

Mia wanted morning to come fast, now, so she could get him to hospital and have the CAT scan done. She needed to know what was going on inside this man's head and if it was dangerous. Reaching for his hand, she took it in hers and just held on.

His gaze lowered slowly to her hand, then he looked back up into her eyes. And she felt it—a need—something very different from the earlier sexual desire she'd seen in his eyes.

Mia was a sucker for a person in need of help. She was a born healer. It's why she'd become a nurse.

Cole turned his hand palm-up under hers, lacing his fingers together with hers, drawing her gently down onto the bed beside him, wrapping his arms around her. Before she even knew what she was doing, Mia had turned her face to his and her lips met his. Light as a feather.

He stiffened for a nanosecond, then moved his lips hungrily against hers, his hand threading up into her hair as he drew her hard against his body. His lips were salty, strong. He parted her lips and Mia opened her mouth, entering the kiss wholly, blindly, swept by a poignancy and sensuality she'd never experienced. She felt the desperate need of his hunger and her nipples turned hard as he gathered her so tightly against himself she thought she wouldn't be able to breathe. Then Mia pulled back, almost a little afraid now.

"Cole?" she whispered.

"Shhh," he said. "Don't talk, just lie here with me." He closed his eyes, spooning her tightly into the curve of his body. And he fell into a deep, calm sleep. As if he hadn't slept in months. Years.

Mia lay quietly, his body warm and deliciously male around hers. And her fear grew.

Because she was falling, being sucked down into something she didn't quite understand, with a man who had no name, no past. No history that he could speak of.

Jagger was roused from deep sleep by a faint beeping. Confused, he opened his eyes. Morning had dawned with yellow light streaming in through the windows. As he came fully awake he realized it was an alarm that was beeping softly in the next room.

Mia was still in his arms, sleeping. Warm. His forearm rested against her breasts. Jagger's pulse quickened as desire stirred hot and low in his gut. He breathed in the scent of her hair splayed on his pillow, golden under the rays of dawn reaching the bed,

It struck him suddenly—that thought he'd had in the diner about sunshine, fresh mornings, sunny smiles, the scent of clean laundry. It was all here, wrapped in his arms. Mia. Like a rare and precious thing that was going to slip through his fingers as soon as she woke.

She'd stayed with him the whole night. She didn't know who in hell he was, but compassion, the healer in this nurse, had kept her at his side, in his bed. And for the first time in over a year, Jagger had slept through the rest of the night like a baby. No more nightmares. No flashbacks. And because of it he felt clear-headed. Sharp. Full of energy. Even the dull pain in his temple, the constant ache in his thigh bone and the scarred muscles where the bayonet had ripped through his flesh, were somewhat eased.

Affection, feelings he couldn't even articulate, blossomed through his chest as Mia stirred in his arms. Her mouth was slightly open as she breathed. Her lashes were soft against her cheeks.

Jagger thought of kissing her again, and heat sharpened in his groin. He thought of turning her over, making love to her, giving in to this woman, and that thought began to consume him with a blinding fire. But he held back.

There was something sacrosanct about Mia, something that couldn't be taken lightly.

He'd been using sex, alcohol, sleeping pills to blunt his flashbacks, to escape the memories. He'd felt no emotion when he slept with women after returning from Afghanistan. But this was different.

For more than a year he'd been running from something he'd learned only recently he'd never be able to outrun. That's why he was here—to find a way to claw back a semblance of life. Work. But now, in her arms, he felt off-kilter. Confused. As if something had brought him here, to this place. To her. For deeper reasons.

Christ, he was being ridiculous.

Slowly, he extricated himself from the bed. Grabbing his jeans and shirt, Jagger tiptoed through the sitting room into the other bedroom where the alarm was bleating softly. He switched it off. On a chair near the bed, Mia had neatly piled her clothes for the day. A slim laptop rested on the desk next to her purse.

Jagger stilled. A real person, a woman with feelings. She was helping him and he was lying to her. He eyed her laptop. He could use it while she slept to access his files which he'd stored in a secure, password-protected online database.

But it felt wrong. Conflicted, Jagger dragged his hand through his hair.

Go back to the basics—this is about a story. About finding justice for a small boy probably long dead.

About finding the truth of what had happened all those years ago.

Truth. And here he was, lying to get it—a little Faustian bargain of his own. Nothing was ever simply black and white, always infinite shades of gray.

One step at a time, he told himself. First thing was going for the CAT scan. He had to follow that through to maintain his cover. The appointment was at 10:30 a.m. Cheyenne was about forty miles out. They'd need to get moving soon.

He padded barefoot to the little kitchenette, filled the coffeemaker with water and opened the fridge.

Mia woke to the scent of fresh coffee, eggs, bacon and toast. Her stomach grumbled—she felt starved. She rolled over in bed, then sat up with a violent shock.

She was in his bed.

Morning sun streamed into the room. Outside, the sky was bluebird clear, the storm had blown through. Images from the night, the sounds of rain and thunder, her sensual dream jumbled through Mia's head as she tried to sort fact from fantasy, terrified for a moment it had been real, that she'd had sex with Cole. She looked down at her body. She was in her nightshirt. It had been a dream. She'd heard him scream and come to him.

She got up, peered around the door.

"Morning." He smiled, teeth stark-white against his tan,

blue eyes sparkling, that dimple showing. He was wearing Dylan's jeans, slung low on his hips. No shirt. And there was no hint in his easy smile, in his twinkling eyes, of the psychological terrors that had haunted him during the night. But Mia knew they were buried in there, possibly hidden from consciousness by his amnesia.

She stepped into the living room, unsure what to say, whether to broach last night at all.

"Coffee?" he said, holding up the pot.

"God, yes, thank you." Her eyes flashed to her open bedroom door, her clothes on the chair.

"I'll be right back."

Mia grabbed her pile of clothes and inside the en suite bathroom she rinsed her face, put on jeans and a fresh shirt. She looked into the mirror and decided, for the first time in a long, long while, to leave her hair loose. She didn't want to think about what that meant.

She went into the kitchenette, pulled a bar stool up to the counter. He set a mug of steaming, freshly brewed coffee in front of her.

She spooned sugar in. "You look good this morning," she said. "I mean—" *Damn.* "I mean, as in, you look like you're doing much better." Her cheeks heated as the memory of their kiss surged through her.

His sparkling eyes caught hers and he grinned again. Hot damn, that smile did her in. But a darker look had also entered his eyes—a warning, to not mention last night.

"I like your hair loose," he said.

He was sidestepping.

She reached for coffee mug with both hands, needing to steady herself. She took a deep sip.

"Cole—about last night—"

His grin faded and she saw the ghost of whatever haunted him cross his features, resurfacing. He reached for his own mug and the movement flexed the inked wings of the tattoo on his pec.

"Look, Mia. I—"

Her pager beeped on her belt.

"Hang on a sec—it's my emergency pager."

She read the name on the tiny screen. "Gray Stark," she said. "The ranch foreman. I need to call him."

Mia used the suite phone to dial Gray's cell. He told her there'd been a dust-up between two employees in the stable. One of them needed medical attention.

Mia smoothed her hand over her hair and glanced at her watch, then at Cole, who was watching her in a way that was so complete it unnerved her.

"I'll be right there," she told Gray.

She hung up and turned to Cole. "I'm needed in the stables. There's been a fight between two of the ranch hands. I don't think it sounds serious, but it's protocol that I respond so Gray can fill out any paperwork that's needed." She made for her room to fetch her things.

"We should still be able to leave on time for Cheyenne, but I'm going to have to skip that breakfast. I'll come back and pick you up."

He set his mug down. "I'll come with you. We can leave for Cheyenne from the stables once you're done."

"No really, it's fine. Finish your breakfast."

He laughed, making for his own room. "I already did. That's yours that you're going to be missing."

She stared at his back, the way his muscles moved under smooth, tanned skin. Mia felt hot. She pressed her hand to her stomach and inhaled deeply. There was so much happening so quickly between them that it didn't quite seem real.

He called from his room, "I can't just sit in here and wait for my memory to return, Mia. I need to move. I need to see my environment. It might help me recall why I came here in the first place."

Mia shrugged into her down jacket. It would be cold out this morning. She pulled her hair back into a ponytail and grabbed her purse. She left her medical bag—there was a first-aid station in the stables. As she came out of the room, Mia caught her breath.

Cole stood in the doorway dressed in a crisp, white, Western shirt, dark-blue denim jeans, cowboy boots and a belt with a buckle she recognized as Dylan's. In his hand he held a down jacket and a cowboy hat.

"That maid, Misty, left a bunch of clothes in the closet," he said, holding out his arms. "Do I look the part?"

Mia cleared her throat. "They fit."

She turned around and grabbed the Escalade keys from the counter, shaken by how much she was attracted to the look of this man. A stranger.

They crossed the gravel driveway, making for the stables.

The morning was beautiful, mist rising from the fields, cattle moving in distant pastures. The clouds had lifted to reveal a white blanket of snow on the distant mountains. Mia walked with long strides, her Western boots crunching on the gravel, her ponytail swinging briskly across her back. Her blue jacket brought out the color of her eyes and the bite of autumn put pink into her cheeks. Jagger thought she was the most beautiful thing he'd seen in a long time.

Yellow cottonwoods and aspens rustled in the slight breeze, and crisp, dry leaves clattered across the ground in small gusts. As they neared the stables the scent of the horses and manure was strong. But it was earthy, grounding. Real. After his sleep, Jagger felt better about the world than he had in months. He owed it to Mia.

As humiliating as it might be, having the tactile comfort of this beautiful woman during the night had both aroused and settled something in him. He had an uncomfortable feeling Mia Sanders was going to be like a drug to him. Jagger didn't want that. He no longer wanted to numb things by drugging himself. But this sensation of reawakening was so fragile, so addictive, it scared him.

As they passed a stand of cottonwoods he saw a ranch hand working a horse on a longe rope. The man waved at them.

"That's Dylan Frick—horse whisperer extraordinaire," Mia said as she returned the wave. "They're his clothes that you've been wearing. It was his mother who was murdered eight weeks ago." She paused as she watched him briefly. "He's not allowing himself to rest," she said quietly.

Jagger was, of course, aware of Faye Frick's murder, but he wanted to know more about her son and their circumstances here.

"Both he and his mother worked here?"

"Faye was a single mom. She started working as the ranch governess when Dylan was still a toddler. She always had a way with children." Mia walked on in silence for a moment. When she spoke again, her voice was thick. "It really shook everyone up. All the staff loved Faye. We all care deeply about Dylan."

"Was Faye here when Cole was kidnapped thirty years ago?"

She looked up. The sun caught her eyes. "Why do you ask?"

"I'm just trying to picture how things pieced together back then. Maybe it'll bring something back about why I came here—or how."

"I think Faye and Dylan arrived about a year after the kidnapping, just after Dylan's first birthday."

Jagger would have liked to have stayed to watch Dylan work with the gelding. It was poetry in motion—the soft thumping of hooves as the horse went around the ring, tail held high, hot breath misting into white clouds, the wrangler in the middle.

They rounded the stable building and both Jagger and Mia stalled briefly at sight of a police car.

"Cops are here," she said as she moved faster. "Must be serious. Gray must have called them."

They entered the stables. This was a high-end business, Jagger thought as he hurried after Mia down the aisle between the stalls. At the end of the row of stalls, near a big barn door, sitting on a tack box outside what appeared to be some kind of office was a tall, dark-haired ranch hand cradling his left arm, his face white with pain. As Jagger neared, he saw the man's lip had been split and there was blood on his shirt.

Beside the man stood two cowboys; one had also been roughed up. His shirt was ripped and he was holding his jaw. A female cop was taking notes.

"That's Jared Hansen sitting on the box," Mia explained quickly as they neared. "And that's Trip Colton holding his jaw. The man next to Trip is Gray Stark, ranch foreman. And that's Officer Karen Locke talking to Gray."

From his research, Jagger knew who Trip Colton was. Trip had lived in one wing of the Colton mansion with his mother, Darla, and his sister, Tawny, ever since Jethro had divorced Darla. What Jagger wanted to know was *why* they continued to live here. Was it wealthy eccentricity? Or was there a deeper reason Jethro kept Darla and her two kids from a previous marriage on?

"Thank you for coming, Mia," Gray Stark said as they approached. "You know officer Locke?"

The brown-haired cop nodded a curt greeting.

"What happened?" Mia said.

"These two had a tussle over some property." Gray did not look amused. "I put the first-aid kit over there next to Hansen. I think he's broken his arm. We'll probably have to send him off for X-rays, but if you could give 'em both the once-over for the records."

As Mia began to examine Hansen's arm, the brown-haired cop's eyes went straight to Jagger. He gave her a nod.

"You our John Doe?" she said.

"Apparently."

Her brown eyes held his for a few beats.

"You seen that bag before?" She pointed.

And Jagger's heart stalled. Besides the tack box upon which Hansen sat, resting on the stable floor, was his duffel bag. Empty. His gaze shot back to the cop.

"Gray Stark says these guys were fighting over it," she said. "It looks like the duffel that people saw you leaving Dead River with the other night."

Jagger's pulse raced as he met first Jared Hansen's eyes, then Trip Colton's. Both gazes were cool, hostile. Had one of these men taken his laptop, ID, wallet, phone?

Had they tried to access his password-protected phone? His computer?

Had one of them tried to kill him?

Chapter 7

"Is that your bag?" Officer Locke prompted.

Jagger kept his features guarded but his pulse raced as the brown-haired cop continued to watch him intently. If they'd gotten into his phone, they might be able to figure out who he was. He wasn't that worried about his laptop—he used it merely to access an online database where he kept all his notes and files under secure password protection.

"I don't know," Jagger said carefully.

"You sure?"

Mia glanced up sharply.

"I can't remember," he said.

Karen Locke said, "You were seen leaving the Dead River Diner carrying a kit bag exactly like that one."

"I was?" He made a move to reach for it.

"Whoa! Please, don't touch," Officer Locke said, stepping in front of it. "I'm going to have to take that in. No one touches it."

"I told you, we weren't fighting over any damn bag," Trip growled, holding his jaw.

"Is that so," Officer Locke said. She turned to Jared Hansen. "That your story, too?"

Hansen grunted, then winced sharply as Mia palpated his arm.

"Feels like you've fractured your radius," Mia said.

"Like I told you," Trip grumbled, "Hansen made a move on Lucy Elton at the Joe Bear's Bar the other night. I just found out—that's all this was."

"And you're dating Lucy Elton, so she's off-limits to Hansen?" Officer Locke said.

"Damn right she's off-limits."

The officer scribbled something in her notes and closed her book. "So where'd the bag come from, then?"

"Found it in the ravine this morning, while I was out riding," Trip said. "I was returning my horse to his stall and was going to call it in to the Dead P.D., because it matched the description. Then Hansen shows up and we got into it over Lucy."

Silence hung for a moment. A horse whinnied down in the stalls. The scent of hay was warm and sweet in the cool morning air. Hansen stared at the ground, jaw tight against pain as Mia strapped on a makeshift splint.

"Is that so," said Officer Locke again. "Because Mr. Stark here said he saw you two fighting over that bag. Hansen was claiming it was his, saying that you stole it from his room."

Mia glanced up sharply, a frown crossing her brow as she narrowed her gaze on Trip.

Jagger caught the odd and sudden look in her eyes.

Trip shrugged. "I don't know what he's talking about. I was going to bring it in to the police, like I said."

Hansen's gaze ticked up to meet Trip's. Their boss was

watching them both. Tension tightened across Jagger's chest. One of these guys, or all of them, knew something and was lying about his bag.

Mia stood up, dusted off her pants. "There's nothing an X-ray and a cast won't fix," she said of Hansen. "You might want to try some ice on your way to the clinic. Want me to look at that jaw, Trip?"

Trip had a dangerous look in his eyes when he met Mia's gaze. As if he was warning her back. His attention flicked briefly down to the bag, then returned to meet Mia's again. She swallowed. The exchange was subtle, but there.

Jagger felt a hot protectiveness rising in his chest. He moved a little closer to Mia.

"My jaw's fine."

"Put some ice on it," she said brusquely, then checked her watch. "We need to leave for a medical appointment in Cheyenne. Gray, are you okay to take things over from here?"

"Go—we're good. Thank you, Mia."

"Officer Locke," Mia said, nodding toward the cop. But then she hesitated, turned to Jagger. "I just want to go into the office and grab my fishing gear that I left here after I found you."

She disappeared into the office.

All the men turned to watch her. Mia was an attractive woman. Heat rode into Jagger's chest, and it struck him—he wanted her. He wanted her to be his.

She came out with an antique-looking wicker creel and a case for fly rods, a fishing vest tucked under her arm. "Okay, let's go."

They moved at a brisk pace through the stalls. Jagger could smell the leather of the saddles hanging alongside bridles on hooks outside the individual stalls. Two grooms were mucking out empty ones.

"Fishing gear?" he said, matching her stride.

"I was going fishing when I found you," she said. "I left my stuff here after bringing my horse, Sunny, back, so I could help Levi attend to you."

He looked at the creel and vest. "Fly fishing?"

She nodded.

"Alone, on horseback?"

"Rivers are best enjoyed alone and a horse is an ideal way to access places you can't by vehicle."

Inside he smiled. Hot damn—the more he learned about Mia Sanders the more she appealed.

"Where'd you learn to fish, Mia?"

"My dad. Since I was little. He was big into the outdoors."

Was. Jagger noted the past tense, but didn't push. For now. He was more interested in finding out about her silent exchange with Trip Colton.

"What was that look about, between you and Trip?"

"I ran into Trip in the employee wing last night when I went to get my things." She slowed her pace a little, frowning. "I could have sworn he was carrying that same bag."

Jagger's pulse kicked. "And it was empty?"

She pursed her lips. "I...don't know. I can't be sure. The lights had just gone out and he'd spooked me so I was unfocused. I was on the female staff floor and—I thought Trip had come out of one of the maid's rooms. But he told me he'd come down from the men's floor." She glanced up. "Jared Hansen has a room there."

"So you think what Gray Stark said he heard could've been true—that Trip had taken the bag from Hansen's room?"

"I suppose. You sure you don't recognize it, Cole?"

Jagger glanced away. He had to find a way to let Mia in

on what he was doing, but he also didn't want her to blow his cover just yet. "No," he said quietly.

As they passed the next stall a massive black stallion inside reared back its head and snorted. Ice shot instantly through Jagger's veins and he froze in his tracks. The stallion had a jagged white streak emblazoned across his chest. It pawed the ground, irritated.

The chill in his veins spread slowly through Jagger's body.

"Mia." His voice came out low, hoarse. "Who does that horse belong to?"

Surprise crossed her features as she stopped beside him. "Why?"

"I…I'm not sure."

"That's Midnight," she said. "He's Jethro's horse. A real handful—like bottled rocket fuel and just as skittish. The last time Jethro rode Midnight he wasn't well and the horse threw him then almost trampled him. Levi saved Jethro that day. It was a turning point in their relationship."

"Who rides him now?"

"Dylan. Midnight is putty in his hands. He's one of the few who can actually handle the horse. You should see them together, it's incredible. Like a man riding the wind."

Jagger thought of the thudding hooves in the dark, the control of the rider aiming at him with a hunting light on his head.

"Are you remembering something, Cole?" she said, watching his face keenly

"I…" He put his hand to the bandage, then swore softly. "I don't know, Mia. You said you thought the gash on my temple might've been caused by a shod hoof, and that there were hoof prints all around me."

"What—? You think it was *Midnight?* Why would you think it was him?"

"That white streak on his chest. I think I remember seeing it with my flashlight."

"That's hardly possible…" Her voice faded as her gaze went to Midnight's hooves. "Dylan's the only one who rides him."

The horse stomped and sniffed, lifting and dropping his head as he regarded them warily with a shining black eye through thickly-fringed lashes.

Worry darkened Mia's gaze. "We can ask Dylan on our way out," she said, very quietly. "Maybe someone else has been working Midnight because Dylan sure as hell didn't attack you."

"What makes you so certain?"

"I know him. He's a good guy. And he's grieving. He's just lost his mother, remember." She glanced up at him. "You sure about that white streak?"

"It stopped me dead in my tracks when I passed his stall. I feel that I've seen that horse before."

As they exited the stable doors, a gust of autumn wind caught her ponytail, and she said, "On our way back from Cheyenne I'll take you the past the field where I found you. Maybe it'll trigger another memory."

Jagger nodded. He was anxious to see the site for other reasons, but he imagined the cops had given the area a thorough once-over and probably trampled their boots all over any prints while they were at it.

Mia went up to the paddock fence and called Dylan over. The man coaxed his horse in, untethered the lunge rope and wound it into a loop as he strode toward them. He was tall with dark-brown hair, and he had a long, easy cowboy stride. He pushed his hat slightly back on his head as he reached them.

"Mia," he said, and there was warmth in his voice. His gaze ticked toward Jagger.

"Dylan, this is—"

"Cole," Dylan said as he appraised Jagger with suspicious eyes. "I heard about you."

"I'm sorry for your loss," Jagger said. "I heard about your mother."

The wrangler gave a curt nod, features tight.

"Dylan, I need to get Cole to a medical appointment in Cheyenne, but we have a quick question—did anyone ride Midnight the night before last?"

"I did, why?"

"What time?"

"Early evening. Why are you asking, Mia?"

Mia said, gently, "Cole might have been injured by someone who tried to run him down with a black horse that had a white streak on its chest."

"You're saying *Midnight* ran him down?" His words were clipped now, his eyes angry.

"We don't know what happened, Dylan. It could've been an accident," she offered.

"Jesus, Mia," Dylan said, eyes narrowing sharply. "No one rides Midnight in the goddamn dark! Mere shadows spook the hell out of that horse, especially since the accident with Jethro. Riding him in the dark could be lethal."

It almost was.

Dylan glowered at Jagger as he spoke. "I heard you had no memory, yet you think you remember a horse with a white streak?"

"Dylan, I'm sorry," Mia interjected gently. "We just passed Midnight in his stall and Cole thought he might have seen the horse before."

"So you jump to the idea that this was the horse that tried to run you down?"

"It was the size and the white streak on his chest," Jagger said coolly, watching Dylan's eyes.

"Is that all, Mia?" Dylan said, still holding Jagger's gaze.

"Thanks, Dylan. If…" She hesitated. "If you hear that anyone took him out—"

"Then I'll speak to the cops." He turned and strode back toward his horse.

Mia exhaled heavily. "That didn't go down well."

She spun round and headed toward an outbuilding that Jagger presumed was the ranch garage. He kept pace with her across the gravel.

"Is it possible that Dylan rode Midnight in the dark, that he could've tried to run me over?"

"I don't know what's possible anymore!" she snapped. "I like Dylan. He's been good to me here. I don't believe he'd do anything like that. I mean, why *would* he?"

"Accident? Afraid to own up?" Jagger gave her leeway to consider options.

"And then he took your gear, wallet, gun? *That* was no accident. Besides, it's not in his character."

"People can surprise us."

"Yeah," she said crisply. "They sure can."

She entered the garage. Several vehicles were parked inside. She made for a gleaming black Cadillac Escalade as she fished keys out her pocket.

"Let me drive," he said.

"You're kidding, right? You're the one whose been bashed on the head and can't remember a thing." She beeped the lock. "Apart from a white streak, that is."

Jagger climbed into the passenger seat, uneasy. He was rousing her suspicions and making her unhappy by implicating someone she liked. Her allegiances clearly came down on the side of Dylan Frick. This was one reason to keep his cover, for now. Jagger felt she'd tell Dylan.

As they drove down a half-mile-long avenue toward an

ornate brass gate that denoted the entrance to Dead River Ranch, the estate gates began to swing slowly open. A dark Lincoln turned into the avenue.

"That'll be Maximilian Finch, Jethro's lawyer."

"The one he called for yesterday?"

Mia nodded, mouth tight.

Jagger turned to watch as the vehicle passed. A uniformed chauffeur sat in front, but the rear windows were tinted. He wondered if Max Finch might be more than just an estate lawyer. He made a mental note to look the guy up as soon as he got his hands on a computer.

Jagger had also noticed the look in the Colton siblings' eyes when they heard that their father had summoned Finch. Any one of them might be worried that the reappearance of Cole might prompt Jethro to write his first-born son into his will. Was that motive enough for attempted murder?

Fields fell away on either side of the road as they drove toward the Laramie foothills. In the distance the mountains were pristine with snow. Jagger checked his watch, then remembered it wasn't there. He wondered how much time he had before Drucker closed in on his ID.

After several miles in the purring Escalade, the road began to twist and turn as they climbed out of the valley. "It's beautiful here," he said, breaking the silence.

Mia cast him a glance. "I thought we'd take this route seeing as we'll be returning on the road through Dead. That way we'll pass through the field where I found you."

She was silent for several more twists and turns in the road.

"Mia," Jagger said, "I'm sorry about what happened with Dylan back there."

She inhaled deeply, then said, "I just don't want to believe anything bad about him. Or anyone on the ranch. It's so hard, you know, to think someone you work with, or like, might be responsible for something so heinous."

"Yes."

"I'm sorry, too, for what I said yesterday about the Colton siblings being mercenary. About them wanting to save their father over finding the truth about your identity."

"What do you mean?"

"It's love. And love is mercenary no matter how you look at it—people will protect what they care about, sometimes at the expense of others." She paused as she took the Escalade around a steep curve. "I'd probably do exactly the same if it was my father. Or mother."

"Mercenary love." Jagger studied her. "I suppose that's one way of looking at it."

Her gaze ticked to his. "I'm not sure there *is* such a thing as altruistic love, when it comes down to it."

A smile curved over his lips. "You're a philosophical sort."

She gave a shrug. "I like to give people the benefit of the doubt. I was tired yesterday. My words came out harsh."

Jagger's heart rate quickened. Would Mia give *him* the benefit of the doubt if he found the right way to tell her what he was doing? If he could present her with evidence that Jethro was guilty of some crime, might she forgive him for the deception, possibly keep helping him?

Her words came to his mind.

If you're not Cole, it should still remain about Cole, baby Cole, even if he's no longer alive, because the crime was never solved. There was no justice done. And justice needs to be done....

Jagger glanced into the side mirror. There was a truck in the distance, but otherwise the road was quiet.

"What made you come to Dead River Ranch, Mia?" he said, watching the truck. It was coming fast.

"Wow. That's out of left field." Mia slowed the Escalade before taking another sharp curve. They crossed a bridge, the escarpment dropping sharply off on both sides now, the ground barren.

He snorted. "I'm tired of talking about the Coltons. I want to know about you."

A strange, wistful look crossed her face and she smoothed a wisp of hair back from her brow.

"I came to get away from the west coast for a while," she said finally.

"Why?"

"Just needed a break."

"Whereabouts on the coast?"

"Near Bellingham."

He waited, but she offered no more. Mia had walls around her that she appeared to guard fiercely. He wondered exactly what she was protecting inside. He thought again about the way she worried her ring finger.

"So you needed to get away, and this infirmary position came up?" he offered.

Her jaw tightened ever so slightly. Another beat of silence.

"Yes," she said after a while. "I saw the job advertised and the pay was phenomenal, for the right person—there's no shortage of wealth in the Colton family. And the ranch was far enough from home. I was also attracted by the openness of the skies, the fishing in the area. The Laramie mountains are renowned for their trout streams."

"You really love fishing."

"I love the outdoors. Fly fishing can take you to the heart of it. The art of tying flies, trying to mimic nature, watching what the fish are biting, it teaches you to see the world in a very intimate way..." Her voice faded and a deeply sad look entered her eyes.

"What did you need to leave behind so badly, Mia?"

Her fists tightened on the wheel. "This is none of your business, Cole."

He sat back in silence, listening to the smoothness of the Cadillac engine, watching the road ribboning by. Then he said quietly, "I wish I knew *what* my business was here." He hesitated, then said, "Drucker was driving your relationship status home, and he was doing it for a reason. I was wondering if that reason had any bearing on what's unfolding with me."

She blew out a breath of frustration. "It has no bearing. When Drucker questioned all of us after Avery's kidnapping and Faye Frick's murder, he asked where I was from and why I'd chosen Dead River Ranch. He and his officers asked everyone the same questions, looking for motive. So I told him and now he's using it to rattle my cage, because that's what Drucker does. He doesn't trust anyone right now."

He glanced at Mia. Her cheeks were flushed, her neck tense. "Your past rattles your cage."

"Jesus. Yes! I applied for the job here because my engagement fell apart, okay? My fiancé dumped me at the altar while I stood there like a lost fool in my fancy wedding gown. I told Drucker that I'd needed to get as far away as I could from everyone who reminded me what a bloody loser I am." Her eyes crackled with the fire. "Happy now?"

Shock rustled through Jagger.

"I...I'm so sorry, Mia."

She gave another quick shrug. But swallowed deeply.

"It really messed you up?"

"Damn right it messed me up. Sent me into therapy, too. You try it some day and see how you feel. My uncle flew from England to give me away. My bridesmaids were waiting with me. The caterers had prepared a feast and were waiting on guests. My mother had spent more money than she had to spend…" Her voice caught.

"It's not just that, Cole, it's the realization that your whole future was being constructed on lies." She paused, gathering raw emotions. "I loved him. I thought Brad, my fiancé, loved me back. I believed him when he said he wanted to build a life with me, have children with me." She gave soft laugh and her eyes glittered. "How could I have not seen through the lies?"

Guilt twisted through Jagger.

"How long were you and Brad engaged?" he said quietly.

A muscle ticked above her eye. She was battling to hold her emotion in now that she'd started to tell him.

"It's okay, Mia—I shouldn't have—"

"Sixteen months," she said, voice thick. "Long enough to plan the wedding. Long enough to plan a life, put a down payment on a small house, get a mortgage, talk about children." She swallowed. "Long enough to believe I was going to spend the rest of my life as Mrs. Brad MacLean."

"Tell me about him—Brad."

Her gaze snapped to him. "Why?"

"Because I like you, Mia. And that makes me want to know you."

Something unreadable flashed through her eyes. "Cole, last night—the kiss—it was a mistake."

He swallowed, nodded. "I understand." He wanted to say more, but it risked bringing up his nightmares. It risked fracturing the fragile thing they'd shared.

"I don't even know who you are," she added, and Jagger knew she was struggling with her attraction to him. Just as he was conflicted over his attraction to her.

He remained silent.

"I thought Brad was a hero," she said after a while. "A big, brave, alpha guy who knew his heart, knew himself, made sacrifices for others." She went quiet awhile. "But he was a coward. Brad Maclean was a yellow-bellied bastard who was terrified of commitment and didn't have the guts to look me in the eye and tell me. He didn't have the balls to call off the wedding before it happened. He just got on a plane that morning and left me standing outside the church."

Jagger stared at her, shocked. "He got on a plane?"

"For Nigeria. He's still there for all I know. He never called or wrote. He never said sorry."

He thought of his own fear of commitment, his inability to ask for Melinda's hand in marriage. Melinda, like Mia, was a good person. She'd dreamed of the same things Mia had just spoken of. House. Kids. Family. But every time Melinda had raised those things Jagger had been unable to breathe. The mere thought of tying himself to a woman and a mortgage on a house in suburbia had given him severe claustrophobia. Until Afghanistan.

Until the ambush and the head injury had changed everything Jagger thought he knew about himself.

But by then it had been too late.

Melinda was gone, married to someone else. Jagger figured she'd been seeing the guy while he was in Afghanistan, if not before. But she had offered him an ultimatum. She'd given him a chance to change his mind.

And he'd run. Like Mia's ex had run.

Jagger got guys like Brad MacLean. Brad was the man Jagger once was.

Guilt, remorse, wrenched through his stomach. He wanted to reach out, touch Mia. Say he was sorry. For her, for himself. For Melinda. For men like Brad who lived empty lives. For every damn mistake he'd made in his life. He wanted to tell her how he was different now.

She quickly rubbed her nose with the back of her hand. "Mia...I shouldn't have pressed. I'm sorry—"

"I should've listened to what my mother was actually trying to tell me from the beginning—that Brad was wrong for me, that he was too much like my father, that I was going to repeat the mistakes she'd made in her own relationship with my dad." Her jaw lifted as she straightened her spine. "And I should be so over it by now," Mia said crisply. "I thought I was. But..." Her eyes met his, briefly, then she returned her attention to the road, leaving the sentence hanging, as if she'd said too much.

"But what?"

"It's nothing."

Genuinely curious now, Jagger said, "How was Brad like your father?"

Mia gave a soft snort. "My father lived for adrenaline, adventure. He was a mountaineer. The dopamine fix that came from risking his life was a drug for him, and he was an addict." She slowed for another bend, following the road higher into the mountains. The snow seemed closer. "The more my father could inhabit that raw place between life and death, the happier he was. And he'd choose it over my mother, over helping her make a home. He'd choose it over being a father." She paused. "In hindsight, Brad was just like him."

Jagger leaned back into the passenger seat and scrubbed his hand over his jaw. Mia could be talking about him. His fix had also been risking his life. In his case it was to get the story. And it had been a drug. Sure, he liked to argue that he was the voice of the underdog, but he couldn't deny that he'd started to live for the thrill of the hunt. Jagger was a composite of everything Mia didn't like in a man.

"Did you hate your father?" he asked quietly, watching the empty black ribbon of road unfolding before them.

"No. I loved him, worshipped him. We all did. Like puppy dogs hoping your superhero will look your way, and feeling so proud when he did pay you attention. Or when he taught you to fish. Or took you camping." Mia inhaled deeply. "In some ways, when he died, my mother was liberated."

"What happened to him?"

"Avalanche on Denali five years ago."

Avalanche. Denali. A beat of recognition drummed through Jagger. "Your father was a guide?"

"Yeah, he was taking five clients up when he triggered a massive slide—an error of judgment. It was a controversy in the climbing community for a while. People blamed him for the deaths. Two of the families sued. Others said that was just the risk of going out there—sometimes Mother Nature won and you died."

Jagger felt a thrill down his spine. *Hal Sanders was Mia's father?*

He knew the incident well, had even written about it. Sanders had been a lion of an adventurer. He used to maintain one of the most popular climbing blogs out there. He had huge following, had written several books. And Mia was right, his taking five climbers to their deaths with him had rocked the climbing community.

Jagger had never thought deeply about the wife and children that Hal Sanders had left behind. He'd been consumed instead with the man himself. Sanders had stood six-foot three-inches tall with a violent shock of white hair and a handlebar mustache, his skin weathered by sun and wind, hands like hams and the thighs of a lumberjack. Jagger had been interested in what drove men like Hal Sanders to take extreme risks. He'd been interested in those echoes in himself.

Jagger knew also that Sanders had been a keen fly fisher. He'd pioneered as stretch of river in Russia's Kamchatka after Soviet disintegration.

Suddenly Jagger craved to drop the facade, to talk openly with Mia about her father and family. He wanted to tell her how Hal Sanders had inspired the romantic in him, too. But he couldn't. He was "Cole" with no memory, suddenly trapped in a cage by his own deception.

He went quiet.

Hills rolled by. A handful of vehicles came from opposite direction. Only one overtook them, going the same way, disappearing into the horizon. Jagger glanced into the passenger-side mirror again. That truck was still behind them, a steady hundred yards back.

"So Brad, your ex, was like your father, then, an adrenaline seeker?" He said, watching the truck. Something about it felt off.

"Smoke jumper," she said.

A chill rushed down Jagger's spine. The echoes between Mia's life and his were eerie. He had an uncanny sense that he'd been brought into this woman's path for some reason.

Jagger had wanted to be a smoke jumper, too, after seeing a poster when he was ten years old—a group of four firefighters staring up at an unconquerable and towering wall of flames, their faces blackened with soot. What had gripped the young Jagger at the time was the look on those men's faces as they stood back, ceding triumph to the stories-high wall of fire devouring a stand of ancient Douglas firs. It was a look not of fear, not of exhaustion. But awe.

And the awe Jagger had seen in those men's faces had changed his life. At the time, he was struggling to adapt to being with his biological family in California. He was skipping school, causing trouble, hitting out at anyone who tried to help him. But when he saw that poster, it had made him hungry to see, to feel, what those smokejumpers were feeling.

Jagger had bought the poster and pinned it above his bed. He'd begun to focus because he had direction. He was going to be a hotshot and fight fires all around the world.

He never did became a smoke jumper, but his first story had been on a wildfire and the hotshots that battled it.

That magazine piece had set him on the road to adventure journalism, which in turn had led to foreign correspondence in war zones, getting stories where others feared to tread. And now he was here, sitting next to Mia.

After some story on a missing boy.

"Do you believe in destiny, Mia?" he said quietly. "Something bigger than us?"

She shot him a hard look, held it. "Why?"

"I wonder if that's what men like your father find in the mountains, in that space between life and death, a way to touch something bigger, to be a part of it."

"Bull. It's a chemical reward system, a drug for men like him. When he was away from risk for too long he'd start jonesing for his endorphins and dopamine."

"That's clinical."

She snorted.

"You blame your father for abandoning you, by dying, don't you? Like Brad abandoned you at the altar. You're so busy hating them for breaking your heart that you're lumping all adrenaline-seeking males in with them."

Her eyes flared to his and she almost crossed the center line. She swung the wheel back and muttered a soft curse. "I don't have to explain myself to you."

"No. You don't."

But I'd like to explain myself. I'd like to tell you how men can change, how sometimes people might benefit from second chances.

Jagger's head hurt and his chest felt tight. He'd resolve that when he got to a computer. He was going to drop Melinda a line, just to ask how she was doing, and to say sorry.

Because he was. Deeply. He didn't want things to be like this anymore. It was why he'd come here for this story—to find a way back into living. He hadn't expected it might be a woman named Mia who was going to help him, in quite another way.

They passed a sign warning of steep gradients and a mountain pass ahead. Mia glanced up into the rearview mirror and gave a soft gasp. "Holy crap, that guy's coming up fast!"

Jagger spun around. The dark-gray, two-door Ford pickup was now racing up behind them at incredible speed. His pulse quickened. Hopefully it was going to pass.

But the truck came right up behind them, tailgating the Escalade tightly round a curve. Jagger could see the driver—black jacket, dark shades and a dark toque pulled low and tight over his head.

His gut tightened and adrenaline pumped like fire into his blood. He swung forward in his seat to squarely face the road ahead. In front of them another sharp bend loomed—they were about to enter a treacherous mountain pass. The ground sheered off into a cliff on their left, and in the valley far below a silver river snaked.

"Slow down, Mia! Let's see if he'll pass." Jagger hoped his gut was wrong.

Mia pulled onto the dirt shoulder, tires kicking up stones, but the truck came up and smashed them from behind. Mia gasped as the Escalade swerved and they were both flung forward against seat belts.

White-faced, Mia pulled farther onto the dirt shoulder, but she was going too fast. The Escalade's tires skidded, dust billowing in a brown-yellow cloud behind them. Again, the truck smashed into them, this time catching the left rear of the vehicle which nearly sent them into a roll.

Jagger swore and reached across Mia, wrenching the wheel back and aiming for the paved road. "Hit the gas. Mia!"

Tires squealed as they hit asphalt and the vehicle kicked forward.

"Get us up and over the bridge ahead!"

Mia swerved back into the middle of the highway, tires squealing, and aimed for the narrow bridge over a gorge ahead, perspiration gleaming on her brow, her knuckles white.

The Ford gained on them again, coming in for another crash. Jagger spun round and saw the Ford's driver's-side window coming down. A gloved hand came out.

"Cole!" Mia yelled. "He's got a gun! Oh, God—he's going to kill us!"

"Keep driving—just focus on the road!"

The driver fired out his window. A bullet sparked off the tar behind them.

He was shooting for their tires, aiming for a blow-out.

If they went over the cliff, by the time they hit the bottom they'd be a mangled wreck, they'd probably go up in a ball of flames. It would look as if they'd had an accident.

"Cole," Mia said, gripping the wheel and leaning to the side as she rounded another curve. "In my purse, on the back seat—I've got a gun…get it!" She lowered his window as she spoke. Cold wind beat inside and whipped their hair. Jagger found her pistol.

"Shoot his tires! Stop him!"

Leaning out his window, he aimed carefully for the

Ford's front left tire, and fired. And again. He missed both times but the truck pulled back, slowing momentarily. Mia squealed the Escalade around another bend.

Their attacker was out of sight for a moment.

"There, Mia!" Jagger pointed. "See that dirt track going in behind those rocks—slow down, pull off into that dirt track!"

She hit the brakes and swung the wheel. They bounded wildly onto the battered track.

"Quick, drive up a little higher then pull in behind that outcrop."

She did.

Below them on the highway they heard the truck squealing around the sharp bend.

"He didn't see us," she said hoarsely. "We lost him." Mia's hands were shaking. Her face was sheet white.

"Let me take the wheel. I'm going to drive us farther up this dirt road." She scooted over as Jagger clambered over her into the driver's seat. He handed her the pistol.

Jagger put the truck into gear and gunned farther up the rutted track, rounding a higher outcrop of red rocks. "Any idea where this track leads?" he asked Mia.

Her eyes were wild, bright. She swallowed hard. "I…I think it's the old highway that was decommissioned years ago. I think it eventually leads down into the Laramie valley."

Jagger veered round a dirt bend, skidding close to a precipitous drop.

"We lost him, Cole, why are we going so fast?"

"He's going to see within minutes that we're gone. He'll backtrack. He'll see our tracks and our dirt cloud." Behind them fine dry sand was blowing high, like spindrift into the wind. "We need to keep moving."

The road grew narrower, steeper, more twisty. "You sure this eventually leads down into Laramie, Mia?"

"No, dammit, I'm not sure." She turned in the passenger seat.

"Oh, God," she said softly. "I can see his dust rising in the distance. He's coming."

Jagger's mouth tightened as he floored the accelerator, his eyes flicking up to the rearview mirror.

"How far back is he?"

"Maybe…a half a mile or more. I can't tell."

There was no escape—he was going to keep coming."

"Who would try and kill us, Cole? *Why?*"

Jagger was silent, concentrating on keeping them on the track.

She stared at him. "He wants you, doesn't he? He wants to finish the job he started in that field."

"Mia, I'm so sorry—you shouldn't be a part of this."

"But I am! That bastard back there doesn't give a damn who you're with! I'm just the collateral damage."

"Do you know who drives a truck like that, Mia? Who it might be behind that wheel?"

She was silent for a moment.

"Oh, God—" she whispered. "Dylan. He owns a gray Ford pickup." She paused. "But trucks like his are a dime a dozen out here," she countered quickly. "*And* he loans his out."

"Does Trip ever borrow his truck?"

"I don't know. I wouldn't put anything past Trip."

"What about Hansen?"

"I think he has his own truck."

Jagger saw what he was looking for, a narrow trail that led off their track. It looked as if it was primarily used by four-wheelers and from what he could see, it switchbacked all the way down to the river into the gorge.

"Okay, we go down here," he said to Mia as he slowed down for the turn. "You got spare ammunition for that pistol?"

"No, I don't carry extra. The gun's for self-protection, not a battle."

He swerved again as they barreled and jounced down the steep, twisting trail, dry grass clacking against the undercarriage, dust still billowing out behind them.

As they neared the bottom of the gorge they saw that the old bridge over the river was unnavigable—slats were missing, water flowing fast underneath.

"It's a dead end," Mia said, her voice hoarse. "We're going to be sitting ducks."

Jagger turned to look at her. Her eyes were red-rimmed and gleamed with adrenaline. Mia was afraid, this was beyond her scope. Meanwhile his heart pounded with the thrill, and fire burned through his blood. He was born to this stuff.

And as he looked at her Jagger was struck with a thought clear as glass—he was under stress, under "attack," and he hadn't buckled mentally—no flashbacks. At least, not yet.

And in his heart, he knew it was because of her. She'd helped him get his first good night's sleep in months. She was showing him that he wanted things out of a future. Mia Sanders was giving him a route out of his own hell. But in the process he'd drawn her down into danger—now he had to get her out. Or die trying.

Because he was not going to be responsible for another death.

Up above the ridge Jagger caught sight of blowing dust. Their attacker was coming.

Chapter 8

"We can't outrun him," Jagger said, watching the approaching dust trail. "So we need to outfox him."

"How?"

Jagger checked the remaining rounds in Mia's pistol. She watched him. "Ambush," he said. "We use the rounds we've got left." Jagger glanced up, scanning the interior of the Escalade, testosterone thumping through his blood. "We need something else we can use as a weapon or distraction."

"Bangers," Mia said suddenly

He shot her a fast look. "What?"

"I've got bear bangers—explosive cartridges to scare away bears—and emergency flares in my fishing gear." She spun round in the passenger seat and reached for her fishing vest on the backseat. Scrambling through the pockets, she handed him first a small box containing six explosive cartridges, then a box with two emergency flares plus two pen-style launchers.

"You carry this stuff with you?"

"It's always in my backcountry kit. I'm a nurse, Cole. I volunteered for Search and Rescue—I *know* what can go wrong."

God, he could love this woman. Mind racing, Jagger studied the surrounding terrain. The river had at some time raged much higher than it was flowing now. The water had receded, leaving enough room along the alder-fringed banks to squeeze a car in and drive it along the bank behind the screen of trees.

On the left of their trail was a rocky outcrop covered with dry scrub. Higher, to their right, was another outcrop of basalt.

Quickly, Jagger put the Escalade in gear and drove right down to the river, making sure he left clear tracks in the dirt. He then turned the SUV in behind a fringe of alders and drove tightly along the bank behind the trees, then he gunned the Escalade back up a hillock of dry grass until he reached the rock outcrop he'd seen higher up. He pulled in behind it. The vehicle was now hidden from the approaching trail, yet facing it for a quick getaway.

"Okay, Mia, here's the plan." He spoke quickly, screwing an explosive bear banger cartridge onto one of the pen-style launchers she'd given him and a flare cartridge onto the other. "I'm counting on him following our tracks all the way down to the river. At first, he's going to assume that we might have found a way across. He'll slow down and stop until he sees our tracks going along the bank. That's where we get him—when he stops. I want you to climb up this outcrop until you have a clear line of sight to the river, but use the rocks for cover. I'm going to cross over the trail and head down to that outcrop over there." He pointed. "As soon as our guy reaches the bottom of those tracks by the water, that's where we get him."

"You…want to *kill* him?"

He handed her the loaded bear banger along with the spare cartridges. He kept the flares and the pistol.

"I want to stop him," he said simply. "When he reaches the bottom, watch for my hand signal. When I raise my hand up high, fire that banger. Aim at his windshield. To him it'll sound like a shot from a 12-gauge shotgun." He spoke faster as the line of dust came slowly closer.

"He'll be distracted by the explosion. If he tries to leave the vehicle, launch another, right at him. Meanwhile I'll try put a hole in his tires and gas tank. On my sign—get back down the rocks and into the vehicle, fast. Start the engine running, open the driver's door for me." He hesitated, watching the trail of dust nearing. "Mia, if things go to hell, just get out, okay? Drive back to the highway without me. Then call the cops."

"Cole—"

"Now! Move— He's almost here. Keep the other cartridges in your jacket pocket. Soon as you've fired one, load another and have it ready. Got it?"

She sucked air in, visibly calming herself, and she nodded, her mouth tight.

Jagger sprinted across the trail and down the hill. He scrambled up the rock outcrop on the opposite side of the track. As he reached position, he caught sight of the gray truck. Then he heard the vehicle's motor, tries crunching over sand as the truck slowed, the driver searching for them. A sharp jab of panic pierced through him, but Jagger focused on steadying his breathing. This was not Afghanistan. This was a different ambush—he was going to stay clearheaded. This time he was in command.

He was going to get Mia out.

No one was going to die on his watch—not this time.

The truck came round the bend. It was coated in a layer

of fine yellow dust, the license plate obscured. Jagger's chest tightened as he waited for the vehicle to come even closer. He could see the driver inside now—the man's features obscured by the sunglasses and tight toque. The man drove the truck under Jagger's rock, crawling down to water. Jagger raised his arm into the air.

Mia fired.

The cartridge detonated against the truck windshield with a violent blast. Stunned, the driver slammed on the breaks and swerved his truck into soft sand. Immediately he threw it into Reverse and stepped on the gas. The truck wheels spun, whined, digging in deeper.

The guy was stuck—Jagger couldn't have planned that if he tried. He aimed Mia's weapon carefully at the back left tire, and squeezed the trigger. The bullet hit with a soft *thwock*. Air began to whoosh out of the tire.

The driver's door was flung open and the man ducked behind it, returning gunfire in Jagger's direction. But Mia launched another banger. It hissed through the air exploding right into the cab of the truck. The man threw himself to the ground and leopard-crawled for the cover of some rocks nearby.

Jagger quickly shot out the truck's left front tire, then the rear right. One bullet left.

The man peered up from behind his rock, this time firing in Mia's direction.

Jagger put his last bullet into the bottom of the truck's gas tank. Fuel began to leak out, darkening the sand and gleaming on blades of dry grass.

The driver spun, fired at Jagger. He ducked, the bullet striking off a piece of rock above his head. His heart hammered and adrenaline rushed hot and fast through his blood. His mind felt clear as glass.

He was staying in the present. Afghanistan was not here to haunt him right now.

Another explosion from Mia forced the man to hurl himself back to the ground.

The puddle of gas beneath the truck was widening. This time Jagger cocked back the trigger on the pen launcher and he fired an emergency flare—right at the leaking gas tank.

The flare ignited fuel instantly. Fire licked up the side of the gas tank. A few seconds later pressure inside the tank blasted it apart, throwing up a ball of flame. Acrid black smoke billowed into the air as fire crackled and whooshed through the truck.

Using the smoke as cover, Jagger scrambled down the rock and across the track.

He reached Mia—her face was white, her eyes huge.

"Give me that last banger," he said. "Get in the car!"

She handed him her loaded device, clambered down the rocks and raced for the vehicle. Jagger peered up over the edge of the rocky outcrop and fired the last banger directly in front of the rocks where the man was hiding.

The explosion echoed against the rocks and up into the hills. Another ball of fire *whooshed* out of the truck as the flames flared and spread to light the surrounding grass on fire, quickly engulfing a stand of dry scrub.

Jagger scrambled back down and sprinted for the Escalade. The driver's door was open, engine running.

He jumped inside, slamming the door shut as he hit the gas. They fishtailed wildly back onto the dirt track. Once he hit it, Jagger floored the gas. Tires spinning, they bounced and rocked up the steep and twisting switchback trail.

Mia was dead quiet, knuckles white as she braced

against the dash. Far below them smoke billowed black and high into the air.

They reached the wider decommissioned road and Jagger inhaled deeply, turning in the direction of the highway. He glanced at Mia. Her features were pinched.

"You okay?"

She nodded but said nothing.

"We'll head back down to the highway the way we came," Jagger said, voice rough, adrenaline still hammering through him. "He's not going to come after us, not now. We'll have a clean run."

She looked at his face, reading something in his eyes. But still she didn't speak. She turned in her seat and faced the front. Jagger noticed her hands were clutched tightly in her lap.

After about a mile along the decommissioned road, Mia said quietly, "It did look like Dylan's truck."

"I couldn't get a read on the plate. It was obscured by dust. When we get back, we'll see if anyone's truck is missing from the ranch."

She was a silent for a while longer, tension rolling off her in waves. They rounded a bend and Jagger saw the ribbon of highway below, twisting into the mountains.

"Are we going to call the police?" she said quietly.

He shot her a glance. "We're not in Dead P.D.'s jurisdiction, are we?

"Does it matter whose jurisdiction we're in?"

Jagger blew out a slow breath of air. This was another complication. With only Drucker and his officers on his case, Jagger still had a little bit of time left to get what he came for. And he needed this time to find a way to tell Mia the truth about his identity before someone else did. Involving state or Laramie police would change things.

"You're leery of police in general, aren't you?" She was watching him intently. "Why?"

"I'm just thinking how it'll start all over with them asking for my ID."

She closed her eyes. Trying to calm her breathing. "I get a feeling," she said very quietly. "You want to delay the DNA test, too."

He shot her a glance.

"We can't just not report it, Cole. Someone tried to *kill* us. My gun was used to shoot out his tires. My explosives blew up his vehicles. He could be the same guy who killed Jenny. This could be a lead the police could use."

Jagger steered down a steep incline, feeling the vehicle slipping slightly on soft sand. "We'll report it to Drucker," he said. "He can take it from there, include whatever law enforcement agencies he wants."

She didn't reply. They neared the turnoff onto the highway.

"Stop the car, Cole."

"What?"

"Just stop, dammit!"

Frowning, Jagger slowed and brought the Escalade to a halt. Dust settled in a cloud around them.

She turned in her seat to face him, eyes burning suddenly with tears. "What in hell is going on here, Cole!"

"What do you mean?"

"You got off on that, didn't you?" She flung her arm in the direction from where they'd come. "You were cool as a damn cucumber even while you had fire in your eyes. And look at you now—you're exhilarated. You *enjoyed* that. I can see it in your face, in your eyes."

"Mia—"

"Where did you learn to be like that, Cole? Are you military? Who in hell *are* you!"

Tears spilled down her cheeks. She tried to swipe them away with a shaking hand. "Who wants you dead, Cole?"

"Mia." He reached for her hands, taking them in his. What he wanted to tell her was, yes, he *did* enjoy that—because it was the first time he'd experienced stress without being plunged straight back into pure mental anguish. He hadn't blacked out, or lost time, or seen dead boys walking toward him, or experienced flashbacks as vivid and terrifying as the real deal.

"I don't know why someone is trying to kill me."

"I...I'm sorry." She swiped at another tear. "It's...it's just the shock." She inhaled a shaky breath. "I've been in some bad situations, Cole, but usually I'm trying to help people live. I've never done anything like that...we could have *killed* him."

"It was either him or us, Mia."

"Us." She repeated the word slowly as the notion seemed to sink in that she was also in some villain's crosshairs now that she'd witnessed him trying to run them off the road, seen his truck.

"Whoever tried to kill me out on that field the other night clearly wants to finish the job, Mia. And I don't know why. If I am Cole, then it's Cole they want dead. If I'm not Cole, they want me dead before anyone finds out I'm not him. Which means, either way, they want people to believe that Cole Colton is dead and gone."

"That doesn't make sense. If you're not Cole, and you're murdered, forensics will show it."

"I know. I don't get it, either, unless they have a plan to dispose of the body before it can be checked."

"That's ridiculous."

He glanced away, watching the black smoke recede up the valley, then he turned back to her. "Think about this

Mia, why take all my ID yet leave me with that blanket and photo?"

"So people would assume you might be Cole," she said quietly.

"Yes. A dead Cole."

She stared at him.

"And if I'm not Cole, that blanket might even have been planted on me. Someone might have tried to frame me as him. And because I didn't die, they're worried my memory will return so they want to finish the job before it does."

"But you did have the photo on you when you came through Dead River," she countered. "*That* wasn't planted on you."

Jagger's pulse kicked. "How do you know this?"

Something changed in her eyes. "Staff gossip," she said quietly, lowering her gaze to stare at her hands. "Tanner, one of the ranch employees, told the others that he'd seen the photo fall out of your wallet in the Dead River Diner."

Jagger watched her face carefully. He knew this, of course, but he wouldn't if he had amnesia—he needed to act surprised. He was going to trip himself up any minute with what he should or shouldn't know.

"The staff also say that Chief Drucker confronted you in the diner." She paused, then slowly her gaze lifted to meet his. "And that he saw your ID."

A hot beat of silence.

"So why the hell didn't Drucker tell me that in the infirmary?" His voice was clipped. "Why didn't he tell me who I was?"

"I don't know," Mia said. "He might be holding back that information for some reason pending his fingerprint checks. Or he might believe your ID is fake, Cole."

"It might well be fake—it's hardly going to say Cole Colton."

"We'll ask him when we go through Dead and report the truck incident," she said. "If he has your name—even if it's a fake you've been living under for the past thirty years—he's got no right to withhold it."

"Mia," he said, leaning forward and taking her hands in his. "Will you help me? I need to get to the bottom of this. I need to know what happened all those years ago. Can I use your computer to look some things up?"

"Like what?"

"Like information on employees, on anyone who might have been on the ranch thirty years ago when the kidnapping took place. Someone in Dead River knows something and wants the past to stay buried, and the police are not making a whole lot of headway in finding that person."

She went quiet, her gaze locking with his for several long, simmering beats, as if she was weighing him up again, reevaluating.

"Of course I'll help," she said quietly. Then she gave a soft snort. "I'm sure you've deduced by now that I'm wired to help. I find it a little easier than trying to kill people. My laptop in the suite—it's yours when you need it."

A smile curved over Jagger's mouth.

She returned the smile, and it lit her eyes. His chest squeezed with affection.

"Come here." He drew her against his body and held on. She was trembling in his arms, the aftereffects of shock, adrenaline.

He stroked her hair. "I won't let them hurt you, Mia," Jagger said as he lowered his head, resting his nose against her soft hair, inhaling her scent. "God, I will not let them hurt you," he murmured.

Mia closed her eyes, allowing herself to just fold into him. He was warm, hard, strong, and he smelled of dust and gunpowder. Yet she could also feel his tenderness. She loved that—male strength, tenderness. She loved his calm under fire as much as it unsettled her. It was an aphrodisiac to Mia. More than anything. And as the adrenaline in her system subsided, she felt the warmth of affection blossoming through her chest. She felt safe—Mia hadn't been held like this in a long while.

"I think we made good team back there," she murmured against his chest.

"Hell, yes." He paused, the tension in his body changing, and when he spoke again, his voice was thick.

"Mia, look at me."

She did. He tilted her chin higher. His mouth was so close. His eyes—a darkness had filled them with dangerous, edgy gleam. His energy had shifted.

Mia's heart began to pound.

He lowered his mouth and soft warning bells clanged in the back of her mind as something whispered...*you don't even know who he is.*

But the thought shattered into a million little sparks as he brought his mouth down on hers. Crushing. Fierce. She melted under him, into him, opening her mouth to his. He slid his hand up her back, up her neck, and his tongue entered her mouth, slick, hot, aggressive.

Mia's world spiraled violently as heat arrowed straight down her belly. Her heart was slamming, furious, fast.

Danger...stop. While you still can...

But Mia couldn't stop.

She slid her hand up into his hair, curling her fingers tightly through the thick, dark strands as she drew him down farther, closer, her tongue tangling aggressively with his. He cupped her breast and fire fanned through her. Mia could barely breathe. Couldn't think.

She was blinded by lust, incapable of forming a rational thought.

Fire spiked through Jagger, white hot and ragged, like nothing he'd felt in years. Her soft, hungry, angry mouth tasted sweet. It tasted of sin. He wanted more, all of her, couldn't get enough. Her hand fisted painfully in his hair as she moved her mouth over his. Her breast was full, soft, the nipple a tight nub under his palm. He moved his hand down her waist and she moaned softly under him as heat began to dissolve his thoughts, sweeping rationality along with it.

Jagger struggled to pull back. To focus. *This was wrong. Not now...not yet. Not when she didn't know the truth...*

He pulled back suddenly, his heart racing, his groin hard, throbbing.

Her eyes were gleaming, cheeks pink, lips swollen. The top button of her shirt had popped open, exposing white lace.

Focus.

"Mia..."

She cleared her throat and a look of panic flashed across her features as her gaze shot to the clock on the dash. "Oh, God, I almost forgot—the appointment! We... we should get to that appointment," she said, flustered, smoothing down her shirt. "We can make it in time—just." She straightened herself in the seat and brushed back her hair. Her hands were still shaking as she tried to rebutton her shirt, but the buttonhole had ripped. Finally she got it to hold.

"Cole—drive, will you?"

Jagger put the vehicle in gear. They began to bounce down the last leg of dirt road toward the highway.

She turned to watch the smoke billowing up from the gorge behind them. "I hope it doesn't turn into another wildfire," she whispered.

Jagger turned onto the highway and pressed down on the accelerator.

He could feel Mia watching him as he drove.

Nerves, irrational, difficult to control, rustled through Jagger as he got out of the car in the Cheyenne Memorial parking lot. He'd had his fill of hospitals, head scans, shrinks. Therapy sessions. Poking, prodding. This was not going to be fun.

"You okay?" she asked coming around to his side.

He nodded. But as Jagger looked up at hospital building, an unspeakable cold speared down his chest and a sharp memory exploded through his brain. The boy. His liquid eyes.

Jagger felt sick.

"You sure?" she said, touching his arm.

He glanced down into her clear blue eyes. Once again, she had his back. She was at his side. He could do this.

"Yeah," he said with a smile. "I'm good."

Mia hooked her arm through his and together they began to walk toward the building.

Jagger felt uneasy about how much he liked Mia at his side, and how he was beginning to want to keep her there. It was not right. He couldn't continue down this road in this fashion.

"We can do this, Cole," she said, reading something in him. "No matter how hard it gets down the road."

"I sure as hell hope so," he answered.

Once inside, the smell of the hospital almost stopped Jagger dead in his tracks.

"You're nervous." A bemused smile curved Mia's lips. "You're as cool as a cucumber while ambushing people and blowing up trucks, but a hospital scares you?"

He smiled. "Maybe."

She looked up at him, compassion and warmth entering her eyes. "It'll be fine. You'll see"

And somehow she made him feel as though it would—that he *would* get well.

Underlying his goal in coming to Dead River had been a desire to heal, to find a way to start living again. Jagger had thought the Cole Colton story would be his ticket. But he hadn't expected it would be a woman like Mia Sanders who would reawaken him, filling him with a desire to build a life in all sorts of deeper, different ways. And as Jagger looked into her eyes he realized his goal had split into two streams.

One was to honor his contracts with the television station and his publisher in getting, and airing, the Cole Colton story. The other was Mia—finding a way to get to know her better over the long term. And as this dawned on him, a sick feeling sank through Jagger, because these two streams might be mutually exclusive.

If he had to choose one over the other, which would it be—his contract, a job, survival, justice for baby Cole? Or risking it all for a faint chance at love?

The image of that tumbleweed outside the diner entered his mind. The same wind that had propelled the tangled ball through the dust had been blowing at his back as he walked the road to the Colton ranch that dark, cold night. Jagger had an absurd feeling that early autumn wind—or a bigger driving force behind it—had blown him across Mia's path.

Or was he truly losing his mind?

"Hey," he whispered, lowering his head. "Your button is undone."

She glanced down, saw her exposed bra and quickly rebuttoned her shirt, cheeks flushing. "Thanks."

She squeezed his hand and led him down the sterile hospital corridor.

* * *

Outside Dr. Ranjit Singh's office, Mia paced up and down the shiny passageway, the antiseptic scents of the hospital familiar to her and grounding. She was unable to sit quietly in the chairs provided in the waiting area. Mia preferred to be out here, moving.

She'd watched through the glass window as they'd slid a hospital-gowned Cole into the CT machine. A doctor on the outside had charted areas of his brain activity on a computer as he gave instruction to the radiologist inside.

After that, they'd taken him and the brain charts through to see Dr. Singh.

Mia checked her watch again. He been in there for almost for almost an hour now.

Her thoughts turned to what it might feel like to not know who you were. Did she believe he was Cole?

It was possible.

Did that matter?

She dragged her hand over her hair. She was no longer sure what mattered. What she did want was the truth, to *know*. Once they had that, they could take the next step.

Baby steps, she thought, and almost laughed at the absurdity. She'd already taken a giant leap and fallen for him. A perfect stranger. And here she was thinking in terms of "they."

The door opened and he came out. He looked pale as he gripped a large envelope in his hand.

Mia's heart skipped a beat at the expression on his face. She went quickly up to him.

"What is it? What did he say?"

Something cool had shifted into his eyes. He seemed different. "There's no swelling," he said. "No physical damage. Just evidence of a previous skull fracture."

"Yes, that's good, right?"

He snorted softly. "And he referred me to a psychiatrist."

Mia was silent for a beat. "Meaning?"

"Meaning my memory loss is all in my head. He did a whole bunch of tests and Dr. Singh thinks my amnesia is psychological. Possibly a result of post-traumatic shock of some kind. A protective mechanism that my mind is using to block something terrible out."

Mia thought of his nightmares. His screams. His scars. Her heart clutched.

A psychological reason didn't make the problem any less real. Or easier to deal with. She knew from her nursing experience that psychological scarring could sometimes be more complicated to treat than tangible, physical damage. It could also be permanent.

He dragged his hand through his hair.

"Are you telling me everything?"

"Yeah. He said my amnesia could have been induced by being attacked on the farm, but it more likely stemmed from some prior traumatic experience and the farm attack was a mental straw that broke my mind. It's all in his report in here, apparently." He raised the brown envelope. "This is for Levi. Dr. Singh said he'd be in touch with Levi by phone."

He looked worried.

"Do you have an appointment already with the psychiatrist?"

"No."

"Do you want to make one, while we're here?"

"Mia, can we just leave it for a few days?"

She held his gaze. In his eyes she could read real anxiety. She reached for his hand.

"Cole. It's okay. Seeing a psychiatrist is nothing negative, it's—"

"Please, don't patronize me, Mia." A spark of something crossed his features, warning her back. "I know exactly what psychiatry is about."

"How do you know, Cole?" she asked quietly.

His eyes narrowed. "What are you implying?"

She heaved out a big breath of air and hooked her arm through his.

"Come, let's get a coffee before we drive back."

They stepped out into bright sunlight. The air was crisp and cool, the sky endless blue over the skyline.

Jagger closed his eyes, inhaled deeply. Inside he felt cold, tight. He'd been through this, too many times. He'd arrived stateside with a big chunk of his memory missing. He'd had some brain damage. When the memories did return, the flashbacks started. They'd sent him to shrinks. In the end, he'd hit the road, figuring he had to do this himself.

Now this. It was all so real, so close to the bone that he suddenly had a fierce and desperate urge to lean on Mia. To share, offload, tell her everything that he'd been unable to share with therapists and that was eating him up inside. He gritted his jaw, hating the fact that he needed anybody at all. That he wasn't man enough to just suck this up by himself.

She reached up, touched his face.

"I'm here for you, Cole. I said I'd help you, and I will. We'll do it together, we'll figure out why you came to Dead River. And the DNA—a paternity test—will prove who you are and whether you're Jethro's son."

His eyes burned sharply with such a sudden surge of emotion it scared him. Her touch, what it did to him. The power she had over him.

Her eyes also shone. With care. Warmth.

She was throwing aside her suspicions, trusting him with her heart, if not her head. The healer in Mia Sanders wanted to help. She knew that he had dark and hidden shadows in his past, that he could even be dangerous, a felon. Yet she was not leaving him alone.

And suddenly Jagger had no idea how Brad Maclean could have left this woman at the altar. Not only did Jagger understand Mia on some fundamental level, he also knew he could love her.

And *that* scared him more than anything he'd ever been through. Because Jagger didn't know how to love, had not allowed himself to love. Truly love. Since he'd been ripped out of life as he knew it at nine years old.

He looked over the skyline, toward the horizon. The landscape—his reasons for being here—all tilted drunkenly on its axis.

"Come, let's go get that coffee. Then we'll drive to Dead River, report the truck incident to Chief Drucker. After that we'll go look at the field where I found you." She hooked her arm through his again and drew him close as they crossed the parking lot.

"We must look at this as good news, Cole. If we know for certain that there's no physical reason for the amnesia, we can start working to unlock your memory in other ways. That field is as good a place as any to start—it might trigger something." She looked up at him. "You already remembered a black horse."

Chapter 9

Cole took the highway off-ramp at the sign for Dead River. Mia had taken off her boots and her sock feet were propped against the dash as she jotted names down in the notebook she'd found in the glove compartment.

She was making a list of people who were either on Dead River Ranch or connected to it thirty years ago when Cole Colton was kidnapped.

"So far we've got Jethro, of course. We've also got Bernice Black and her husband, Horace. Agnes the head cook. Mathilda the housekeeper."

"What does Horace do?"

"He's a general handyman and an ordained minister. He gives services from time to time in the small church on the ranch. They live in a cabin on the property—they basically predate Jethro's tenure on the ranch. He kept them on when he bought it, from what I understand."

"Hmm. And Agnes—she was a cook back then?"

"She worked as kitchen help. Mathilda said something once that made me wonder if Agnes and Jethro might have had an affair."

Cole gave a soft whistle. "This is one tangled setup. What about Mathilda—what's she about?"

"Mathilda has basically run the house for the past three decades—she's been like a mother to the three Colton sisters. She's very protective of Jethro and his kids." Mia laughed. "She's like a mother bear—I wouldn't want to cross swords with Mathilda Perkins. There's also an old ranch hand, John Selwick, who's still around. He used to be a top wrangler back in his time but he had some kind of injury and just handles small jobs now. And there's Hilda Zimmerman who lives in town but shows up several days a week to work as a maid. She and Mathilda don't seem to get along."

"Why not?"

"I don't know. Agnes told me that Hilda doted on the Colton girls when they were babies, in part because she could never have her own children. Maybe there was rivalry there because of it?"

Jagger shot her a look. "You think she was, or is, obsessed with babies? Enough so to have paid Duke Johnson to kidnap Cheyenne Colton?"

"Hilda?" Mia dusted dirt off her knee from where she'd knelt on the rock outcrop. "I don't know, Cole," she said thoughtfully. "If so, how would she connect with the attack on you, the truck incident, the other murders?"

"She'd need a partner—a male. Someone with enough strength and skill to handle Midnight, and who could have driven that truck today."

"Who could also shoot Jenny Burke in the face?"

"What if she did that herself? A 9 mm handgun is an easy weapon for an older woman to handle."

A chill darkness ticked at Mia's mind, something coming to the surface. She turned and looked at Cole. "How did you know Duke Johnson was responsible for the kidnapping?"

His jaw tightened, ever so slightly. "You must have told me."

"I don't think I did."

He glanced her way. Her eyes were dark and cool.

"You must have."

Mia turned to watch the road. After about another mile, ranchlands unfolding on either side, fences keeping land apart, she said quietly, "You know, whatever brought you to Dead, it can't be good."

Jagger kept his eyes dead ahead, hands firm on the wheel.

"How so?"

"Either you came in search of your biological father and the answers to an old crime, and something buried in your lost memory is threatening someone here. Or you came here in connection with the old kidnapping. Because you had that photo with you when you arrived in Dead, you were asking questions about the Coltons and looking for work on the ranch. Your being here is not random."

Tension whispered through Jagger. She was getting close. Mia was nobody's fool. And the closer she got, the more he felt required to come fully clean with her. Jagger swore softly to himself. She was going to hate him when she found out the truth. It was already too late. How had he gotten himself into this bind?

"If I'm not Cole, what do you think I might have come for?" he said quietly.

His gaze shot to her.

"I don't know," she said, turning to watch the land flashing by. "Answers. Either for good or bad."

"Meaning?"

"Well, you could have wanted to use what you'd come to learn to blackmail someone in the family. Maybe you got the idea from seeing all the news coverage. Or...maybe you wanted justice for some reason."

"Would that be a bad thing?"

She frowned. "I believe in retribution, Cole." She hesitated. "But I like it to be done through the legal system."

Jagger turned off the highway onto a smaller road, following the signs to Dead River. Clouds had started blowing in from the north. "Can you think of any more names for our list?"

Mia returned her attention to the notepad, chewing the back of her pen. "Well, Desiree Beal, Brittany's sister, was on the ranch at the time," Mia said, thinking of more names. "She's the one who embroidered the blue blanket, but she's dead now."

"What happened to her?"

"She left Dead River after her sister's funeral and went to Jackson where she got a job in a diner. She was shot dead in her Jackson home almost a year later. They never found her killer."

Cole whistled quietly. "Now there's something interesting."

He made a mental note to look up and contact the detective who was on that case.

"Put her name on the list, Mia." He paused. "Was Drucker also around back then?"

"He was the rookie who helped with the initial investigation."

"Put his name down, too. And what about Darla, Trip and Tawny—why does Jethro keep his ex and her kids around when clearly no one enjoys their company?"

"Mathilda has intimated that Darla has something on Jethro."

"As in something from his past that she could use as blackmail?"

"Possibly—that's the idea I get, but it might just have come from staff speculation."

"What happens to her when Jethro dies, which won't be long now?"

"Either he's written Darla and her kids into his will, or he dies and there goes her blackmailing power. Unless she's got—or gets—something else she can use, the Colton kids will probably evict her. And there goes her Botox and cushy life."

"Ouch."

Mia gave a shrug. "They're hard to like, Cole. I don't think anyone on the ranch really gets on with them."

"Well, you better add Darla, Trip and Tawny to the list, then. Trip could have driven that truck, and that could've been my bag that you caught him with in the employee wing. Put Jared Hansen down, too. Who knows where he got that duffel bag before Trip got his paws on it. Either he or Trip could be doing someone's bidding." He hesitated. "And put Dylan Frick down."

"Oh, no, not Dylan. I just don't see it. I mean, the guy's mother was killed. He's grieving, deeply. He's not involved in all this."

"Still, he's the most likely to have ridden Midnight, especially in the dark. We might find out when we get back that Dylan's truck has gone AWOL."

"Doesn't mean he was driving it. Like I said, he loans it out. Besides, what would his motive be?"

"Protecting the memory of his mother. Perhaps Faye was involved in the abduction of Cole herself."

"Faye arrived *after* Cole was abducted."

"So did Darla—still, they might have learned something that implicated Jethro, or someone else, after the fact. And think about this possibility—what if Faye's death was *not* an accident? Maybe, like Jenny Burke, Faye Frick came across something incriminating and someone needed to silence her."

Mia reluctantly wrote down Dylan's name. "Damn," she said softly. "There are so many people on this list. It's more a case of who *doesn't* have motive of some sort."

"Well, it's a start."

Mia rubbed her face, looking suddenly tired. She turned and grabbed her purse from the back, found her water bottle inside and took a deep swig.

She held the bottle out to him

"No, thanks, I'm good."

She closed the cap and leaned her head back against the seat.

Jagger turned into the small town of Dead River and stopped at the first red traffic light.

"You need to take a right here," Mia said. "The police station is just down the road."

He put on the indicator.

"Mia," he said carefully, watching the light. "Back in the suite you mentioned there had been talk about how Jethro came about his wealth. You said there were rumors."

She looked away from him again and began worrying her ring finger, as if deciding how much she wanted to let him know or how much she could trust him.

"I guess the rumors are common enough knowledge around these parts," she said. "So I don't feel I'm stepping over the line by saying that he's had what some would call questionable business dealings. And I can't imagine he made billions from ranching alone. He has mineral rights on the land…but…" She turned to face him. "The emotion I saw in Jethro's eyes, when you walked in through his bedroom door, Cole, that was real. I've known this guy for over two years now and believe me, he's not a sentimental sort. Those tears were genuine. It means everything to him right now to have his son back."

"Guilt, relief, absolution before he dies?"

The light went green. He took a right.

"That's harsh."

"Is it?"

She glanced away, still debating something internally, then looked back into his eyes. "Jethro said something to Levi last month. I overheard them talking about Desiree. Levi had learned that when Desiree first arrived in Jackson, she'd been seen with a baby."

Jagger's pulse quickened. Desiree again.

"Levi asked Jethro about that incident and the old man clammed up, clutching his chest and going into apparent medical distress. But when Levi left to get medication, I saw Jethro sit up just fine and reach for the phone. I didn't hear who he called."

Jagger's instincts prickled the hair up his neck.

"After she was murdered, the Jackson police along with the FBI investigated this claim, but there was no sign of any baby, if there ever was one. They began to believe the initial report had been false or in error.

"Jackson," he said, frowning, thinking. "What was Levi's interest in Desiree?"

"I think it had something to do with his mother, but I don't know what." Mia was quiet for a while. "I shouldn't really say this, but it's become too key not to. Levi appears to have suspicions about his own father's involvement in the kidnapping of his son."

Jagger's brows raised. "Why?"

"Because of the way Jethro avoids certain questions, the

way he reacted to that question in particular. Levi thinks, at the very least, Jethro knows something about what happened. Over there." She pointed. "Dead P.D. station. Next to the fire hall."

Jagger turned into the parking lot.

No clouds of dust in Dead River today. Brown leaves rustled across the cracked paving in the breeze, and a United States flag flapped above the building.

Two police cruisers were parked outside.

Inside the station, a receptionist sat behind a counter. Behind her was a small bull pen with metal desks. The chief's office was at the back, glassed in. Drucker was in there, working at his computer.

"Let me do the talking, okay?" Mia whispered.

Jagger wondered why—protecting his fragile mental state? Or something deeper? He let her go with it.

The chief caught sight of them immediately, got up, opened his door and swaggered past the empty desks toward them. His voice boomed against the walls. "It's okay, Elaine. I got this." Drucker came up to the counter.

"Miss Sanders." He nodded at Jagger but did not call him by any name. "What can I do for you?"

"It's *Ms.* Sanders," Mia replied with a false smile. "Or you can call me Mia, if you like."

He didn't return her smile. His narrow-set eyes bored into her—the chief was drawing his line in the sand.

"We'd like to report an attempt on our lives," she said.

His eyes did not blink. There was no surprise at all in his face. A typical veteran cop, thought Jagger, practiced at not revealing any emotion.

"What do you mean, 'attempt on your lives'?"

"Someone tried to run us off the road repeatedly and fired a weapon at us."

The chief eyed her for a moment, then leaned over and opened the low door in the counter, admitting them into the bull pen area.

He picked up a clipboard with forms from one of the desks and led them through to an interview room, indicating they should take seats at the table, which was bolted to the floor. Drucker took the plastic seat opposite them.

"What happened?" he said, clicking his pen, eyes fixed on them.

Mia explained the events of the morning.

"And you didn't report it right away?"

"Medical emergency," she said, her glance flicking toward Jagger. "I was worried about a possible hematoma on his brain—we went straight to Cheyenne Memorial where we had an appointment for a CT scan, then we came right here."

Drucker's eyes narrowed. "You could have called it in on your way to the hospital."

"My cell battery is dead."

Jagger inwardly raised a brow. She was fast. And he'd be lying if he didn't admit to secret thrill in aligning with her against this balding cop. He found her sexy right now. Jagger reached under the table and put his hand on her knee, squeezed. Her spine stiffened but she didn't look his way.

He repressed a smile.

"I guess it's state jurisdiction?" Mia said as she looked at Chief Drucker with doe eyes. "Or Laramie's. Perhaps we should have gone there."

"You did your best," Drucker said brusquely. "I'll handle it from here and bring in whoever is necessary."

Inwardly Jagger grinned. Drucker was territorial. Mia had read and played him well.

Drucker took down the details of the truck chase, shooting, location and descriptions of the vehicle and driver, then he asked Mia if she had a carry permit for her hand-gun. She produced it from her purse. Drucker examined it, then looked up from his paperwork directly at Jagger. "You done this before?"

"What?"

"Ambush. Firebombing. Shooting out tires."

Jagger blinked, momentarily assailed by sounds and scents of an ambush of a very different kind.

"Not that I know of."

"But you're practiced with a weapon."

"It would appear so."

"Why do you think someone is trying to kill you, sir?"

But Mia sat forward, heading him off. "How can he know that if he can't recall why he came here in the first place? Or who he is? The neurologist we saw today explained that his memory might take some time to return, if ever," she said, embroidering slightly on the prognosis. "You can speak to Dr. Colton about that. I'm sure he'll confirm it, although it's patient privilege."

Drucker pulled his hand over his mouth, drawing his lips down into a frown as he eyed Jagger. In turn, Jagger met the man's scrutiny with a cultivated blankness.

"Why do *you* think someone might be trying to kill me, Chief?" asked Jagger.

The chief didn't answer. Instead, he abruptly pushed his chair back from the table and stood.

"Can you leave your weapon with us, Ms. Sanders? We'll need to take it into evidence."

Mia hesitated, then took her gun from her purse and slid it over the table toward the chief. "Any word when your DNA technician will be able to do the test?" she asked. "The sooner we know, the better for our patient."

This time Jagger did see something flicker through Drucker's watery gray eyes. And he now felt certain

Drucker was delaying the test in his own interests. He clearly wanted control, and he wanted all his legal ducks in as clean a row as possible. Jagger wondered how long Drucker would take to tell Laramie or state police about the truck incident, if at all. Or if he was going to try and handle it solo first, from the Dead River end.

"He should be finished testifying and back here tomorrow. I've informed Jethro Colton, who'll be providing his own DNA, to see if there's a paternal match. I'll be bringing my technician out to the ranch—he can take blood samples there. The D.A. has recommended blood over saliva. It'll be better in the event of a trial down the road."

Irritation flashed through Mia's eyes. "Well, thank you for letting us know. How long until we get results after the samples are taken?"

"It'll depend on the lab schedule." His tone brooked no further discussion. "If that's all?" He held his hand toward the door.

"Chief Drucker," Mia said sweetly, staying seated. "One last question—you've seen this man's ID. He showed it to you in the diner. Why have you kept this from us?"

The Chief's mouth flattened, his eyes inscrutable. "The case is under investigation."

She got to her feet abruptly "You can't tell him the name on his own driver's license?"

"We're checking to see whether the identification is fraudulent. Once we have DNA test results we can match—"

"What about the prints?"

"Ms. Sanders, this is a police matter. Now if there's nothing further, I have an investigation to run."

The chief showed them out in silence.

"He's an ass," Mia muttered as they exited the station.

"He's a cop."

"Not all cops are asses," she said grumpily as she strode over to the parked Escalade.

Jagger beeped the locks and opened the passenger door for Mia.

"First stop, I'm getting a new weapon," she said as she climbed in. "There's a store down Main Street, across from the Dead River Diner."

He got behind the wheel.

Half an hour later they had a Glock and a Smith & Wesson in their possession, along with plenty of spare ammunition. Mia also bought new bear bangers and flares.

"Make sure you keep that pistol and spare ammunition on you," Jagger said quietly as they walked back down the sidewalk to where he'd parked the Escalade.

"Hey," Mia said, stopping suddenly and grabbing his arm. "Isn't that Grace, the diner waitress, across the street in the parking lot?"

Jagger turned to look. Grace was leaning against the wall smoking. "I don't know," he lied.

"I'm sure it is," she said, squinting to see better. "Tanner said it was Grace who served you that night, and that you spoke to her for a while." Mia glanced up at him, her eyes suddenly bright. "Maybe she remembers something, Cole. Come, let's go talk to her." Mia started across the street without waiting for a reply.

Jagger followed. Mia was right—Grace might be of help, but for different reasons. Her boss, Maggie, had shown a keen interest in him from the moment he'd walked into her diner. Maggie might have even called Drucker on the phone after she'd seen him. Jagger wanted to know why.

"Grace!" Mia called, waving, as the waitress stubbed out her cigarette and began to head back to the diner.

The waitress spun round at the sound of her name, and

surprise showed on her face. "Hey," she said, coming over, hugging her arms against the chill.

"Grace, my name is Mia, I work as the nurse on Dead River ranch."

"I know," said Grace. "Nice to meet you." She glanced at Jagger. "I served you the other night but I guess you don't remember, huh? They say you might be Cole Colton. I figured that's why you were asking so many questions about Jethro and the ranch. At least, that's what I told the police."

"They questioned you?" Jagger said.

"Basically interrogated anyone who might have crossed your path that night."

"Do you have a second, Grace?" Mia said. "Can we ask you a few questions?"

The waitress cast a quick backward glance toward the diner windows. "Better be quick—Dragon Lady will be watching. Come over this way. It's warmer against the wall, out of the wind."

They followed her to the wall where the sand was still piled in soft drifts. Grace took a package of smokes out of her deep apron pocket and lit another cigarette. She blew out a long stream of smoke, and said, "What do y'all want to know?"

"Anything that might help trigger the return of Cole's memory," Mia said. "Like, what did he order that night?"

Jagger saw where Mia was going—starting with the easy questions. She'd have made a good reporter, building trust slowly.

Grace flicked another glance toward the diner. "Uh-oh. She's watching, like I told you."

Maggie was standing in the window.

"That's Maggie-Jane Draper, she owns the joint. Always on my case." She took a drag. "I have five more minutes on my smoke break." She waved brightly, and Maggie sifted back out of sight.

"Okay, let's see…you had a burger—the ranch special, with fries and two beers." Grace paused, studying Jagger. "You really don't remember, do you? You said we might meet up at Joe Bear Bar later."

"I'm guessing I didn't show?" Jagger said cautiously.

"'Fraid not. Might've saved your bacon had you come," she said with a seductive smile.

Jagger grinned. He liked Grace. She was worn around the edges but she was real.

"I'm told I had a photo of Brittany Colton on me," he said. "Did you see it?"

"Uh-huh. Fell out of your wallet and landed right onto the table. Maggie was telling everyone after you left that it was a picture of Brittany with the kidnapped Colton baby, and that you were a spitting image of Jethro when he was younger. She's the one who first said that you could even be Cole Colton yourself."

Jagger's pulse kicked. Mia shot him a glance.

"Maggie knew Jethro when he was younger?" Mia said quickly.

Grace took another long drag and blew smoke out the side of her mouth. "Maggie and her husband used to work on Dead River Ranch. They started shortly after Jethro Colton bought the place, but didn't stay long."

Jagger's pulse went up another notch.

"Maggie helped in the kitchen. That's where she got started cooking the crap she has them dishing up in the diner." She paused, looking weary all of a sudden. "I'm sorry—I didn't mean they serve crap on the ranch." She dropped her cigarette and stubbed it out under her black shoe. "I'm a single mom with a five-year-old son. I hate the job, but I need it."

Jagger felt a stab of compassion for her.

"The word among the old-timers in Dead is that Maggie and Mr. Colton, you know, had a thing. I don't know whose skirts old man Colton *didn't* try to get under back then, a regular breed bull he was."

Then she blushed. "Oh, God. You could be one of them, a Colton. He's your father. I'm really sticking my feet in my mouth now, aren't I?"

"It's okay. I'd rather know."

"Yeah, well." She scuffed the dirt with her foot. "Maggie had a hard time with her husband. He used beat her before he went and killed himself. Shotgun in the mouth. Some say Maggie did it, and no one cares if she did. He was a mean piece of work, that husband of hers."

"What was his last name, also Draper?" Mia asked.

"Nah, his name was Mitch Radizeski. Maggie changed it back so she could start fresh. He used to work as a hand on the ranch. Either they both saved up all their money, which I doubt because Mitch used to drink it all away each month, or Maggie got cash from somewhere else after they left the ranch, but she had enough to buy this diner."

Jagger thought of Jethro. Money. Criminal connections. Paying people off.

"Did Mitch Radizeski ever do time?" he asked.

Her brows arched right up. "Why?"

"Just wondering."

"Well, yeah, he did. He was part of a petty theft ring called the Dalton Gang or something. But he cleaned up after, you know, before he went to work the ranch."

"Where did he do time?"

"Wyoming Medium Correctional from what Maggie says."

Jagger felt his skin prickle—the kind of feeling he got when he knew he was onto something. Wyoming Correc-

tional was where Jethro Colton had served his sentence
before buying Dead River Ranch. Jagger made a note to
look up this Radizeski's case as soon as he could get his
hands onto Mia's computer.

"When was Radizeski's suicide?" he asked.

"About ten years back." Grace threw another glance
over her shoulder. "I reckon that's when Maggie and
Drucker started their affair."

Mia caught Jagger's eyes again.

"Drucker and Maggie were seeing each other?"

"They were until Drucker's wife, Harriet, found out."
Grace checked her watch. "My break is up. I need to get
back in there."

"Grace, before you go, what else did Cole tell you in
the diner that night?" Mia said.

Grace hunched her shoulders against the cold and
rubbed her arms. A strand of brown hair blew across
her face and Jagger saw silver in it. Her makeup showed
streaks in the stark outdoor light. Again, he felt sorry for
her.

"Well, he'd told me he'd seen the news about the Colton
kidnapping on TV in Casper."

Mia's eyes narrowed. "Casper?"

She nodded. "And that he'd come looking for work on
Dead River Ranch." She turned to Jagger. "You were asking questions about Jethro, and about Cole Colton—like,
whether I thought that old kidnapping case was connected
to the recent Cheyenne one."

"Apparently he showed Drucker his ID," Mia prompted.

"Yeah. Montana driver's license. I didn't see it, though.
One of the ranch hands did—Tanner, I think it was. Look,
I really should get back," Grace said. But she hesitated
then looked up into Jagger's eyes. "It was good to see you
again. I hope it all works out." She glanced at Mia. Then

turned. Shoulders hunched against the cold, her brown skirt ugly, she made her way back to the diner.

"I feel bad for her," Mia said as they got back in the car.

Jagger started the ignition and pulled out into the street.

"So—Casper, Montana—ring any bells?""

Jagger inhaled deeply, shook his head.

"And what was that about prison and doing time, why did you ask that?" Mia said. Jagger could feel her eyes boring into him, but he focused on the road.

"I don't know…just a feeling."

"Like a *memory?*" There was bite to her voice. Impatience.

"I don't know, Mia. Maybe I was drawing a connection between what she was saying, and what you intimated about Jethro possibly having a criminal past. About him coming into sudden money. And Maggie coming into money to buy the diner." He stopped at another red light. As far as he could tell, Dead River was a two-stoplight town.

"We need to look up this Mitch Radizeski," he said. "And add both his and Maggie's names to the list. Put Hank Drucker's wife, Harriet, on there, too. She might be holding a deep grudge—not that I can imagine how it might connect to the Coltons."

The light turned green and Jagger made a left turn, heading down the valley he'd walked on his way in. He hadn't seen the road in the daylight—evidence of the wildfires was everywhere along this section of the foothills.

Mia sat in silence all the way back to the ranch. Jagger wondered what she was thinking, if she was even more suspicious now, after having listened to Grace.

"Turn there," she said as they neared the back end of

the Colton spread. "We'll go in via the employee entrance, then turn back to the field where I found you.

A few minutes later they were traversing the track that Jagger had been walking in the dark. This area had all burned and looked bleak, depressing. The Colton mansion was just visible in the distance and Jagger realized how close the fire had really come.

"Stop here, this is it."

He drew the Escalade to a halt. Ashen dust settled around them.

"I was riding across there—" she said, opening the door and getting out of the car. Mia stood with her arms tight across her stomach as she waited for Jagger to get out and come round to her side.

"That's the ditch." She pointed. "You were lying in there, unconscious. Your hat was over there."

There were still hoofprints in the ground. And lots of human prints. Probably cops, he thought as he dropped to his haunches to study them.

Mia was standing over him, watching him with such intensity it unnerved Jagger. There was a need in her eyes— a need for him to remember, to be whoever it was that she wanted him to be.

His chest ached suddenly to meet that need—her *every* need.

And he realized he had a big decision to make. Being undercover was one thing, but lying to Mia was another. He couldn't do it. Not now.

Now it had become personal.

He was going to tell her, everything. Tonight.

Hank Drucker stared at the name on his computer screen. He'd gotten a hit on the prints. Not only did this guy have a record, he was also linked to a military database for which Drucker would need higher clearance to access.

He sat back in his chair, adrenaline trilling soft and hot through his blood, his brain racing.

Jagger McKnight.

And the man's photo matched the mug shot on the fake Montana driver's license.

Checking his watch, Drucker called his wife. "Harriet, I won't be home for dinner," he said when she answered. "Something's come up." He paused as she ran through her usual set of questions. "Yes, it could be an all-nighter. I've got a major break in the case. I'll be here in my office, call me if you need me."

He hung up, knowing Harriet would call later. She checked up on him ever since he'd broken it off with Maggie. But she didn't know about his other lover—he was more careful about things now.

Drucker did a basic internet search using the name Jagger McKnight. You never knew what might show up in Google these days.

He got hits instantly, and the list of links was long.

Drucker clicked on the first link. A page opened and shock rippled through him. Quickly he opened the next link, then the next, and the next. His heart hammered loudly in his ears.

Leaning back he smoothed his hand over his pate as he tried to absorb the weight of his discovery.

Jagger McKnight was a journalist. Not just a simple reporter; he was one of the world's top print foreign correspondents. He'd most recently written stories while embedded with a United States military unit in Afghanistan where he'd been the only person found alive after an ambush by Afghan militants that had lasted nineteen days.

What was a top gun like that doing here in Dead River, asking questions about Jethro Colton?

Drucker searched deeper into the internet. The clock ticked, but he didn't notice time passing.

Then he found something that sent a chill through his blood. Jagger McKnight had been kidnapped when he was three months old, the same age and same year Cole Colton was abducted. McKnight had been found when he was nine—he'd been living under a false identify secured by the woman who took him.

Drucker frowned. Was this some kind of link?

There was no way he was going to inform Laramie police about the truck incident—not now.

This was his to handle, and fast.

Chapter 10

Heavy clouds were cutting out the sun and lowering the sky. Mia rubbed her arms against the increasing chill as she watched Cole. He was crouched down among the blackened stalks of grass, his gaze going toward the house and stable buildings in the distance.

He got up suddenly, moved across the field and dropped quickly back to his haunches.

"What is it?" she said, coming up to him.

"A gold pen," he said, picking it carefully out of the grass and holding it up for her to see. "It's engraved with the Dead River P.D. logo."

"They must've dropped it while they were searching the site."

"But they missed this," he said, reaching into the soil and carefully picking up a dull gold shell casing. He twisted it between his fingers. "It's .45 caliber."

Cole looked up toward the mansion and stables again,

his eyes going distant. A gust of wind suddenly lifted a fine cloud of black soot.

Mia turned her head away from the wind, blinking against the grit. She knew from the earlier investigation into Jenny Burke's murder that Jenny was shot with a 9 mm, and she knew that Dead P.D. cops carried .45s. Everyone on the ranch had been discussing calibers at that point. Drucker had also asked Cole if his missing pistol had been a 9 mm, because he said he'd found 9 mm casings here, too. There must have been an exchange of gunfire out here—two different guns.

"I was shot at that night, Mia," he said suddenly.

"You're remembering?" she whispered, dropping down into a crouch beside him.

"The horse came from out of the dark over there." He pointed in the direction of the house. "Huge black horse with that white streak on its chest—I must've had a flashlight to see that streak because everything else was pitch dark. But the rider, he was all dressed in black, black ski mask, and he had a light on his head. Bright as a hunting spot."

"Cole," she said. "Your memory is returning—coming to the field has triggered something!"

He turned away from her, suddenly unwilling to meet her eyes.

"Who on the ranch hunts, Mia? Who would have a hunting spot?"

She placed her hand on his forearm.

"Cole, look at me."

He rubbed his brow and glanced up at the sky instead, as if clouds and heavens might part and give him the answers he needed. Then slowly he turned and met her gaze.

A dark and haunted look filled his blue eyes. Conflict

creased his brow. Her chest squeezed. Wind gusted again, whipping strands of hair across her face.

"Cole, you should call that doctor."

"You mean the shrink."

"Psychiatrist."

He got to his feet, walked a few paces farther into the blackened and denuded field. It was a depressing landscape that made him appear even more alone, lost. And Mia suddenly wanted to take him away from this place. It was upsetting him. The human mind was a fragile thing. She knew that from experience, from her work.

She got up and called to him. "It's not a negative thing, Cole. It's nothing to be ashamed of. A psychiatrist has professional tools he can use to help unlock your memory. If you can remember these things now, by coming back to this field, other triggers should work, too."

"I want to go see Jethro," he said, his back to her. "Then…then we'll talk, Mia."

She frowned and went up to him again. "What do you mean, 'talk'?"

He faced her and Mia's heart skipped a beat. Something in his features had changed fundamentally. A chill sense of foreboding rustled through her.

"Cole, you're recalling something else, aren't you?" she asked quietly. "What is it?"

He didn't reply. He walked past her, heading back to the SUV. He opened the passenger door for her. "Who would have a hunting spot, Mia—who on Dead River ranch hunts at night?" he asked again as she climbed in.

"A lot of the guys hunt. But a bright headlamp is also accessible to all of the ranch hands. Sometimes they have to ride out at night if there's a problem with an animal. Amanda has one, too, in case she has to attend to an animal out in the dark." Mia paused, anxiety mounting. "You remembered something else. Cole, why won't you tell me?"

"It's nothing, Mia."

He got back in the Escalade and they drove down the farm track toward the house, an uneasiness growing between them now. It made Mia tense. He seemed to have locked her out from whatever was going on in his head and there was suddenly a chasm yawning between them.

He parked the Escalade out front of the house and sat in silence for a moment, the weight of everything that had happened this day suddenly heavy between them.

"I should get this medical report to Levi," Mia said, reaching for the envelope on the dash.

"Yeah." He gave a soft snort. "You can tell them all that I'm a head case."

"Is that what you're worried about?"

He didn't smile.

"Look, nothing changes with this diagnosis—psychological or physiological, your amnesia is real."

"It's not the same, Mia. People don't see it as the same. There's this underlying idea you should be able to man up, snap out of it."

Mia frowned as she looked deep into his eyes. It was as if Cole was talking from a place of prior experience, as if he'd been struggling with this memory loss before he even got here.

"You can't just snap out of amnesia. Where did you get this idea from, Cole?" she asked quietly.

He scrubbed his hands hard over his face.

"Look, don't go all macho male on me now and think that you can—"

"Here comes Catherine," he said, motioning with his chin.

Mia turned to see the Catherine running out of the mansion door toward their car, her long blond hair flying in the wind. Her cheeks were pink and her eyes were bright.

"Mia! Cole!" she called out as she came up to the car.

Mia opened the door quickly and got out to meet her. "Is everything okay?

"Yes! Yes! My father has agreed to see a specialist!" Her eyes danced in light. She was breathlessly happy. "The oncologist—he's one of the best—has agreed to come over *tonight* after he's done with his other patients."

The power of money, thought Mia.

"Dad wants to talk to Cole." Catherine went round to the driver's side where Cole was getting out the SUV. She reached for his hand, took it in hers. "I can't tell you what your coming here has done for us all, Cole. You've changed everything. Come!"

He glanced at Mia.

"I'll go put this medical report in the infirmary and see if Levi is around," she said. "I'll catch up with you later."

He had an odd look on his face as Catherine pulled him off into the family mansion.

The door swung shut behind them and Mia stood alone on the gravel outside, staring after them, wind cool against her face. She felt suddenly like the outsider she really was and that empty hole of loneliness in her stomach grew bigger. She'd glimpsed something golden with Cole, the possibility of a second chance in life, but it was as if a tide had turned suddenly in him, and it had happened in that burned and blackened field.

Besides, if Cole really was a Colton, there might be no place for her in his new life, in that big house, with that family. Did she even want that?

Mia knew in her heart she didn't.

She dropped the thought and made for the employee wing around the side of the house.

* * *

Mia left the report in the infirmary. There was no sign of Levi. She called his cell phone and left a message that they were back, and that Dr. Singh's report was on his desk.

Slipping her gun into her new concealed holster at the waistband of her jeans, Mia made her way past the kitchen. She intended to head out to the stables to find Dylan. She wanted to make things right after confronting him about Midnight earlier. Deeper down, she wanted to know that he hadn't lost his truck today.

Outside the pantry Mia ran into Mathilda coming out of her small administrative office.

"Mathilda, do you happen to know where Levi is?" she asked the housekeeper.

Mathilda's gaze lowered, taking in the dirt on Mia's jeans.

"I tripped," explained Mia, her mind going back to the terror of their ambush. But she kept the incident to herself. She was no mood to hand Mathilda more fuel for staff gossip.

"Levi and Kate went into Laramie today," Mathilda said. "They went with Gabby and Trevor to look at something for Gabby's wedding. But Levi will be back this evening so he can be here when the oncologist arrives. The others will overnight in Laramie and return in the morning."

The wedding—Mia had completely forgotten about Gabby and Trevor Garth's Christmas wedding plans. The sudden thought of their love, their dreams, their hopes— a marriage—made that empty hole in her stomach ache suddenly.

Mathilda hesitated, then reached for Mia's arm. "Nurse Sanders, do you mind if I have a candid word with you?"

"Why, what is it, Mathilda?" she asked as the head

housekeeper drew her aside into her small alcove of an office near the pantry. The pantry itself was still boarded up after Jenny's murder, and being near it still sent chills up Mia's spine. She rubbed her arms again, unable to shake the increasing sense of cold and the feel of dark foreboding that had come upon her in the burned-out field.

"You're worrying me, Mathilda. What is it?"

"You need to be careful, Mia. You shouldn't get involved with him."

"You mean *Cole?*"

"Yes."

Mia bristled. "Who said I was 'involved' with him?"

"The staff are talking."

"I don't believe this—I'm ordered to stick with our John Doe 24/7, move into his suite, drive him to Cheyenne, now I get accused of a *relationship* with him?"

"Mia, please." Mathilda's voice was gentle, but no less authoritarian. "It's my role in this household to guide staff and to enforce the rules, you do understand?"

Yes, thought Mia, and Mathilda was old school—she liked to make sure that the lines between upstairs family and downstairs staff were clear as glass. And that staff stayed in their place.

"I thought you didn't believe he was a Colton, anyway, Mathilda," she said crisply.

"I don't. In my humble opinion he's a con artist after the Colton money. But I've lived long enough to know that anything is possible, and for the moment, Mr. Colton has included him as family. If you're looking for a way to land yourself a fortune, Nurse Sanders, be warned, the Coltons stick to their own."

Indignation flared hot and fast in Mia and she couldn't help what came out of her mouth next. "Is that what you think? That I'm a gold digger? And what about Gabby marrying Trevor Garth—now there's an example of a Colton not sticking to 'their own.' And how about Levi Colton taking up with Kate, your kitchen help?"

Mathilda's eyes narrowed sharply. "Sex might be one thing, Mia, but believe me, the Coltons do stick with their sort over the long run. You'll be sorry."

Mia's jaw dropped. "Oh, and are you speaking from some past experience, then, Mathilda?"

The woman's eyes shrivelled with anger.

A warming bell clanged in Mia's brain but she was unable to pull back her own outrage. "Sex with Cole Colton might be all I want, Mathilda," she replied curtly. "He's pretty damn hot, don't you think?"

Mathilda cheeks flushed red at the impertinence. Mia turned and stormed off toward the mudroom, her boots sounding a sharp tattoo along the tiled floor.

"I think he could be dangerous, Nurse Sanders!" Mathilda called after Mia. "Someone is up to no good on this ranch, we all know that already!"

"I'll bear it in mind, thanks," Mia called back as she entered the mudroom.

She stomped out the door and over the gravel path to the stables, her blood racing, hot.

She was furious she'd even reacted to Mathilda's accusations at all. It was not her style. Until now Mia had managed to keep herself at a distance from all the staff gossip. Now she was the subject of gossip herself, being accused of trying to sleep her way into the Colton family. She cursed under her breath as she approached the stable doors. If she knew Mathilda, the housekeeper would now be gunning to have her fired, in the interests of family, of course, and Mathilda's opinion tended to hold weight—Mia's employment here at the ranch could now be in jeopardy.

Cole's words rang through her mind....

Why do you stay on, Mia?

She was no longer certain she *did* want to stay. But that left the future a scarily blank slate.

As she stomped into the stables, a stubbornness settled firmly into her chest—she almost wanted to make a move on Cole, have hot monkey sex with him, just to defy Mathilda. To defy herself. Her self-imposed isolation and resistance to intimacy were finally ganging up on her. No-strings sex might just be where it was at. Perhaps it should have been her revenge against Brad from the beginning.

But it was not her. Mia knew that. It just wasn't.

In the stables she asked for Dylan. They told her he was out in the back paddock.

Mia tromped across the fields.

From Jethro Colton's bedroom window Jagger watched Mia's blond ponytail tossing in the wind as she marched with deliberation over a ploughed field toward a cowboy working a horse in a distant paddock—a woman on a mission.

His attention shifted to the cowboy. Dylan, he thought. Mia was going to speak to Dylan Frick. A twinge of something akin to jealousy pinged through Jagger. Mia liked that wrangler, a lot. That Dylan also had an affection for Mia was obvious.

Jagger could not have anticipated this—that a personal investment would tear him away from the very story he'd come for. He rubbed his hand across his jaw. It'd be all over by tonight. He was going to tell her the truth of his identity and why he'd come to Dead River. Then he could only wait to see how the cards would fall. If Mia was angry enough with him to immediately spill the beans on his ID, all hell would break loose. And worse, he might have killed any chance of a longer-term relationship with her completely. Talk about a double bind.

"Cole."

A spark ran through him at the sound of Jethro's voice coming from the bed behind him.

He turned round.

"Beautiful view, isn't it?" Jethro asked, his eyes watery.

Jagger gave a soft snort, Mia still on his mind. "Yes, Jethro. It is."

Morphine was feeding slowly from the drip into the sick man's arm—like a timer, counting down the minutes until his mind grew foggy and he'd drift into a pain-free sleep. Jagger had only a small window to get what he needed out of the patriarch.

"I built this ranch from scratch, you know, almost two thousand acres of it. Those heads of cattle you see out there in the fields now—when I bought the place there was nothing. My own sweat and blood I put into this place."

And money that came from somewhere.

Jagger sat on edge of the sick man's bed. The oxygen concentrator hummed noisily beside Jethro. His cheeks were gaunt, and he was pale with pain. Catherine had left them alone at Jethro's request. Jagger got a sense Catherine sat with him often. She loved her father and Jagger was envious of that kind of love. Again he thought of how his inability to give it had hampered his ability to receive it for most of his life.

"What did the doc in Cheyenne say?" Jethro said.

"Levi will have to take a look at the report and interpret the medicalese for you. Bottom line, I still don't remember why I came here or who I really am."

Something darkened in the old man's eyes, as if ghosts were swallowing him up from the inside. Part of Jagger felt sorry for him.

"Is that why you wanted to talk to me?" Jagger said.

"I wanted to tell you that I had my lawyer come in."

"Max Finch?"

Jethro's gaze sharpened slightly, then he coughed, pressing his fist tightly against his chest. "Yes—Finch handles some of my estate stuff along with...a few other things. I got him to change my will. I want you to know that as soon as the DNA paternity testing is confirmed you'll receive the first of your inheritance cut that's due all the Colton children on their thirtieth birthday." He coughed again—a wracking and wet sound. "Chief Drucker said he'll be here with his tech first thing tomorrow morning to do the blood sampling. We'll have results by nightfall tomorrow—Drucker's guaranteed me top priority with the lab."

Tension whispered through Jagger,

"And if paternity is not confirmed?" he said quietly.

Jethro waved the idea away with his hand. "Then the clauses I've added to the will do not kick in. The girls have expressed the same concern...they..." Another wave of coughing seized him. He was silent for a minute as he gathered his breath. "They don't have to worry. If you're not Cole, you get nothing."

"I don't believe I came here for money, Jethro."

"Then what? Everyone wants money...my money."

"I don't remember what I came for. Maybe it was to find out where I was born, to find a sense of belonging, home, family." All things Jagger imagined Cole would want, if he was still alive. "Answers to why my father stopped searching for me."

The old man's eyes flared to Jagger. "I never stopped— The leads ran cold."

Jagger nodded, thinking of his own parents, how they hired one P.I. after another, never gave up. Until they found him. Not that it resulted in the big happy ending everyone had hoped for.

The old man stared at him for several beats, his features pained. Then he closed his eyes, breathing in deeply from the cannula in his nose. The oxygen machine hummed into the silence.

Jagger glanced at the meds bag hanging from the drip. The contents were slowly going down.

"We came back from Cheyenne through Dead River," he said carefully. "Maggie from the diner there used to work on the ranch, I believe?

Jethro frowned slightly and slowly opened his eyes. "Maggie Radizeski?"

"She goes by the name of Draper since her husband killed himself."

Jethro turned his head away, eyes red-rimmed and rheumy. He said nothing.

"Her husband worked here, too, didn't he?"

"Where you going with this, Cole?" His voice was weakening.

Jagger got up, walked to the window, put his hands in his pockets.

"It's weird," he said slowly, staring out the window, "Not knowing who you are, having no memory. You grab on to anything to try and understand the past, to figure out why you might have come here. Maggie seemed startled to see me from what I am told." Jagger turned. "She thought I looked like you when you were young."

Jethro's watery gaze met his. Silence filled the room, apart from the old man's wheezy machine-aided breaths and the hum of the oxygenator.

"I had a relationship with Maggie once," he said finally. "It was just physical. A man can understand that."

"Chief Hank Drucker certainly would."

"What do you mean?"

"He also had an affair with Maggie."

Jethro stared at him, eyes going a little unfocused as morphine continued to feed *infinitesimally* into his veins. Tension wound tighter in Jagger. He could feel the clock ticking.

"Maggie was a very, very attractive woman," Jethro said quietly. "And a good woman. She gave Desiree Beale a job at her new diner...." His voice faded.

Jagger's interest piqued and he came forward. "When was that?"

"Around the time of Brittany's death. But Desiree didn't stay long after Brittany's funeral. She took a job at a diner in Jackson."

Jagger shot another glance at morphine drip. The meds were making the old man loquacious, but a tipping point would come any second now, and he'd go downhill as he drifted off into drugged sleep.

"Where did you first meet Maggie?"

Jethro closed his mouth, and through his nose he carefully inhaled a lungful of oxygenated air.

"Mitch Radizeski." He closed his eyes, inhaled again, slowly. "I knew him from...long ago."

The penitentiary? Or further back? Had Jethro been somehow connected to Radizeski's petty theft ring? Had the money used to buy the ranch land been stashed away somewhere, the proceeds of crime? Jagger needed to get his hands on that laptop Mia said he could use—he needed to look up Radizeski's case.

"I want you to know, Cole, I did love your mother." The old man's voice was very weak now.

Jagger seated himself again on the side of the bed. "That blue baby blanket I was wrapped in when I was abducted,

you said that was given to my mother by her sister, Desiree, right?"

He nodded. "Distinctive embroidery—I'd know it anywhere."

Jagger figured that whoever had planted that scrap of
blanket on him had to know what had happened to Cole all
those years ago. And that person was here in Dead River
somewhere, maybe even on the ranch.

"I'm told that Desiree was seen in Jackson with a baby
not long after she left Dead River."

Jethro's gaze ticked to his. Jagger could read caution in
the man's eyes—warning bells were going off somewhere
in his mind despite the woozy effects of the medication.

"What…do you want with this, Cole?"

Jagger got up and paced slowly to the window and back.

"I'm trying to piece together what might have happened
to me, Jethro, and who might have taken me without wanting ransom. If my memory doesn't return…I'll never have
any idea. The mystery will never be solved. So *anything*
you can tell me would help."

The wariness lingered in the old man's eyes. "She was
murdered," he said quietly. "And there was no baby. It was
a rumour that was disproved. The detective investigating
her death—Novak—he looked into it carefully and found
no substance." Jethro closed his mouth and inhaled slowly
through his nose.

"So many rumours, red herrings, false leads came in
after you were taken. Everyone wants to help at a time like
that. They all want to be the one who solves the case, but
it can just confuse the process."

Taken.

Again Jethro had chosen to use that word over *abducted,*
or *kidnapped.* Was there a subliminal reason? Did it feel
softer somehow, less violent or less criminal?

"Why do you think no ransom was ever demanded?"

The man's eyes glazed over. Jagger's gaze flicked back to the drip.

"They...all waited for a note...never came."

"They" waited.

Not Jethro?

Perhaps the morphine was responsible for his choice of phrase. Or perhaps Jethro's mental defences were dropping because of it. Urgency rippled through Jagger.

"Tell me about it the abduction itself, Jethro."

He shook his head, face going white suddenly as he gripped his fist tighter against his chest, eyes watering.

"Please, I need to know."

But the old man lay mute as the machine hummed, his eyes going distant. Finally he said, thickly, "I...showed them...the police...how it looked like...robbery."

"Robbery," Jagger said, then threw a quick glance at the door, lowering his voice. Catherine might be coming back any second.

"Wasn't that what you and Mitch Radizeski did time for?"

Jethro's eyes fluttered weakly as he struggled to pull himself out of the haze clouding his brain.

"Damn...meds." He fisted the duvet, tried to pull himself up, but succeeded only in dragging the bedding up off his feet. "Damn illness. No...time for illness." He looked away. Frustrated.

Jagger's pulse quickened. He leaned forward. "*Who* took him, Jethro?" he whispered urgently. "Do you know who took your son? Is that why you didn't need to wait for a ransom note? Did you help make it look like a robbery?"

Jethro's eyes closed, his breathing changed and his mouth slackened. The old man had gone to sleep.

Jagger stood up, adrenaline buzzing through his blood.

This was all he was going to get out of Jethro Colton, but more than ever now, he felt Jethro knew something. And was hiding it.

But why?

And how did it connect to what was happening on the ranch now?

"Dad?" It was Cath, at the door.

"He's gone to sleep," Jagger said, stepping back from the bed. "The meds have finally kicked in."

She came up to Jagger. "Thanks for sitting with him. I…" Her eyes filled with emotion.

"Hey," he said, hooking his arm gently around her shoulders. "It's okay." And as he comforted Catherine Colton, guilt bit into him. It was not a comfortable or familiar feeling for Jagger. He'd never felt guilty for going after a story before, but this was different. It was in a family's house, up close and personal. This was not a battlefield or war zone, there were no political treachery or global implications. Why in hell had he been so consumed about getting this story, anyway?

As he walked out with Catherine, Jagger reminded himself, it was about a stolen baby. A child never found. A father who stopped looking. Cole Colton—the little voiceless victim who could have been Jagger himself.

That was the bottom line—always had been. And yes, it was intimate, because someone connected with this family had done an innocent child wrong. But after he told Mia the truth, that all might be tossed to the wind.

"I hope you don't mind that there won't be a family dinner tonight, Cole," Catherine was saying. "Gabby, Trevor and Kate are overnighting in Laramie, and Levi will be with the oncologist who'll be arriving later." She smiled. "But I've asked Agnes to prepare something special for when the others do get back, a feast. All of us together.

Maybe we can manage to get father down, too. We could bring his drip and all." She looked up at him, hope in her eyes.

"Maybe we'll even have reason to celebrate after your DNA results come in tomorrow. A proper welcome-home dinner."

Mia found Dylan leaning with his arms on the fence as he watched his latest pride prance in the field. She leaned on the fence beside him.

"Hey, Mia," Dylan said, his eyes meeting hers briefly.

"She's gorgeous," Mia said as she watched the chestnut mare trot across the grass, her coppery-red mane and tail ruffling in the wind. Against the backdrop of the mountains and the stormy sky the horse looked like a painting and Mia was reminded that this was beautiful place. It had also been a place of peace for her. Until recently.

"How did the scan in Cheyenne go?" Dylan said, eyes on the mare.

"Okay. There's no immediate medical concern but his memory might take a while to return. Dylan, I'm sorry about earlier. I didn't mean to imply anything—"

"Midnight was taken out by someone that night, Mia," he interrupted. "I questioned the grooms. One of them had returned to the stables that night to look for his watch, and he'd noticed Midnight's stall was empty. He didn't say anything because Midnight was back there in the morning. He assumed I'd taken the stallion somewhere." He turned to look at her. "I checked Midnight out—there's a small cut on his shoulder that no one can explain."

Mia stared at him.

"And you don't know who it was that took him out?"

Dylan shook his head, his mouth set in a grim line. "Could've been any one of the better riders. Damn risky, though." He went silent as he returned to watching the horse in the field. "I just don't see any of them doing this, Mia, taking Midnight, running a man down." His face darkened as he thought of something.

"I don't know what in hell is going on here. Dead River Ranch can never be the same again, not after all this."

"Yeah, I know."

"I'd like my own place," he said. "Been saving."

"You'll get it, Dylan. I don't doubt it."

He turned to her. "How about you, Mia?"

"I...I'm thinking of moving on, too." She hesitated, then said quickly, "That's between you and me, okay? Besides, I have no idea yet where I might go."

He offered her a smile. "Gotcha."

Mia thought about how best to phrase her next question. She watched the horse for a while, then said quietly, "Someone tried to run us off the road in the mountain pass this morning."

"What?" His gaze flared to hers.

"Someone tried to kill us, Dylan. He rammed us from behind with his truck and shot at us. We've reported it to the police. We think whoever tried to run Cole down with the horse is trying to finish the job and silence him."

"Silence him— Why?"

"We don't know."

Dylan stared at Mia, a strange look entering his eyes. "Who would do this...what kind of vehicle?"

"Gray Ford pickup. Two-door—the plates were obscured by dust."

His eyes narrowed sharply and his features turned hard. "So that's what you came out here for, to know if it was my truck?"

"Dylan—" She touched his arm. "I *know* you. I trust you above everyone else on this ranch. You were the first one to help me feel at home. You set me up with Sunny. But I also know you loan your truck out."

"You think someone borrowed my truck to run you off the road?"

"Where is it now?"

"Behind the storage barn, where I parked it twenty minutes ago."

Relief washed through Mia. She was right. Dylan Frick had nothing to do with this.

"The police are investigating this incident?"

She nodded. Wind whipped hair over her face and she pushed it back.

The horse in the field whinnied and trotted over to where they were standing. Dylan gave her a treat from his pocket. She nuzzled his hand, taking it, and he softly stroked her nose. Then, with a whinny, she trotted off.

"First time she's done that," he said, pleasure in his voice. "She was real skittish when we got her. Takes patience to build that trust."

Trust.

Trust was one thing Mia had lost with Brad. Dylan Frick was going to make a woman very happy one day. He was damn fine wrangler and an even better man.

"Do you like him, Mia?" he said suddenly.

Surprise washed through her. "You mean Cole?"

"Yeah."

"I...I don't know who he really is, Dylan."

"But there is something about him that you like."

"I...yes, I suppose. Is this about the rumours?"

He smiled, a little sad. "No. It's about your eyes. I can see it in your eyes."

She blew out air. "You can read people like you read horses, Dylan."

Clouds were darkening the sky as dusk crept over the

ranch lands. Mia felt a few flecks of fine rain against her cheeks. "Look, I should go. Thanks for hearing me out."

"No worries." Then he said, "Be careful, Mia."

His words played over and over in her mind as she made her way back to the mansion....

Be careful, Mia.

Then it was Mathilda's voice....

He could be dangerous, Nurse Sanders! Bernice Black's words joined the chorus. *Things—people here—are not what they seem.*

And that deep, cold sense of foreboding sifted deeper into Mia. As she neared the mansion, she resolved to pull back from her involvement with Cole. They were all right—she didn't know who he was, where he'd come from, what he might have done. Their visit to Cheyenne Memorial had confirmed that he was not in any physical danger from his injury. He no longer needed her to watch 24/7. She'd go up to the Blue Suite now, gather her things, move back into her room and keep her distance.

At least until the mystery of his identity was solved. And that would happen by tomorrow night. Nerves ate at her as she entered the mansion, a sense of time closing in on her.

"He's a *reporter!*" the voice hissed, low, angry, urgent. "He's a goddamn journalist pretending he's Cole Colton. He came to Dead River for a story and I hope to God he hasn't filed anything yet. Where did you put his computer?"

"I told you, in the root cellar."

"Did you look at it?"

"No, what for?"

"Listen, a story could bring us *all* down. This is a worst-case scenario. I don't care how you do it, but stop him. *Kill him.* Before his blood can be taken for DNA tomorrow morning. No more messing around with subtlety or attempted accidents. The man must die, before it's proved he's not Cole Colton."

"Hey." Cole glanced up as Mia entered the suite. Fresh out of the shower, he was sitting at the table shirtless, and his hair hung damp over his brow. He was working on her computer.

Mia froze, staring at her laptop.

His smiled faded and he stood up. "Mia, I hope it's okay, you said any time—"

"It's fine," she said crisply, tearing her attention away from his half-naked body, the way his tattoo flexed across his chest, trying not the think of the heat suddenly washing into her belly. She brushed past him, making for her own room.

"How was your visit with Jethro?" she called out as she opened her gym bag on the bed and began tossing her few belongings into it.

He leaned against the doorframe. "Jethro gave me the name of the detective in Jackson who looked into the claim that Desiree Beale was spotted with a baby."

"And?" Mia continued packing—unable to look at him. Her heart rate was going up despite her intent to distance herself. He had a magnetic sexual power over her and she was quite simply weak against it. *He could be dangerous... Be careful, Mia... All is not as it seems....*

"I called the detective. His name's Novak."

Her hands stilled. She stared at her gym bag.

"What did he say?" Still, she wouldn't look at him.

"Mia."

Slowly she raised her eyes, met his gaze.

"What are you doing?"

"I'm packing. I need to move back into my room."

He came up to her and took her by the shoulders. His touch was firm, yet gentle, controlling. Panic washed through her as her skin turned red-hot. Her gaze flicked to the door, to escape.

"Mia, please, just stay the night, until the DNA test is done. Besides, I want to show you what I've found." He paused, a strange look entering his smoky-blue eyes. "And I need to talk to you."

She swallowed, emotion surging up into her throat. "Cole." Her voice came out husky. "I…I need to step away, step back. From this— Us. Until I know…until we know what's going on."

He held her gaze in silence for several beats.

"Okay," he said quietly, his hand sliding down her arm, encircling her wrist. "But first come see this." He drew her away from her half-packed gym bag and into the living area. Pulling up a chair besides his, he said, "Take a seat."

Mia did, slowly. He sat beside her, too close. She could feel his body heat and she wished to heaven he'd put a shirt on. He reached for the mouse and the eagle talons on his forearm stretched as his muscle moved under them, as if readying to grasp prey.

And that's exactly what she felt like right now, prey, mesmerized by the glare of a hungry eagle.

Cole clicked on a link and the website of the Jackson P.D. opened onto her screen. Mia concentrated on inhaling a long, slow breath of air. *Just listen to him, then pack your bags and go down to your room…it'll be fine.*

As he clicked a link on the web page, he said, without looking at her, "How'd it go with Dylan?"

"How do you know I spoke with him?"

"Saw you from Jethro's window."

Unnerved, she hesitated. "It wasn't his truck."

Cole met her gaze, his face so close, his lips. The memory of their kisses swelled hotly through her mind. Mia swallowed against the lump of desire building painfully in her throat.

"I... Dylan...also said that a groom confirmed Midnight was not in his stall at the time you were attacked, and that he found an unexplained cut on the stallion's shoulder."

His gazed dipped briefly to her mouth, and his breathing changed subtly. "Doesn't mean it wasn't him who rode the horse, Mia. Did you see Dylan's truck for yourself?"

"I... No." She felt herself leaning toward him, aching for the feel of those lips against hers again. Mia pushed back her chair abruptly and launched to her feet. She went to the kitchen, grabbed a glass from the cupboard. "Want some water?"

"No. You okay, Mia?"

"Fine. I just hate you implicating Dylan like this. Tell me what the detective said." She shoved the glass under the ice dispenser, and cubes clattered into the glass. She filled it to the top with cold water and took a deep sip. She stayed behind the counter. He watched her intently, a strange look on his face—a mix of hunger, regret, something else Mia couldn't place.

It did nothing to quell her nerves or the edginess riding hotly through her.

"The detective, Luke Novak, is a police chief in Jackson now." Cole stood as he spoke and came over to the counter. He drew up a stool and sat opposite Mia. She was glad for the counter between them and she remained standing.

"Novak confirmed that he found no irrefutable evidence of a child at the time, but he believed there was one."

Mia lowered her glass slowly and set it on the counter. "Really?"

"Yes. Shortly after Cole was kidnapped, Desiree Beale arrived in Jackson and took a job at a diner. One of the waitresses who subsequently bought the diner—Marnie Sayers—drove Desiree home one day, and when Marnie dropped Desiree off, she thought she heard a baby crying inside Desiree's room."

Cole leaned forward, bare arms resting on the counter. Mia resisted stepping back, out of the reach of his darkly sensual aura. Again, she wished he'd put his shirt back on. Her gaze lowered to the tattoo across his chest—the dog tag and wings. *Death before Dishonor.*

"Marnie apparently asked Desiree about the crying and according to her, Desiree acted weird. Then someone else saw Desiree getting into a cab with a small child wrapped in a blue blanket. According to Novak, the cab driver confirmed that he did give a woman with a baby a ride that day, but she paid cash and he couldn't confirm that it was in fact Desiree Beale—she'd been wearing big sunglasses and a scarf over her hair." He reached for the glass of water Mia had left on the counter, and he took a deep swallow. She watched his Adam's apple move and she focused on taking in another deep breath, her world narrowing, logic skittering away at the edges.

"Are you saying you think *Desiree* took Cole with her to Jackson? And that Jethro knew about it?"

"I think he might have condoned it, Mia. And I think Jethro helped make it look like a robbery and kidnapping. He knew all the time that a ransom note would never come."

"But *why?*"

"I phoned Marnie Sayers—she still owns the diner. But the woman got real cagey when I asked who had owned the diner before her. She said it was a woman named Faye Donner. And that it was Faye who had initially given both her and Desiree waitressing jobs. But I haven't been able to come up with an address for any Faye Donner."

"Another Faye?"

"I know, Faye Frick, Faye Donner, it's an interesting coincidence. Come take a look at this."

Reluctantly Mia went back to seat herself beside him at her laptop.

Cole pulled up an old photograph of Faye Donner posing with Desire Beale and Marnie Sayers at the diner. "Novak sent this pic to me—he's keen to help. The fact that Beale's murder was never solved has been dogging him for years."

Mia leaned sharply forward as the picture filled the screen. The resemblance was uncanny.

She looked slowly up at Cole, her heart rushing. "It could be *her*—she looks like Faye Frick, the Colton nanny. I… Faye Frick's hair was black, and she was at least forty pounds heavier than the woman in this diner photo, but add a few decades…" Words failed Mia as the possibility sunk in.

Faye Donner looked like Faye Frick. She could be Dylan's biological mother.

Chapter 11

Mia stared at Cole. "Okay, let's just take a step back here. You think there *was* a baby in Jackson with Desiree?"

"That's what Novak believes, he just couldn't nail the proof at the time."

She leaned forward, studying the image of Faye Donner on her laptop screen again. A chill trickled down her spine. "All right," she said quietly. "For argument's sake, let's say that Desiree Beale was the one who took baby Cole, and that Jethro knew what his sister-in-law had done. Desiree then goes to Jackson where she's hired as a waitress in a diner owned by this Faye Donner. Next thing we know, Desiree has been shot dead, the baby goes missing, the diner is sold and a woman named Faye Frick shows up in Dead River with a seven-month-old baby boy, and she says she's looking for work on this ranch." Mia glanced up. "Could it be possible? Could Faye Donner have taken baby Cole after Desiree's death and come here, claiming Cole was her own biological child?"

"Hypothetically, it's possible."

"Which could also explain how the piece of blue baby blanket ended up here."

He nodded, pupils darkening as his gaze locked with hers. Sexual energy swelled like a tangible force between them.

"That…that would mean Dylan Frick could be Cole Colton."

"Yes," he whispered, his lids lowering slightly. His lashes were so dense, so long. His mouth so close. Mia could hardly think straight as she met the intensity of his dark-blue eyes. He smelled so good, of shampoo, a touch of aftershave. She could feel the warmth radiating from his bare skin. And these startling revelations, the weight of them, were being clouded by something physical that was rolling so powerfully through her body that logic was blurring along the edges of her mind.

She needed to back away. That had been her plan.

But Mia was also compelled to finish hearing this out.

"If Dylan is Cole," she said, softly, "then…who are *you?*"

He swallowed.

"That DNA test tomorrow—it's not going to be a paternal match, is it?" she whispered.

He raked his hand through his still-damp hair, the movement flexing his chest muscle. Then he got up suddenly and went to fetch the remainder of her water from the kitchenette counter.

Mia turned to watch him. He stood with his powerfully muscled back to her as he drained the glass and set it down with a clunk. He stood like that for a while.

Something akin to anger, defiance, rose in Mia's chest as she realized she *wanted* to think he was Cole. That was the simple truth. She was no better than the rest of the Coltons, because she was afraid of the truth now, and what it might mean to her.

Mia got up and went to him. She placed her palm flat against the back of his shoulder. He tensed. His skin was hot. "You could still be him," she said. "This is all just conjecture."

He didn't answer, did not turn to face her.

"Why?" she whispered, lowering her hand to his waist. "Why would Jethro let go of his own son?"

"Perhaps he struck some kind of Faustian bargain with Desiree," he said, his voice thick, husky. Still, he wouldn't turn to face her. "Maybe Desiree knew something and she wanted her sister's baby in return for secrecy."

"And when you arrived in Dead River with that photo of Brittany and her baby, asking questions about the Coltons, and you looked so much like Jethro himself in his younger days—someone thought to frame you as Cole, and kill you?"

Slowly, he turned. His gaze lowered to her lips. Mia's mouth went bone dry and her heart started to jackhammer against her ribs. She fiddled with her empty ring finger and that gaping hole in her stomach began to pound with an almost painful need to be filled, with him, all of him. Mia ached to open herself to him fully, wrap her legs around him, take him into her, hold him tight against her body. Before it was all shattered. Before she found out who he really was.

"I still don't understand why someone would want it to appear that Cole had returned, and then been killed."

"To stop all the questions, maybe." He put his hand on her arm. Electricity sparked through her. He moved his palm slowly up to her shoulder. Mia tried to swallow, tried to breathe.

"Mia—" His hand crested her shoulder and slowly he

slid it up to the bare skin of her neck. He cupped the back of her neck with his fingers, so strong yet gentle. Her vision began to narrow. "I need to tell you something. I—"

But she quickly pressed two fingers against his lips. She didn't want to hear. Whatever it was. Not now, not yet. By tomorrow night this could all be changed, over. And this thing between them that felt so secret and intimate and precious would be forever shattered. This might be the last time she'd be with him like this, have an opportunity. And right now she wanted sex—with this mysterious dark stranger. She wanted sex, hot and fast and hard.

She wanted to feel deliciously female and wicked. She wanted to claw back all those things she'd lost, or been fighting against, since Brad abandoned her. Since she'd allowed shame to claim and inhibit her. She thought about the condoms she'd seen in the bathroom cabinet and her lower body turned hot.

With his thumb, he tilted her face up. A muscle pulsed fast at his jaw. The urge to kiss him was fierce. Consuming. Overwhelming

Panic surged hot and sudden in Mia, riding on the back of her lust. Would she be able to do this and walk away tomorrow if it all went to hell in a handbasket? Her eyes began to burn, and inside she began to tremble. But her body had already overtaken her mind.

Reaching up, Mia curved her hand behind his neck and drew him down to her. She pressed her mouth over his lips. Warm. Salty. A wave of molten desire swamped Mia's brain wholly as she moved her mouth over his, her tongue flicking, licking, teasing, seeking the crevice between his lips.

Something cracked in him, and he yanked her up against his bare chest, opening his mouth under hers, kissing her back hard, furious, his tongue running along her teeth.

Mia met his fury, desperate to obliterate the wasted years, to push away the past. To be woman. To be Mia again. She ran her hand down his flat stomach, feeling the ridges of muscle, the delicious coarseness of the line of hair that disappeared into the waistband of his jeans. The memory of him naked on the cot in the infirmary flashed in her mind, the flare of hair between his thighs. The size of him. She moved her hand lower, cupping the hard bulge in his jeans. He groaned against her mouth, then pulled back suddenly. He looked unfocused, dangerous.

"Mia…" His voice was hoarse. "Are…you sure…"

She silenced him by aggressively pressing her mouth back over his while she used both hands to undo his belt buckle, then his zipper. She pushed down the front of his briefs, sliding her hand in. His erection swelled hot and hard into her hand and she could barely breathe. She began to stroke, caress, milk the quivering length of him, as a wild kind of fury built dangerously in her chest.

Quickly, Mia crouched, drawing his jeans over his calves, and her lips met his erection. She teased him with her tongue as his jeans pooled on the floor. Taking him into her mouth completely, she traced the rigid scar that ran up the inside of his thigh, up to his groin.

He moaned, his voice low and feral in his chest as he dug his hands tightly into her hair, guiding her motion.

As she worked him, Mia could feel him beginning to vibrate, the muscles in his legs shaking. Suddenly, his hands fisted in her hair and he stopped her, pulling her head back. And in a sudden powerful movement he swung her up onto the kitchen counter and fumbled wildly to undo her jeans. He yanked her jeans down her hips and slid his hand into the front of her panties, cupping her hard. Mia gasped, throwing her head back as his fingers pushed up into her.

He found her sensitive nub, scoring, caressing, twisting

his fingers inside her. Mia opened her legs wider, drawing her knees up. With his free hand he yanked off her boots. They clattered to the floor. Raising her up off the counter, he pulled off her jeans. Kissing her deeply, he unbuttoned her shirt, unclasped her bra. He moved his mouth down her neck, taking her nipple between his teeth, encircling it with his tongue as he moved his fingers inside her. Somewhere in the back of her mind she heard the delicate lace of her panties ripping.

"The bathroom," she whispered. "Protection, in the bathroom cabinet."

She sat naked on the counter, her body shaking with need while he walked buck naked toward the bathroom. Her heart jackhammered. She could—*should*—stop right here. Get off this counter, pull on her clothes, leave this room.

But it was too late. He came out of the bathroom, walking toward her, his eyes consuming her, his erection sheathed and gleaming between his massive thighs. His face was etched with hunger, his lids low. Mia tried to swallow as he neared.

Next thing, his hands were under her buttocks and he yanked her up off the counter and down onto the length of his erection. It went in hard, deep. Mia gasped, throwing her head back. Her stomach swooped and her vision swirled into shades of scarlet and black.

Hooking her ankles behind his waist, her arms around his neck, Mia rocked her hips against his, every nerve in her body singing, raw, screaming for release at the feel of him inside her. Her muscles began to tremble; her hand fisted in his hair. A vase of flowers went crashing down from the kitchen counter, scattering water and blooms across the floor.

Holding her tightly, skin to skin, he carried her through

to his bedroom while still kissing her aggressively. Her foot connected with a lampshade and the lamp fell off the table. In the bedroom the drapes were open. Outside the light had grown dim as twilight crawled in from the shadows of the mountains.

He dropped her onto the bed, and Mia flung backward, hair splaying out over his pillow as she spread-eagled across the sheets.

He stood there, staring down at her, naked as the day he was born, his erection powerful. His eyes looked black, dangerous. A dark thrill arrowed down through Mia's chest into her belly.

He leaned over her, bracing his hands on either side of her body. Kneeing her thighs open wide he bent his head down, kissed her mouth again, thrusting his tongue. She arched her pelvis up, desperate, screaming inside for more of him. But he didn't give, not yet. Instead, he moved his mouth slowly down the column of her neck, flicking his tongue softly into the hollow at the base of her throat, trailing his lips down so achingly slowly and gently she felt a scream of desperation building in her chest.

He teased her belly button with his tongue—wet, warm. Mia thrust up her hips, quivering as his lips moved lower, lower until he found her folds, and his tongue entered her. She sucked air in sharply at the sensation, her fists balling the sheets at her side as he moved his tongue rhythmically inside her, his teeth scoring her swollen, sensitive nub. Mia's eyes began to burn, filling with tears as her body began to shudder.

"No…" she whispered. "No…not yet…please…."

He stopped, brought his body over hers, holding up his weight. Then even more slowly, he pressed just the tip of his erection against her folds. Mia was unable to breathe.

He teased her, pushing just the tip into her, before sliding it out. With the next thrust he gave her just a bit more, then a tiny bit more. Mia went almost blind with need. She lifted her hips high, desperate for all of him, and with a sudden thrust he was inside her to the hilt, the weight of his body pressing her back down into the bed. He ground his hips urgently against hers.

She matched his rhythm, his movements, writhing, her skin going slick and hot against his. He opened her thighs even wider and she raised her knees, allowing him to go even deeper. Suddenly Mia froze as every muscle in her body went rigid as iron. Then, with a sharp gasp, she shattered around him, wave upon powerful wave shuddering through her. Tears of sweet release streamed down her cheeks.

Mia held him tightly against her, her fingers digging into his firm buttocks, not wanting to let go as small aftershocks continued to tremble through her. She felt weightless, free. She could do anything. And the thought brought a fresh surge of emotion to her eyes.

Jagger felt her tears wet against his cheek and he pushed himself up, worried. But she smiled at him through the emotion streaming down her face, and his heart clenched.

"Mia…"

She shook her head, her eyes telling him it was beautiful as she wrapped her arms around him, pulling him down against her breasts. The tenderness Jagger felt in her arms, the soft weightlessness, the enveloping sensation of her care, was so exquisite, so painful, he thought he might burst. He hadn't wanted it to come to this. He'd needed to talk to her first. He'd tried to pull back, not once, but twice. He should pull away now.

But she began to move her hips under his, a soft circular motion, and it cracked any vestige of control. Fire shot through his groin and seized hold of his brain. He thrust into her, moving harder, faster, friction increasing his temperature to a searing heat, his breathing going ragged, his vision blind as he dug down deep, trying to reach something he couldn't articulate, didn't understand, drowning all his darkness and guilt and shame in the deep pure sweetness of her arms.

And he came inside her, an explosive release that blew the terrible memories into thousands of glittering shards that tinkled away into some hidden part of his brain.

His world spun as she gathered him tightly against herself, just holding him there, inside her. He could taste her tears on his lips. Or were those his? And in this moment, Jagger knew he'd be able to love this woman. Wholly. Forever. In a way he'd never been able to love before.

He'd finally found his way back, he'd seen which road he wanted to take into the future, however hazy it might look right now, however challenging and littered with obstacles it might become. Jagger wanted to go down that road, with her hand in his. But now he stood to lose it all. He was standing on the crumbling edge of an abyss.

He rolled onto his side. It was almost dark outside now, the sound of rain ticking softly at the undraped window. Her skin looked alabaster in the haunting light, her hair a tangled halo of pale gold on his pillow. Jagger trailed his finger along her collarbone, over the swell of her breast, her nipple. He felt it contract under his touch and his eyes met hers in the faint light.

"You're beautiful, Mia," he whispered. "In every possible way."

Her eyes glittered and she said nothing.

"You're sad?"

She shook her head. "Just…overwhelmed." She smiled at him, and he watched as the light of her smile reached her eyes. His chest squeezed with emotion—with love, affection, a powerful desire to protect, cherish. He'd kill for this woman. He knew that now. He wished he could use the sudden feeling of physical power and energy to crush this other thing he had to deal with now, force it away. It was a sword of Damocles hanging over their heads.

But all he could do now was tell her.

Whatever shape things took from here was not in his control.

Jagger glanced at the bedside clock. They had a little more time, he told himself. It was a still a long, long way from morning—the night could yet be theirs. He trailed his finger lower, down her waist, her hips. She gave a quivering sigh. He grinned, desire stirring in him again.

She rolled onto her side, hooking her leg over him. Her hand moved to the scar down the inside of his thigh. His erection began to swell.

"I wish you could tell me how you got this scar," she whispered. "It's like a roadmap, something from your past written right onto your body, yet the piece is missing from your mind. Do you not remember at all?"

Jagger inhaled deeply. She was pushing him into a corner with her questions, because he couldn't lie to her now. He kept silent instead.

She studied him for a while, her gaze probing, dissecting in the gloom. "Do you remember anything more about what happened in that field?" she said.

Jagger cleared his throat. "Mia, I need to tell you something."

Worry entered her eyes.

He sat up, reached for his jeans, desperate for some distraction, a way to avoid what he knew was coming down the pipe.

"What is it?" she asked, propping herself up on her elbow, an edginess entering her voice.

"Mia, you know how—"

He froze as a terrifying scream cut the air.

Mia bolted upright, eyes wide.

"What was that?" she whispered.

Another scream came through the walls of the mansion, the words unidentifiable, the sound bloodcurdling.

"Sounded like a man!" Jagger said as he raced out into the living room and flung open the suite door. Mia lurched out of bed and scrambled for a robe in the bathroom. She came up to his side, belting the robe.

This time they heard someone call, *"Help!"*

'It's from down the passage!" Already in his jeans, Jagger grabbed his Glock from the counter and sprinted down the passage toward the source of the sound.

At the end of the hall he saw a figure—a man, all in black with a black ski mask. He was clutching a bundle against his chest and he froze when he saw Jagger. The man raised a gun with his free arm and fired.

Jagger flung himself behind the wall as a bullet buzzed like a hot hornet past his cheek.

"Mia," he yelled. "Stay back!"

He ducked out from behind the wall and gave chase. The man had reached the top of the stairs and was starting down, boots clattering against wood.

Jagger braced on banister and hurdled over it, swinging his legs wide and bringing his shins across the man's face.

The man was flung backward onto the stairs. With horror, Jagger saw what fell from his arms. He heard the cries at same time he saw the tightly swaddled bundle roll down one stair, then another. Jagger lunged, dropping his weapon as he caught hold of Cheyenne with both hands. He heard his gun clattering down the steps and falling onto the landing below. Clutching the baby close to his bare chest, balanced with one knee on the step and one foot farther down, Jagger glanced up. The man had his gun pointed at Jagger.

He was defenseless, could not drop the baby.

"Don't. Move." The female voice came from above.

The man's gaze flared upward to the banister. Mia stood in her white bathrobe, her new Smith & Wesson aimed directly at the man's head.

"Move one muscle and I'll shoot your goddamn face off," she growled. Her hands were steady, her eyes clear— she was focused with such an intense yet controlled fury, Jagger hardly recognized her.

"Now, drop that weapon and put your hands up above your head where I can see them."

Jagger swallowed, moving slowly backward and down a step, his priority the baby.

He reached the second landing. He'd seen a phone earlier, down the hall. He backed slowly around the corner. Then he sprinted down the hall to where a statue was set on pedestal in a slight alcove. Carefully he laid Cheyenne behind the statue. Then he went for the phone, hit 911. Leaving the receiver off the hook and the baby crying, he tore back down the passage to retrieve his gun and go help Mia.

But as Jagger neared the second landing, he heard a shot.

Grabbing his gun from the floor, he dashed around the corner in time to see the man fleeing. Mia fired after him, but the man ducked around into the passage.

"Leave him!" he ordered. She froze at the sound of his voice.

"Don't go after him, Mia," he yelled as he ran up the stairs. "You're not trained for this. Go get Cheyenne." The baby's crying could be heard loudly now, coming from downstairs.

Jagger dashed down the darkened passageway into the

next wing of the house. He rounded another corner just in time to see man disappearing out a broken window at end of the hall.

Dashing to the window, he looked down. A portable fire-escape ladder swung against the outside of the house as a figure ran across the lawn and disappeared into the darkness of shadows. Jagger fired. But the man was gone.

Jagger swung round and raced back to where they'd heard the screams coming from.

He burst into Cheyenne's nursery. Mia was already there, Cheyenne crying in her crib as Mia knelt in front of Cheyenne's guard sitting on the floor, blood pouring from a cut on his face.

"He got away," Jagger said, sheathing his gun in the waistband of his jeans. "What happened here?"

"The attacker…he came out of the blue, surprised me with a blow to the head," the guard said, clearly distressed. "I didn't see him coming at all. Got me from behind, knocked me out cold for a second. Then I came round in time to see him taking Miss Cheyenne. I went for him and he sliced me with a knife. I should have seen it… I should have heard him coming. I shouldn't have—"

"It's okay, Tom," Mia said as she pressed a wadded baby blanket against the cut on the man's face. "Hold that tightly against the wound," she said. "And we'll get you down the infirmary where I can stitch it up. Where's Miss Amanda?"

"She's with her father. So is Dr. Colton. After the oncologist left, Mr. Colton went into medical distress and he lapsed back into a coma."

Mia's gaze flicked up to Jagger.

"Call Amanda from that phone on the wall over there," she said. "Just press the extension for Jethro's suite."

Mia helped the guard get to his feet while Jagger dialed Amanda and told her what had happened.

"Are you steady enough to walk to elevator, Tom?" Mia asked.

He braced his free hand on the crib and looked inside, desperate to see for himself that Cheyenne was okay, in spite of her screaming protests. His eyes were pained. "I should have seen him, heard him. Stopped him."

"Shh," Mia said. "It's going to be okay. The baby is fine. Let's get you and Cheyenne down to the infirmary where I can get a good look at you both just to be sure."

Amanda appeared in the doorway, breathless and white-faced. "Oh, my God, Cheyenne." She rushed forward, gathering her baby up into her arms. "What happened!"

"Someone tried to kidnap Cheyenne," Jagger said. "He got away."

"I didn't see him, Miss Amanda," Tom said, pressing the bloodied blanket against his cheek. "I'm so sorry."

"Where's Trevor Garth?" Jagger said.

"He's still in Laramie," Amanda answered, rocking her baby against her chest, her eyes gleaming with emotion. "Oh, God, the kidnapper must have known they'd all be away. Levi has been trying to reach them, bring them back," Amanda said, her voice catching. "My father went into distress right after the oncologist left. He…he's unconscious, in a coma." She seemed overwhelmed. "We… we should call the police, too."

"I already dialed 911," Jagger said. "I'll follow up with a direct call to the police station. But they should already be on their way. What else can I do to help?"

"You could help by taking Tom to the elevator and down to the infirmary," Mia said, taking charge. Jagger went over and took Tom's arm.

Mia turned to Amanda. "Go be with your father, Amanda," Mia said gently. "I'll take Cheyenne down to the infirmary, check her out and then bring her right up you."

Amanda hesitated, tears suddenly spilling. She was a strong woman, Jagger could tell, but she was broken right now. He felt a pang in his heart.

"Come, this way," he said to Tom. "Tell me exactly how it went down, what did you see?"

Jagger watched in quiet admiration as Mia calmly contacted Levi on the infirmary intercom and told him to stay with his father. She could handle Tom Brooks and baby Cheyenne.

Jagger sat in the wingback chair under the window cuddling five-month-old Cheyenne against his bare chest. Mia had examined the child and reswaddled her in a soft blanket patterned with little yellow bears and fluffy clouds. The redheaded maid from the kitchen had warmed a bottle of formula and brought it to the infirmary at Mia's request.

"Feed her, please," Mia told Jagger in a cool, collected tone. She'd gone into efficiency mode. Bemused, Jagger took the bottle and seated himself in the wingback while Mia got to work suturing the cut on Tom's face. The old guard had suffered no broken bones, but his pride had taken a devastating blow.

Jagger realized suddenly that the baby's eyes were watching his face intently as she sucked at her bottle.

He glanced down and met the adoring little gaze. His heart did a funny little tumble in his chest.

"You managing okay?" Mia said, throwing him a glance as she worked.

"Uh, yeah, I think so—I mean, how hard can this be?"

She smiled. "Hard enough. Sometimes. Are you warm—you need a shirt?"

"I'm fine, Nurse," he said with a grin. "This little kiddo is like a hot water bottle."

But Mia had already returned her attention to suturing.

"Hey there, sweetness," Jagger whispered, looking down into the baby's face. Cheyenne stopped sucking for a moment and stared at him, listening to his voice.

"You not hungry?" He nuzzled the teat against her little rosebud lips and she gave what he could swear was a smile and a giggle before she latched firmly back on to to the nipple and resumed sucking, her gaze locked onto his. Something cracked inside him, spilling an indescribable warmth through his body, swelling emotion into his eyes.

Was this what it was like? To be responsible for a little human who was otherwise so helpless, so dependent? That feeling of protectiveness, the same fierce feeling of fire that had filled him after making love to Mia, after gently holding her naked and warm in his arms, came over him now, ten-fold.

He watched the milk in the bottle going down and he was almost afraid to look up lest Mia or Tom see the sappy emotion he was certain was written all over his face. When he did dare to glance up, Mia was watching him, and she looked quickly away.

No matter how you sliced it, thought Jagger, this precious little baby that they'd saved from a masked monster was a bright and shining light in the middle of all the darkness this family had been experiencing—and still was. She was a metaphor for life, the very essence of they all needed to protect. New life.

Mia's words sifted into his mind....

I loved him. I thought Brad, my fiancé, loved me back. I believed him when he said he wanted to build a life with me, have children with me....

Suddenly Jagger wanted this Colton thing to be over, and fast. He'd already made his choice when he'd decided to come clean with Mia. He was going to break his contract with the television station and the publisher. He'd buy it all back, no matter how much it cost him. Because he'd chosen Mia. He was ready to gamble with the faint possibility of true love. A wife. A family. And, yes, he wanted children. Jagger wanted to give Mia all those things her ex had denied her.

The idea—the desire—was suddenly so fierce in his mind that it had physical power. Jagger had never ever dreamed he'd come to this. But his past, his brutal experiences with life, with death, and his struggle back from brain damage, had altered him. Or perhaps Mia had. Or maybe he'd just finally matured enough to come to terms with something way back in his childhood.

The image of that tumbleweed sifted into his mind, the crossroads he'd stood at after the diner. Jagger wasn't sure about Destiny, but this felt an awful lot like the hand of some greater guiding power in his life. He'd been brought into her life for a reason. Now he had to find a way to tell her the truth.

She was helping Tom off the bed. "You'll be fine," she said. "But you must get some rest. Mr. Garth will be back any minute and he'll take security matters over from there."

She opened the door. "And don't even think about going up there," she said mock-stern. "Nurse's orders. I'll get Liz in the kitchen to bring you some tea."

Mia closed the door and stilled for a moment, her back to Jagger. And he thought he saw her shoulders sag slightly, as if releasing the pressure of holding everything together with utter calm. Jagger thought of the way she'd handled that gun, cool and commanding as she'd stared into that kidnapper's eyes, not flinching for an instant.

"I can see why you must have been good in E.R.," he said quietly.

She turned to face him, gathering her bathrobe tighter

over her chest, and resecuring the belt. Her complexion was pale and she looked tired, but right now she was more beautiful to him than ever. Her eyes met his, then lowered slowly to the baby against his bare, tattooed chest.

"Looks surprisingly good on you," she said quietly. Jagger heard the wail of police sirens in the distance, coming closer. The cops were finally on their way.

She came up to him, holding her arms out for Cheyenne. "Thank you. I'll take her up to her mom now. If you could meet with the cops when they arrive—show them nursery, and take them to see Tom Brooks if they ask?"

"Where will I find Tom?" he asked, placing the little cherub into Mia's arms.

"Employee wing, men's floor. Someone there will be able to point out his room." She hesitated, baby against her chest, then she bent down and kissed him lightly on the cheek.

Before she could move, he grabbed her arm and whispered in her ear. "I'm falling in love with you, Mia."

She froze, then swallowed slowly.

"When you're ready, we need to talk."

Her eyes caught his, and he caught a glimpse of fear. But she turned quickly and made for the door.

Jagger stared at the vacated doorway for a moment, and a thread of fear curled into his heart, too. He'd finally found the woman of his dreams. He'd finally decided what he wanted out of life. Yet a few words could dash it all.

Anxious, he went down the hall to meet with the police. And to find a shirt.

Exhausted, Mia entered the Blue Suite and flicked on the light. Her plan was to take a quick shower, find some clothes and then head back down to see how the family was faring with Jethro.

Mia knew Jethro had told them all that he didn't want

to be admitted to hospital if he became unconscious again. This was going to be a trying time for the family. At least they had each other.

As she entered the living room Mia's thoughts turned to the man she'd made love to—she didn't know if she could think of him as "Cole" now that he'd raised the specter of the two Fayes and the possibility of Dylan being the missing baby. But that just raised deeper questions, even more confounding ones, about who their John Doe was. She picked up the fallen lamp and set it straight, readjusting the lampshade before going into the kitchenette to clean up the flowers dying on the floor among shards of porcelain.

She smiled to herself as she gathered up the wilted blooms and broken pieces of vase before mopping up the water. She could call a maid to do this, but she'd rather keep the explanations—and lovemaking—to herself.

I'm falling in love with you, Mia...

Her hand stilled as his words curled like dark and sensual smoke through her mind

When you're ready, we need to talk...

Mia quickly dumped the pieces of vase in the trash with the dead flowers. She was afraid of what he was going to say—there'd been something ominous in his eyes, in his tone. She didn't like the anxiety she'd glimpsed in his eyes, either.

As Mia walked past the table with her laptop she noticed that her computer was still on. Memories slammed through her again, kissing him, wrapping her legs around him, tangling in the sheets... Her skin heated all over as she reached and moved the mouse, bringing the screen to life so she could properly close her laptop down.

A page flickered to life on the screen as the mouse moved—the website of the Jackson P.D. Mia clicked the page shut. Behind it was another web page, an online storage site.

Frowning, Mia leaned a little closer. On the page was a list of files with names like: "Colton Kidnapping," "Jethro Colton—Criminal History," "Dead River Ranch Timeline," "Court Case Archives" and "Newspaper Archives."

He'd done a lot in a few hours, Mia thought as she moved her mouse to close the storage site. But a name listed on the top right of the page caught her eye. *Jagger McKnight*.

Her frown deepened. Mia glanced over her shoulder then sat down and pulled her laptop closer. Clicking on the name revealed a drop-down menu that showed an email address for a Jagger McKnight.

Mia's pulse quickened and a strange chill crawled over her skin. Quickly she scrolled farther down the list of files on the site. There was more than one page. She clicked open the next page. On this page the files had names like: "Afghanistan," "Bosnia," "Sudan."

Her heart beat faster, nausea rising trough her chest as she clicked open a file named "New York Times." A subfolder opened and Mia clicked on the top file.

It was a story from the *Times*. The byline under the headline read, "Jagger McKnight, foreign correspondent."

Panic, a cold kind of madness, rushed through Mia. Quickly she pulled up a Google page and typed in the name Jagger McKnight, then clicked "images." Hundreds of images of a man named Jagger McKnight came up, page after page.

A buzz began in her head. Like tinnitus—a ringing in her ears. She couldn't move. Just stared. All pictures of him. One of him standing with a cameraman against a backdrop of jungle foliage. Another of him in a flak jacket. Another where he was sitting on a tank with United

States soldiers around him in a desert. In Africa. In Bosnia. Almost madly, blindly, Mia began to click, opening link after link after link. She stopped at a photo captioned "McKnight returns from Afghanistan."

Mia followed the links through to a story. As she read, a cold dread sank right into her bones. He'd been with a unit that had been ambushed by Afghan insurgents. They'd been trapped nineteen days. All the soldiers had been killed. Jagger McKnight, the reporter, had been the only man to make it back stateside alive.

But he'd been badly injured. Shrapnel had cut into his skull. A bayonet had ripped open his thigh and he'd had amnesia when he returned. Almost frantically, Mia brought up more stories. There'd been official debriefings, inquiries into what had happened. After eighteen days of fighting, a small boy had approached the burned-out bunker where the unit had hunkered down against the attack. When McKnight had regained his memory of the event, he'd testified that the boy strapped with explosives had come into the bunker and blown himself up. The last soldier alive at the time—Cpl. Lance Russell, who'd been immobilized by injury—had been killed in that blast.

Heart speeding, Mia went back to the page of files. She opened a file that said "Colton—Contracts."

With shock she found herself staring at a legal agreement between Jagger McKnight and U.S. Global Television—a deal for the Cole Colton story.

Mia sat back, staring, her hands shaking uncontrollably. She moved her hands up to her face and pushed her hair back. She held on to the top of her head, as if trying to grasp what was staring her in the face.

He was a lie.

I'm falling in love with you Mia...we need to talk.

Damn him! He'd faked his way into this family, right into this house, into her bloody heart...for a story?

Mia lurched up to her feet, marched to her bedroom, then spun back. No.

*No, no no...*it couldn't be.

There *had* to be another explanation. She felt in her gut that he wasn't the sort of person to do this, to brazenly lie and deceive like this. He was a top-notch foreign correspondent by all appearances. Why on earth would he be interested a remote Wyoming ranching family and the mystery of Cole Colton, anyway?

And surely he wouldn't have slept with her if he was deceiving them all, especially not after she'd confided her deepest relationship issues, her fears over rejection. Or was she a flat-out stupid female?

You never were a good judge of men, Mia....

Mia jerked forward and, leaning over the chair, she typed into the Google search bar the words *Jagger McKnight kidnapping.*

Shock stabbed through her as another list of links came up—much older links to newspaper digital archives.

Jagger McKnight had been a kidnap victim himself. He'd been the same age as Cole Colton and had gone missing in the same year. All of a sudden the unanswered questions, the pieces of information came flying together and slotted into a bigger picture—like the explosion of a glass vase being played in reverse.

His nightmares, his scars, his brain injury. His interest in the abduction of Cole. His talk of justice. But there were holes. Plenty of little unexplained holes.

What did he want here? To put to bed some ghosts that haunted him about his own kidnapping?

Okay, Mia thought, so he'd come here for a story he'd already sold to a television network. According to the people who'd seen him in the diner, he was looking for work at the ranch. So maybe that was to be his cover.

Then he'd been attacked on his way to the ranch. Maybe he really did lose his memory. Maybe he hadn't been blatantly playing her, using her emotions, conning everyone else in this house. Maybe he'd forgotten why he'd come.

Dr. Singh had said that the attack in the field could have been an emotional straw that broke the back of his mind—a mind that Afghanistan had already wrought damage upon. But he'd been looking at his own online storage page, his own files. That would mean...

Mia froze at a sound behind her. She heard the suite door open.

"Mia?" His voice was rough.

She tried to swallow, breathe. Her heart pounded against her eardrums. She was afraid to turn around, to see his face. To face what must be faced.

She felt him coming up behind her and her eyes began to burn. He stopped as he saw what she had up on the screen. Silence swelled thick and dangerous in the room.

Mia waited, heart kicking so hard against her chest that she thought she might faint.

"Mia," he said hoarsely. "I was going to tell you."

Her heart sunk and her stomach felt as though a cold hard stone had dropped right through it.

He was going to tell her. He did know who he was. Very quietly, without turning around, she said, "You never did have amnesia, did you?"

Chapter 12

"Mia, I can explain. Please, look at me."

She turned slowly and lifted her eyes. He'd found a shirt in blue flannel and he looked so good it made her hurt. But his eyes were dark with shadows.

"A story," she whispered. "You came to profit from this family's misfortune, so you could broadcast it all over television—tell me this can't be true."

"I came to find out what happened to a three-month-old baby boy, Mia. I came to find out why his family stopped looking for him. I came because I want justice for Cole. I didn't count on being attacked." His eyes bored deep into hers. "I didn't count on meeting you or on what happened so fast between us. By then I was already in too deep. And I was about to tell you everything, the whole truth when—"

"When you'd already slept with me?"

He swallowed.

Mia lurched to her feet, her hands fisting at her sides

as she fought back the raw desire to punch him, hurt him, beat her fists against his chest, kill the hurt ripping through her chest.

"How could you? How could you abuse my compassion like that, make me care for...for a lie? For someone who didn't exist? While at the same time you kept pressing me for information on the Coltons." Her voice caught as nausea surged through her stomach. "I can't believe I was so stupid, that I didn't see the signs—"

"Mia—" He took a step forward, raising his hands to touch her, the need in his eyes ragged and real, and it just cut her even more.

"Don't." She held her palm out. "Do not come near me. I know what you're going to say—I took my own risks. I made the move on you. I could have waited for the DNA test first, I should have listened to my own logic." Emotion balled low and thick in her throat and her eyes filled. "Instead, my heart wanted to believe you really needed me. That you were lost and hurt and I wanted to *help,* and it's my own goddamn fault because it doesn't make me any better that the rest of the Colton family who needed to believe you were Cole for their own purposes!"

Tears slid down her face and Mia hated the fact she couldn't control herself now. Or ever. She was a wretched judge of character, of men. Especially men who looked like him—big and dark and dangerous with hints of hidden pain and wounds. Damn him to hell. All of them.

She spun round and made for her room.

"Mia!" he yelled after her. "I was going to tell you I'd made a choice. That—"

"You told me you were falling in love with me," she said as she stopped in the doorway, her back to him. Her voice caught and she struggled to get the next words out. "You didn't have to do that."

"I *am* falling in love with you, Mia." He came up behind her, his voice low, urgent. She could feel his warmth, his aura of kinetic energy, and inside she began to shake all over again.

"I never planned on running with this amnesia thing. I never planned on being knocked unconscious, or on someone trying to kill me. All I knew when I came around after the attack was that someone had tried to kill me, and I couldn't trust anyone, not even you. I didn't know who you were, or whether you could have planted that blanket on me. So I did what I do when I land in any foreign territory or war zone. I used what was handed to me and improvised. That just happened to be amnesia, and the belief that I was Cole."

"I am not a foreign territory. This is not a goddamn war zone. This is my heart."

He reached for her shoulders, and he turned her to face him.

"Mia, you said yourself that you believe in retribution. You believe justice was never done for this abducted child. You thought this family was mercenary—"

"Until this," she said, holding his gaze, the power of their attraction shimmering with regret between them. "What you have done here takes mercenary to a whole new level...*Jagger McKnight*."

He flinched at the sound of his own name on her lips, the way she'd said it.

"What was this to you?" She waved her hand between them. "You and me—the sex. A private joke? A bit on the side? Did you think you could get more out of me by saying you loved me?"

His eyes flickered and his features turned dark. He took her by the shoulders again but she shook him free.

"Just...get out."

Tears burned into her eyes again, but this time she held them in. She would *not* let him see her cry again. Would *not* let him see how badly he'd hurt her.

"Mia, you're going to hear me out, whether you like it or not." He pointed at her laptop. "Do you think I would've left my online filing page open on your computer if I was so desperate to hide things? I was busy showing you what I had found, so you would understand what I—"

"I said get out. I don't want to see you again."

"Mia." He came up to her. "I made a decision. I'm going to drop—"

She held up her hands. "Don't, please." Her voice cracked. "Please just get out. Leave me alone."

His features twisted with anguish, his eyes pleading with her. But she backed into the small bedroom, blindly groping for the door handle at her side. "If you're still here when I come out, I'm going to call security, the cops, whatever it takes. Just get out of my life."

She slammed the door shut.

Mia turned and slumped backward against the door. She could feel him on the other side. A man she'd started to fall in love with. What a goddamn fool—she hadn't even known who he was.

He was a journalist.

He'd used them all. When he was finished with this it would be all over national television. The story of Cole Colton and his notorious billionaire rancher father...told by an ex-kidnap victim himself. Way to milk your own tragedy.

Shaking like leaf, her skin going hot and cold, Mia clutched her arms tightly across her stomach and sank slowly down the length of the door to the floor. Hugging her knees up to her chest, she thought of Jagger's screams in the night.

The realness of his pain.

How she'd fallen for something fundamental in him that was still there. That hadn't changed. But Mia had done it again.

He was wrong for her. Even if she could get beyond this, Jagger McKnight was *exactly* the kind of man she desperately needed to avoid. It felt like a double betrayal, and it pulled up every hurt from her past.

Somewhere she heard a door shut. And she knew he was gone.

Putting her head to her knees, Mia let it all out— everything that was bottled inside—her body wracked by huge, wrenching sobs.

Jagger found an empty suite down the hall. He lay on the bed inside, staring at the ceiling as night worked its way toward dawn and a pale violet light began to push into the sky. There'd been no use pressing Mia further. He'd forced himself not to bang on her door, harass her. It would backfire.

She needed time to absorb the shock of all this—Jagger understood that.

He understood, too, the reasons for her pain and her anger at him. He was also furious with himself that he'd gotten so entangled so fast he'd been unable to disengage himself before it had come to this.

By the time he'd realized what was happening, that he was falling for Mia, he'd been twisted into a Gordian knot of lies.

Oh, what a tangled web we weave, when first we practice to deceive....

He cursed out loud. It might have been different if he'd been able to finish what he'd been saying to her after making love, if she'd heard the truth come from his own lips as they'd lain naked in bed together, open to possibilities. If he'd had a chance to tell that he was going to drop the story, tell her that he could never, ever profit from, or abuse, the compassion and care and help she'd shown him, it might be different.

Emotion pricked hot and wet in his eyes.

Instead, some bastard had tried to kidnap little Cheyenne.

When the sky turned a pearly gray, Jagger got up and went quietly to the Blue Suite. He knocked gently on the door.

There was no answer.

He pushed open the door, and went inside. There was no sight of Mia. She'd packed her bags and gone.

She must have returned to her room in the employee wing.

Jagger showered quickly and changed, then he headed down to the infirmary. But it was early and there was no one there.

He made his way to the dining room where he found a pale Amanda conversing quietly at one end of the long dark-wood table with her sister Gabby and Gabby's fiancé, Trevor Garth. Beside Amanda's chair was a baby stroller and in it Cheyenne was a pink-faced cherub, sound asleep with her fuzzy bear blanket tucked up to her chin. A giant and rather grim-looking oil painting of Jethro lorded over the room.

They all looked up sharply as he entered. He scrutinized their faces for signs that Mia had already revealed his true identity to them. But all he detected was worry and fatigue. Trevor stood up and pulled out a chair for Jagger.

"Morning," he said, and there was a respect in Trevor's voice as his eyes met Jagger's. "We have a lot to thank you for, Cole. There's coffee and tea and breakfast on the buffet."

Jagger poured a coffee and joined them at the table, anxiety eating at him. He had to find Mia.

As he seated himself, Amanda said, "We were just saying that you saved Cheyenne from your own fate," her voice was soft, the look in her eyes vulnerable this morning.

Jagger snorted softly. "Ironic."

"It is," Trevor said.

"How's Jethro doing?" said Jagger, taking a sip of coffee.

"He's still unconscious," Gabby answered. Her voice was tired, her eyes glassy with emotion. "The specialist and Levi are still with him." Her voice caught. "It's not looking good."

Amanda reached out and placed her hand over Jagger's. Her skin was cool. "Thank you, again," she said quietly. "For what you and Mia did last night. You saved my baby—I cannot begin to tell you what that means."

Jagger fell silent. He wanted to come clean with them right now. He was in no mood to be called a hero. Right now he felt more like a coward in hiding.

Mia's words sifted into his mind.

...he was a coward. Brad Maclean was a yellow-bellied bastard who was terrified of commitment and didn't have the guts to look me in the eye and tell me the truth....

He was no better than Brad Maclean. Jagger's heart sank even deeper as he realized he was never going to stand a chance with Mia Sanders now. She was going to see in him the things she'd said she hated in men—a risk-seeking adrenaline junkie who hadn't looked her straight in the eyes and told her the truth.

He was no hero. He was a fake.

"Thanks for handling the Dead P.D. before I got back," Trevor was saying. "I should never have left the ranch. Whoever tried to abduct Cheyenne had to have been watching—he knew when to take the kid. I made a mistake— I hadn't realized we were so vulnerable. I thought Tom Brooks was up to the job."

"He was," Amanda countered. "He's devastated by what happened—it could have happened to anyone."

"Did the police end up finding anything?" Jagger said.

"They got some footprints in the dirt outside the window below the fire escape ladder." Trevor took a bite of the croissant on his plate. "They'll be looking again at first light and bringing a tracking dog out."

"We shouldn't have gone to Laramie," Gabby said, hanging her head down. "We should have all stayed on the ranch. Dad might not have gone into the coma, Cheyenne might not have been attacked. I feel so damn guilty." She put her face into her hands.

"We have to live our lives, too, Gabby," Amanda said, gently, reaching for her sister's hand. "You're getting married—please don't think of putting that on hold, not for a moment. It's something precious that we can all hold on to at this time." As she spoke, the phone on the sideboard rang.

Trevor got up to answer it.

"Yes, he is," he said glancing up at Jagger. "I'll let him know."

Replacing the receiver Trevor said, "That was Chief Drucker. They're coming in early to do the DNA sampling. He and his tech should be here and waiting in the infirmary within the hour."

Trevor returned to the table and reseated himself. "The good news, and Lord knows we need some around here right now, is that the laboratory has set time aside and will be waiting on the sample. They'll rush the analysis and have results by the end of the day."

Tension kicked through Jagger.

"Is Mia around?" he said. Before these people threw him off this ranch as a fraud, he had to see her again, talk to her. If anything, just to say sorry.

A strange look was exchanged between Amanda and Gabby.

"What is it?" Jagger said.

"It's rather unexpected," Amanda answered. "But Mia Sanders has tendered her resignation. She's taking the remainder of the sick days and vacation days owed to her, and she's leaving Dead River Ranch."

Jagger's spine snapped straight. *"What?"*

"She resigned, early this morning," Gabby said. "And who can blame her after what happened last night? Who can blame any of the staff for thinking of leaving after the murders and all the mischief that has taken place. As it is, Levi had basically taken over the infirmary from her."

Jagger's heart pounded so loudly in his ears he could barely hear himself think.

"When is she leaving?"

"I think she's gone already. She called for a rental at the crack of dawn and packed up the car right away."

Jagger set his mug down slowly, adrenaline surging through his system. He tried to swallow. "Where…where is she going?"

"She didn't say."

"Did she not leave a forwarding address?" he snapped.

"She might have left one with Mathilda—"

Jagger got abruptly to his feet. "Where will I find Mathilda?"

Surprise rippled through their eyes. "She has a small office off the kitchen—" Amanda started saying, but Jagger was already on his way out, running down the passage toward the kitchen, his heart hammering in his chest.

The small office was empty and the only people in the kitchen were Agnes, the head cook, and Liz, the redheaded assistant.

"I don't know where Mathilda is," Agnes said when Jagger asked.

"I think I saw her heading down past the stables earlier," Liz offered.

"Did Mia say where she was going when she left?"

"No, sir, not to us she didn't," Agnes said.

"She didn't look right," Liz offered. "Real pale and really upset by what had happened last night."

"Probably in shock, poor girl," Agnes declared, wiping her hands on her apron. "Not every day you get to aim a gun at a masked kidnapper, now, is it?"

But Jagger didn't wait for Agnes to finish, either. He raced into the entrance hall and flung open the mansion's front door. The blast of morning air that hit him was cold and clean.

The sun was just breaking over the mountains, the dawn rays casting a soft golden glow over the valley and surrounding ranchlands. Mist rose in wisps from the fields. Jagger ran toward the stables, his breath coalescing into white clouds, but as he passed the ranch garage he caught sight of a bright red Chevy Impala parked outside—a vehicle that wasn't there before.

He stalled and went over to it. The car had a rental sticker on the bumper. It was packed full, with bags in the backseat.

Mia.

She hadn't left yet.

Jagger spun around as he scanned the surrounding area. He saw her coming from the stables with a clear purposeful stride, her legs long in slim-fitting denim and cow-boy boots. She wore a down vest and her hair gleamed golden in the dawn light.

His heart began to jackhammer in his chest.

She caught sight of him and froze dead in her tracks, staring at him as if undecided whether to continue forward or turn back to the stables.

But she resumed her stride, chin set in determination, her hands clenched at her sides.

As she neared, Jagger saw that her complexion was wan, her eyes red-rimmed and a bright, fragile blue that contrasted with the color of her jacket. Tendrils of hair escaped her braid and hung soft and loose around her face, and she'd never looked more beautiful or desirable to him. He ached to hold her, just wrap her up tightly in his arms, never let go. It was such an acute desire his muscles hurt with the need.

"Mia." His voice cracked.

"Please, Jagger." She paused, as if still having trouble with his real name on her tongue. "Don't say anything. Don't even try to explain. It doesn't matter anymore."

"I *have* to talk to you Mia. I can't let it end like this."

"But I can, Jagger. I need to. Please, just let me go."

"Mia…I love you."

His words went through her like a visible quiver of electricity. She swallowed and glanced at the packed-up Impala behind him. He was in Mia's way, standing firmly between her and her vehicle.

"Don't do this, Mia. Don't quit your job because of me, not without thinking this through. It's rash—"

"Jagger," she said quietly, her gaze meeting his, clear and direct. "I had a lot of time to think through the night, and I'm not doing this lightly. It's time for me to leave Dead River. I realized that by coming here, by cutting everyone out of my life that I used to care about so that I wouldn't have to feel the shame of my humiliation— I was running. I was not facing up to my problems. I myself was being a coward. I'm going to stop running, Jagger. I'm going to go back to the coast to see my mother. Reconnect with some old friends."

Anxiety, desperation, tore through his chest. He could feel her slipping away through his fingers like grains of fine, golden sand.

"And then?" His voice came out hoarse.

"Then, I don't know."

In the distance, over the field, Jagger saw the glint of a vehicle in the sun and a line of dust rising. *Drucker.* He was almost here.

"Mia, will you wait, please, until after Drucker has been here, and let me explain…just talk."

"No way. I'm not going to be a part of this. I'm done with your Cole Colton ruse, and with the Dead P.D., and with this whole family and all its dramas. I'm getting on with my own life now."

It struck Jagger—she hadn't exposed him to the family, and she had no intention of exposing him to the cops, either.

"Why?" he asked quietly. "Why haven't you told them who I am?"

"You know why."

"Justice?" he said quietly. "You still want justice for Cole?"

"You have a small window until that DNA hammer comes down tonight," she said, pushing past him and beeping the lock on the Impala. She opened the driver's door. "Use it well, Jagger. I hope you get out of it what you really need. I hope you find justice for Cole."

She swung her leg into the car.

He lunged forward and grabbed her arm, hope flaring hot inside him. "Mia, look at me, listen to me— When Drucker and his man get here, I'm telling them that I've remembered who I am. I am *not* doing this story. I will not profit from the pain I caused you. It's over."

She stilled, stared at him.

The cop car was coming closer. Her gaze flashed toward it.

"What about Cole?" she whispered. "What about the answers...about Desiree, Jackson, the baby she was seen with? Jethro hiding something?"

"I'm ditching the story, Mia. I'm buying back those contracts. I'd already decided that yesterday, and I was going to tell you. Once I'd started falling for you I couldn't go through with it anymore. I had to make a choice—the story, or a chance, a faint hope, that I could build something with you. I was about to tell you last night when we heard that scream."

Emotion tore sharp and fast across her face. She knew he was telling the truth, he could see it in her eyes.

She shot another glance at the cop car coming down the avenue toward the house.

He took her hands in his, and she seemed unable to pull away. "I've decided to stop running, too, Mia. And I'm not too male to say this—I haven't loved anyone since I was nine years old when my life was torn apart. I was too scared. I'm still scared, but I'm ready to try...if you can ever see your way around forgiving me for this." He paused. The police sedan was coming closer.

"I never intended to betray you, Mia."

She swallowed, tears filling her eyes.

He could hear the crunch of tires on gravel now, and his pulse started to race.

She pulled away suddenly. "See? You're doing it again.

I'm letting you suck me in. Just like I let Brad suck me in with his promises and lies. Whatever it is that you're working through, Jagger, and I know there's a lot and that you have a long way to go, I need to make a choice of my own now. I need to silence the nurse inside me who thinks she can heal a broken alpha male with her love. That's some sick subconscious fantasy I've had since childhood, God knows why. That's what the therapist told me. So I'm doing it, finally. If this experience with you has taught me anything, it's that I need to grow the balls to look after myself for a change, to turn away from what I *know* is wrong for me."

She paused, inhaling shakily as she squared her shoulders.

"And Jagger, you're the wrong kind of man for me."

"Mia, I'm not Brad. I'm not going to abandon you. I'm not your father."

"But you're just like them, cut from the same cloth, wired to roam around the world in search of one adrenaline fix after another. Unable to settle in one place."

The police cruiser drew to a stop on the gravel. He heard doors open, bang shut. Footfalls crunching toward them. He saw her glance at the approaching men behind him.

Desperation engulfed Jagger. He knew in his heart if he let her go now, she was gone from his life for good.

"Mia," he said quietly, urgently. "I might have been that man once, but I have changed."

"People don't just change, not fundamentally like that."

"You, of all people, should know they do. War changed me. Being responsible for the death of a good man changed me. The fact I could have shot that small boy before he came inside our bunker and blew himself up changed me. It made me question everything I thought I knew to be true. And so did a head injury change me, and losing my fiancée to another man because it took so long for me to see what I was missing in life."

Her eyes met his. Conflict tore through her visibly.

"Who would I be, Mia, if I couldn't learn from all those things? Who would you be if you couldn't learn from Brad's rejection? But I can tell you one thing, running away from what I *know* exists between us is exactly that, running. You're not going to be facing your real fears by going home. You can face them right here. And so can I. We can do this together. Baby steps."

Emotion sparkled in her eyes, and her nose pinked. She tried to swallow.

"Cole Colton," Drucker said from behind him. Jagger cursed and turned slowly to face the cop.

"You ready for that blood test?"

"Chief Drucker, there will be no—"

"Yes," Mia said suddenly, slamming the Impala door shut behind her. "We're ready." She started toward the house. "You can come through to the infirmary this way."

"What are you doing, Mia?" Jagger whispered urgently into her ear as he caught up to her.

"You're going to do this," she hissed softly through a clenched jaw. "You're going to buy whatever small amount of time you have left and find out what the hell is going down here. Because Drucker is up to something—if *I* could find out who you are, why hasn't *he?* He's hiding something and you need to figure out what he's up to."

"And you'll stay?"

"Until the test is done. Then I have to go, Jagger. I have to go back home and start from there."

Mia stood next to the Dead River police chief in the infirmary while his technician got ready to draw Jagger's blood.

Mrs. Black's words curled again like mist through her mind. *Nothing is as it seems....*

Yeah, it sure as hell wasn't.

She watched Jagger and thought of his words. Mia had no doubt he was sincere. But even though she believed him, and she loved him, she also believed he was fundamentally wrong for her, that all those things he'd just said outside would be dust in the wind once he got strong again. Once the hunger inside him returned.

I've changed, Mia.

Conflict warred in her chest. She knew a head injury could profoundly alter personality. So could trauma. She smoothed her hand over her hair, perspiration breaking out over her skin. She was at a crossroads. She was being faced with a choice, too. But if she went down the wrong road again... She forced her attention back to what was happening in the infirmary.

"Do you already have a blood sample from Mr. Colton to compare it for a possible paternal match?" Mia said as she watched the technician laying his phlebotomy tools out on a tray.

"Yes," Drucker answered gruffly. He'd moved closer to the door and was standing with his hands behind his back. His attention flickered to the window. Outside the morning was crisp and bright.

"And did you get any hits from the fingerprints you took yet?" she asked.

He shot her a cool look. "Before the night's end we should have a full picture," he said brusquely.

Jagger caught her eyes.

A full picture.

Drucker knew who Jagger was, Mia was suddenly certain of it. So why was he going through with this paternity test? Did he still believe, perhaps, that Jagger McKnight could actually be Cole Colton?

He'd been kidnapped the same year, was the same age… her eyes shot to Jagger. Was it remotely possible that the P.I. and cops back then had made a mistake when they'd found Jagger?

The technician finished washing his hands and snapped on his gloves. "If you could sit on the chair by the table over here, please, sir."

"I think it would be better closer to the light," Drucker countered. "Where we can all witness what's being done."

Everyone glanced up at him and the technician raised a brow. "Well, we can move the chair over, if that's what you want."

Jagger's brow knitted into a V as he dragged the chair over a few feet. Taking a seat, he held out his arm. The technician applied the tourniquet and swabbed the inside of Jagger's elbow with an alcohol swab.

He then inserted a needle into a vacutainer holder and screwed it tight. Tension in the room felt strangely thick. Drucker seemed edgy.

Then, just as the technician was about to insert the needle, an explosive crack shattered the tension as a *thwock* sounded in the cabinet behind Jagger. Glass fell from the window.

"Get down!" Jagger yelled, lurching up off his chair and lunging for Mia. He hit her with the full brunt of his body weight and slammed her onto the carpet as another bullet pierced the medical cabinet behind where Jagger had been sitting seconds ago.

"Someone's shooting at us!" he yelled at Drucker.

The chief drew his gun and froze. Then he spun around and flung the door open, giving chase. Mia heard the cop's boots hammering down the corridor.

Jagger scrambled off Mia and lurched to his feet as he reached for his own gun tucked into the concealed holster at the back of his jeans.

"Stay in the house!" he ordered Mia. "Alert the rest of the household."

And he was gone, on the heels of the police chief.

Mia turned to look out the now glassless window and she saw a flash of color through the trees. The shooter was heading across a ploughed field toward a densely vegetated ravine out of sight from the house.

Within seconds Mia saw Jagger and Chief Drucker racing over the gently rising slope in hot pursuit of the shooter.

Galvanized, Mia fled out the infirmary and dashed down the passage, bursting out the front door as she sprinted for the stables.

"He went that way!" Chief Drucker yelled at Jagger as they sprinted toward a fence. "Across the ploughed field toward that gulley. You go to the west, head him off that way. I'll come around from the east!"

Jagger hesitated a split second, part of his brain registering that a cop would not ordinarily ask a civilian to help in a chase and takedown. But this was make-or-break. And Jagger wanted that shooter as badly as Drucker did. He veered west, scaling the fence and racing over the ploughed field in the direction of the gulley. It was steep and choked with gold-leafed alders and poplars that shimmered in the autumn breeze.

He caught sight of a movement through the trees—a man in a blue shirt ducking down the bank and heading into the brambles. Jagger veered farther to his left, planning to come down around the man's flank. But when he reached the lip of the ravine, there was no sight of the shooter, just dense trees and bush.

narrow alder trunks. The shooter would more likely try to make it up out the back side and head toward the foothills.

Jagger saw Drucker puffing along the field toward him from his right. They were out of sight of the house and out-buildings now, tucked below a slight rise.

"He went down that way!" Jagger yelled to the chief. "You're going to need backup if we want to get him on the other side."

"I've already radioed for help," Drucker said, panting as he approached. Sweat sheened over the chief's face, and his shirt was wet with perspiration under his arms.

Jagger pointed. "If I go in down—" He froze, ice sliding into his veins as he realized the chief was aiming his sidearm at him.

"Drop your weapon, McKnight," Drucker said, his voice strange, deep, as he came closer, his weapon trained on Jagger. "Now!"

Jagger's mind raced wildly as he slowly moved his hands out to his sides, away from his body, but he held on to his Glock. The chief knew he was Jagger McKnight.

"What do you want, Drucker?"

"I want 'Cole Colton' dead. There's going to be no story. No more questions. It's all going to die right here. Drop your weapon and step backward into that gulley, McKnight."

"Why are you doing this?"

"You should have died in the field that night."

Jagger swallowed. There was no one in sight. For all

he knew, right? ... ink. "So it was you—on concert with
his we... You tried to run me down."

...e snorted. "I'm no cowboy. But I'm not alone in this,
either, McKnight. One of my accomplices is down in that
gulley. He's got his weapon trained on you as we speak.
Step back, head down."

*One of his accomplices. That meant there was at least
one other....*

"Was it Maggie who called to tell you that I'd walked
into the diner that night? Did you get someone to follow
me? Whose idea was it to frame me as Cole? Who had the
baby blanket?"

Drucker laughed harshly.

Out the corner of his eye, Jagger saw dust rising from
the direction of the house. Someone was coming. He had
to buy more time. Taking a slow step backward, he asked
again. "Who had that baby blanket, Drucker? Was it Maggie? Was she a friend of Faye's—did she get it from her?"

"I said drop that weapon, McKnight, or I shoot you right
here!" Ducker's finger curled around the trigger.

Jagger released his gun. It fell with a soft thud to the
dry grass.

"Killing me isn't going to solve anything. You can't possibly believe that people will think I was Cole who died.
A post mortem will reveal that I wasn't."

"You forget that I am the police, McKnight. This is
small town with a tiny force. We're isolated from the rest of
the world out here. Your body will disappear before it ever
gets to the morgue. And Wyoming is a vast state, plenty
of places to dispose of a body. In the Laramie Mountains
the wolves and coyotes and bears and crows will recycle
your remains before anyone will ever find you."

Loreth Anne White

sound and ..... the dull thudding of horses' hooves
ger. His pate gleamed in the ..... riders. Coming closer. Several
clouding at his mouth. ..... flickered toward the
..... and the trig-
..... breath

"It wasn't you who abducted baby Cole Colton,
Drucker—I'm certain of that. You were just a rookie on
the force at the time. So who got to you? Who are you
doing this for? Who are you trying to protect?"

"The things people do for love, McKnight."

Jagger took another step back and faltered, stumbling
a little as the ground behind him gave under his heels,
crumbling away into the steep ravine. He heard loosened
rocks clattering down the slope.

Love— So Drucker was doing this for a woman, someone who was masterminding all this?

The sound of horses drew closer, dust billowing over
the ridge now. Suddenly a bay mare crested the rise.

Mia! Riding like the wind, hair flying behind her.

"This way!" she yelled to the riders behind her, kicking her horse to pick up speed.

Behind her an army of horses and cowboys appeared,
and they thundered toward the gulley.

Drucker's head spun and he turned his weapon on Mia.

Jagger's heart dropped like a stone. "Mia, stay back!"
Jagger yelled just as Drucker fired.

Jagger watched horrified as the scene seemed to play
out in slow motion—Mia's horse rearing up, pawing the
air, her gold hair flying out, catching the sun's light as
her body was flung like a ragdoll from her mount. In the
corner of his eye he saw Drucker turning the gun back on
him, squeezing the trigger.

Jagger felt the impa... ...ing him ...nable to breathe,
heard the shot. It sla... ...ing to his chest. His foot
backward and si... ...or and he tripped, catapulting back-
Jagger sta... ...lumping and tumbling down the steep slope,
caught ... ...shing through brambles and dried berry bushes, autumn
leaves spiraling above him, and behind them, blue sky. He
hit the bottom with a slamming thud, his skull cracking
against something sharp, pain sparking through his head.

And as Jagger lay there, he knew Mia had been shot,
had gone down. The image of her tumbling from the horse
played through his mind, over and over, then faded slowly
away. Jagger's world went stone cold and black.

Chapter 13

Jagger woke to the sound of a soft, rhythmic beeping. He lay very still, unsure of where he was, or what had happened, or even whether he could move.

He tried to open his eyes. His lids felt thick, stuck, and when he managed to get them open the slice of white light into his brain was blinding. He shut them again and tried more slowly. It took a while to see anything at all.

He was in a hospital room. A memory cut like a knife through him. Drucker with the gun. Shooting him. Falling down into the gulley. Jagger tried to move his legs but couldn't. Pain—he could feel pain. Dull and heavy in his shoulder. That was a good thing right—feeling pain? Did it mean he wasn't fully paralyzed?

Another memory cut like glass through him—Mia, riding like the wind, coming over the ridge on a beautiful bay mare, her hair flying free. Cowboys—a whole damn ranch army of them, thundering behind her as she showed them where to go.

Then the shot from Drucker's gun. Her horse rearing up and pawing at the air. Mia—she'd been shot.

Dead?

Where was she?

Panic began to suffocate him. Jagger tried again to move. This time he managed to turn his head.

He saw her.

In a chair next to his bed. Sleeping. A soft blanket covering her. Jagger tried to make his mouth work and his voice come. He couldn't. He struggled to lift his hand, hold it out to her, but it was as if lead weighted down his bones.

"Mia?" the word came out in soft croak, startling him.

But she heard. Her eyes snapped open, then went wide. She lurched up from her chair.

"Oh, Jagger, thank God. Nurse!" she yelled. "He's awake." Her voice cracked and tears began to sheen copiously down her face. She cupped his cheek, kissed him, shaking like a leaf. He noticed her left arm was in a sling.

"Jagger, I thought you weren't going to come back to me. Thank God. Nurse!"

Two nurses came scurrying in, followed by a doctor. One of the nurses took Mia's arm, gently asking her to leave.

"I know you're a nurse," Jagger could hear the woman saying to Mia, "but you need to give the doctor some room to run some tests. You can watch through the window from there."

As Mia was led out, she stared back over her shoulder, and the raw look on her face tore at Jagger's soul. His eyes followed her as she went out of the room, and he waited until he could see her pale face behind the window. She placed her palm flat against the glass.

She mouthed, *I love you.*

For a moment Jagger couldn't breathe. He felt as if the heavens had opened and he'd heard the sound of angels.

He tried to lift his left hand to her, but it wouldn't move. Pain washed through his body, radiating out from his shoulder. How long had he been out? What had happened?

The doctor checked him out, doing a battery of tests, checking reflexes. When he finally stood back, he said, "You're one lucky bastard, McKnight. We almost lost you a few times, there."

Jagger's right hand went to his shoulder.

"Bullet went straight through the deltoid," said the doc. "Again, you were lucky. It did some nerve damage along the way and you might not regain full range of motion. But we can go through it all in detail later." He smiled. "I think there's someone who needs to see you first."

The doctor waved Mia in, and she came rushing to his bedside. Taking his hand in hers, she gave him a smile. He could feel she was still shaking. She seemed so much younger, smaller, more fragile, thinner.

"I'll leave you two alone for a few minutes."

"Thank you, Doctor," Mia said.

Turning to Jagger she said. "You have *got* to stop banging yourself on the head like that, McKnight, because next time you're not going to be so damn lucky." Emotion caught at her voice.

Jagger cleared his throat carefully. "Thick skull," he said, then tried to smile as he squeezed her hand. "I've got a thick skull."

Tears gleamed afresh in her eyes, and she gave a shaky laugh.

"You look thin, Mia," he cleared his throat gently again. "You've lost weight. What happened? How long have I been out?"

"Fifteen long days," she said as she used her good hand

to raise the back of his hospital bed so that he was in more of a sitting position. She brought a glass of water to his lips and helped him drink.

"Your arm?"

"Broke it when Sunny reared and threw me. The gunshot spooked her."

"He didn't hit you— I thought he hit you. I thought he'd killed you."

She shook her head.

Jagger tried to take the glass in his hand, and almost spilled the water. She took it from him and returned it to the stand beside his bed.

"I feel so weak, clumsy. Confused," he said.

She nodded. "It'll take a while, and some physio on that left arm, but you're going to be fine."

"Drucker?"

"I do wish you'd been around to see that."

"What happened?"

"After you took off behind Drucker, I ran back to the stables, yelling for help. I didn't know at the time the chief had turned on you. I just didn't want that shooter to get away. Everyone available came running, got horses, a Jeep. I led the way on Sunny. When Drucker fired at me and Sunny reared, I lost it—I was riding bareback and wasn't used to it. I went down. And when Drucker shot you, the ranch hands just barreled at him en masse. He tried to flee but they surrounded him. One of the guys lassoed him and they took him down like a calf at a rodeo. They trussed him up, tossed him over the back of a horse like a sack of potatoes and took him back to the stables. We didn't know if Pierce Deluca and Karen Locke were involved so Trevor called in the state police, and they took it from there."

Jagger felt a smile curve over his mouth. "Oh, that's rich—bet that drove Drucker wild. State police. His turf."

She nodded, a smile in her eyes.

"Where are they keeping him?

"He's out on bail."

"Bail? You've got to be kidding me."

"The judge didn't seem to think he was a flight risk. He set bail at almost one million, and someone posted it for him. We don't know who. A trial date has been set, and the town of Dead River has already brought in a new police chief. He comes from the Jackson P.D.—"

"Novak?"

"No, Novak's still Jackson P.D. chief. The new guy is Harry Peters. It's a promotion for him. He's sweeping clean—already fired Deluca and Locke and hired two new officers, Mike Harriman and Patrick Carter."

"He's wasting no time."

"No, he wants to solve this. He says because Drucker was corrupt, all his files are suspect and no one can be trusted. Which is why he moved so quickly to clear out Deluca and Locke."

"What about the shooter?"

Mia inhaled deeply. "He got away. They've got some leads, like his bootprints, which match the prints that were found under the fire escape ladder. And the bullets he fired into the infirmary are a ballistics match to the shell casings that were found in the field after your attack. Peters is thinking that the shooter is the same person who attacked you on horseback and who tried to kidnap Cheyenne."

"Drucker didn't give up his name?"

"No. He claims this is all just a big misunderstanding, but they're going to try to strike a plea bargain with him before his case goes to trial. If not, we might learn something when the case gets heard."

"Drucker said something, Mia, before he shot me. He

said that he'd done it all for love. I think there's a woman involved."

"A woman? Who?"

"Someone he's trying to protect, or help. Perhaps some-one from his past."

"We can talk to Peters. I know he wanted to see you if…" Tears welled again and slid easily down her cheeks. She swiped them away. "At that point we didn't know if you would come around."

Jagger reached for her hand. "What about the truck—did Peters look into that?"

"It was found to be stolen from a ranch near Laramie. No fingerprints or DNA could be taken from it, because of the fire. Anyone could have been driving it. And Dylan still doesn't know who took Midnight that night."

Jagger fell silent. "Whoever he is, he's still out there."

She nodded.

"What does the Colton family say, Mia, about me?"

Mia gave a wry smile. "Mixed emotions would be the diplomatic way to put it. They're under the assumption that your memory returned after the kidnap attempt on Chey-enne. They realize now that you'd come to town for the Cole Colton story, and while they're irritated with that, the sisters are still thankful that, because of you, their father went into a coma believing his son was still alive. What-ever happens to Jethro now, they like to think that this belief has given their father a small measure of peace."

"So he's not come out the coma."

She shook her head. "Prognosis is not good."

"And the staff?"

Mia laughed. "Well, Mathilda's busy lording it over ev-eryone. She says she knew you were an imposter right from the get-go, and that they should have listened to her. But all of them—staff and family—were deeply rocked by news of Drucker's involvement. Everyone's still living right on a razor's edge because there's still a killer among them."

Jagger laced his fingers with Mia's. "Thank you for staying, Mia." He hesitated before asking the next question burning into his mind.

"Are you still going to leave?"

She was silent awhile, then she met his gaze. "Will you tell me, Jagger, what it was that broke you out there in Afghanistan? While you were unconscious, I read more of the news coverage of the event." She flushed slightly. "Okay, I confess, I read everything about you that I could possibly lay my hands on, including a lot of the pieces you wrote yourself." She paused. "You're a damn fine journalist, you know that. You helped a lot of people over the years. You went into places where human beings were crushed by oppressive regimes. You gave them voices. You presented all the faces of war, sometimes controversially so. You didn't take sides—you let your stories and the situations speak for themselves. What went so wrong in Afghanistan?"

"The boy," he said simply.

Mia watched his face intently. "You mean the suicide bomber who killed Cpl. Lance Russell?"

"Not a suicide bomber—he was a goddamn kid, Mia. He was nine or ten years old."

"That's what you saw when he approached strapped with explosives. A child?" There was no judgment in her voice, so why was he feeling defensive suddenly?

He looked up at the ceiling, avoiding the scrutiny in her eyes. "I saw a kid who should have been in school. A child who needed a mother. A child who should be playing ball with friends. Instead, he was an insurgent's pawn. A little human weapon sent out like a homing device, and I let him come right into the bunker." Jagger's eyes filled and his throat choked. "I had a rifle. Cpl. Russell had been injured and he couldn't move. Everyone else was dead. The smell in that place…" He cleared his throat. "Russell scooted his weapon over to me, across the dirt. He told me to fire, to shoot to kill.

"I looked down that rifle scope and I saw the boy's eyes so clearly it was as if he was right in front me, looking into me. Big, liquid-brown eyes with dark lashes. His face was so young, so innocent. He was scared." Jagger inhaled deeply. "And at that moment he wasn't Afghan, or insurgent, or a suicide bomber…just a human kid with skinny brown legs and a tattered robe."

Jagger blew out a big breath of air.

"I…I couldn't think. I was in the country as a journalist. And as a journalist I was ethically compelled to observe and report the news, not to make news. It's an ethic that goes to the very foundation of my beliefs in the profession, and I'd lived by it for years—to remain as objective as humanly possible, to bring the true story home. And here was a child who was being murdered by the people who controlled him. A victim." Jagger swallowed. "I froze. I could not shoot that victim—that child—in cold blood. I could not cross that journalistic line. I'm not a soldier, Mia. I am not sanctioned to kill. It was murder."

"Defense, Jagger, it would have been self-defense."

He tightened his mouth, and nodded. "Yeah, that's what Mrs. Lance Russell said when I went to visit her. That's what letters to the editor said, and comments on Twitter and Facebook." Jagger was quiet a long time. "But they weren't there. They never had to look into the kid's eyes."

"So he came into the bunker."

"He got close enough to self-detonate."

"The tattoo on your chest, that's in honor of Lance Russell?"

"Right across my heart. So I'll never forget what I did to him."

Death before Dishonor.

"You felt dishonored."

He looked away from her eyes for a moment. Then he gave a soft snort. "Guilt. Shame. Yes, dishonor. You name it. I wanted to die."

"If you were faced with that again, would you shoot him? The boy?"

He moistened his lips, feeling drained suddenly. "I don't know, Mia. Maybe. It's why I'm done. I can't go back. I don't know if I can be objective anymore."

She stroked the tattoo on his arm, and he felt her love, her care. Jagger didn't even know right now if he deserved that.

"So you just kept walking those highways, until you saw the TV news about the kidnapping, and you learned about the Cole Colton mystery?"

He met her eyes. "It resonated with me. It was personal, and I was desperate for something to grab on to." He paused. "Can you understand, Mia? Can you forgive me?"

"You need to forgive yourself, Jagger. You need to let the burden of guilt and shame go." She paused, looking down at his tattoo under her hand.

"What was this one for?" she asked as she stroked her finger along the eagle.

"For my country."

She looked up into his eyes and he saw love. He saw forgiveness. And it nearly broke his heart.

"You didn't answer me," he said, voice thick. "Have you still got that red Chevy Impala packed—are you still leaving?"

She bit her lip and nodded.

"Thank you for waiting." It was all he could manage.

"What will you do now, Jagger?"

He didn't reply until he was certain he could control his voice, be able to hold back the emotion simmering dangerously close to the surface.

"My plan," he said quietly, "was to take you away from here. Take you home where I could meet your mother and your friends. Then maybe head into Montana, fish the streams. Perhaps go farther north, over the border, into Canada."

Her eyes went wide, and she stared at him, her lip beginning to quiver.

"What do you say, Mia?"

She bit down on her lip, then smiled sadly and squeezed his hand. "You should get some rest, Jagger. They're going to want to give you another scan in a few minutes, just to be sure everything's still okay in that head of yours." She glanced at her watch. "I'll come back later."

She bent down to kiss him softly on his lips.

But he curled his fingers tightly, not letting her go. "I want you in my life, Mia. I want you in my life forever. I want to give you those things Brad wouldn't—home, children. Marriage."

Blood drained from her face and nerves flickered through her eyes. "Jagger. You need rest."

"No. I need you. I need time to get to know you better, and to show you I mean what I say. And I need to take you away from that ranch. It's not safe."

"Jagger." She sighed heavily and her eyes swam with emotion. "It won't work. You'll get well again. You'll run the Colton story, write your book. The next freelance assignment will come up, and...you'll hunger for it. You'll start missing it, that adrenaline, that risk. That punch that comes from nailing a big story that no one else could. And that's fine. But not for me. I don't want that life. I don't want my mother's life—"

"You didn't hear me, did you?" His voice was ragged now, rough. "That life is not for me anymore, Mia. I told you, and I meant what I said. I've axed the Colton story. I'm going to buy back the contracts. It's over. Cole can get his justice from Peters now. Because the only story I want out of this now is our story. You and me."

Mia swallowed and nerves chased through her eyes. Then her cheeks flushed and Jagger caught the glimmer of exhilaration before she quickly tamped it down.

"It's the medication talking, Jagger, the shock—"

Desperation surged through him.

"No, it's not. I wanted to say these things the other night. I mean every damn word."

A nurse popped her head in the door.

"Mr. McKnight, we're going to be around in two minutes for your scan."

"Wait, wait. Nurse, don't go, I need you to do something for me. Please."

She frowned.

Jagger gripped Mia's hand tighter and he turned to her. "You said Horace Black was an ordained minister."

"Yes, why?"

"Nurse, will you call the Dead River Ranch, get them to find Horace Black? Tell him to get his ministerial butt over to the hospital stat. I have a woman to marry!"

Her eyes went round and wide. She shot a glance at Mia.

Mia's jaw dropped. Then a flare of panic and excitement chased through her features.

"Jagger, no! You can't. This is not the time—"

"Goddamit, Nurse, I'm not going to be able to keep this woman here by force much longer, please fetch the minister!"

"Mia." He turned to her, gripping her hand as tight as he could, desperation pumping through him. "I promise, the ring will be beautiful, and it will come later. And I promise, no one is ever going to jilt you at the altar again. I'm going to prove to you right now that I'm a man of my word. I love you. I want you in my life. Marry me. Say yes."

Tears began to stream down her face. She opened her mouth, but was unable to speak, overwhelmed.

"Jagger…" Her voice caught, and she gave a sob, then a smile.

"And don't try telling me that I'm wrong for you, Mia. We both know how to run away from things that scare us. You get that same adrenaline rush, that same life-death kick out of E.R. nursing that I get from nailing a story. You said so yourself. You told me about that rush you got when you could fix someone, save their lives. And at the end of the day, the satisfaction that you *conquered* something, it's what made your job, your life worthwhile. We're cut from the same cloth, Mia. It's all about perspective. And if there's love, we will find a way to face the challenges, all of them."

Mia kissed him, her tears wetting his face. She smoothed hair back from his brow, and fear entered Jagger's heart.

"You're going to say no," he whispered.

She nodded and cupped the side of his face with her hand, looking right into his eyes.

"I won't marry you," she whispered. "Not like this."

A small spark of hope lit somewhere deep beneath his fear. He held on to it.

"Like how, then?" he whispered.

"We'll go west," she said, voice soft and husky. "You can meet my family and my old friends. I'll show you where I come from. And then we'll go to Montana, like you said. Maybe farther north over that border. We'll ski and hike. We'll fish and explore the mountains. Get to know each other. You'll get well and strong again. Then... then if we still feel the same way, come spring, if you still love me—we do it. Okay? We find a little chapel in the mountains and we marry."

Emotion glittered in his eyes and a tear escaped down the side of his cheek. Mia leaned forward and kissed it away. "Is that promise enough for you, Jagger McKnight?"

He drew her down and held her against his body, and he thought his heart would burst. "Yeah," he whispered into her hair. "That's promise enough—more than I really can ask for."

And in all honesty, Jagger couldn't ask for more than a chance at love. But he had it, a second chance. And so did she. The road ahead was shimmering and full of promise.

When she stood back, she was crying and smiling through her tears.

Jagger said a silent prayer in memory of Cole Colton, wherever he was. He'd brought them together.

Five days later, Jagger and Mia were back in the Dead River P.D. station, this time sitting in the glassed-in office now belonging to police chief Harry Peters.

"I'm up to speed with the Desiree Beale case," Chief Peters was saying. "And to rule out the possibility, we ran ballistics for the bullet that killed Beale against Drucker's weapon and against the bullets fired into the infirmary. There was no match. It was a different gun. No match to the bullet that killed Faye Frick, either."

Mia put a piece of paper on Peters's desk and slid it across to him. "Here's the list I told you about, the one we compiled of ranch employees and residents of Dead who either were around when Cole was abducted or who might have links to the case."

Peters took the list, scanned it. "Thank you. We'll be working through this list systematically."

"And this is my file," Jagger said, setting a fat manila folder on the man's desk. "As promised. Everything I've dug up to date on the Coltons is in there. Including a transcript of my conversation with Chief Novak from the Jackson P.D. and a transcript of my chat the diner owner, Marnie Sayers, who used to work with Desiree before she bought the diner from Faye Donner. Also in there are my theories about Faye Frick and Faye Donner. And about Jethro Colton's prior criminal activities and friendship with an ex-con, now deceased, named Mitch Radizeski."

The chief glanced up at Jagger. "You're dropping the story?"

Jagger reached for Mia's hand under the desk, squeezed. "Yeah. We've got new stories to chase."

The chief flicked his gaze to Mia before returning his attention to Jagger. He smiled. "I'll be happy to do an interview once this is over."

"No—that story is dead, at least from my point of view. I've already paid back the advance. Get justice for Cole, Chief Peters. Nail the right people, that's resolution enough for me."

"What about Jenny Burke?" Mia said. "Any leads there?"

The chief rubbed his brow. "Everything Drucker had on file about that case is suspect. We're having to go back and start from scratch. I sent my two new officers to go over the scene again with a fine-tooth comb. They found another slug, 9 mm, lodged in the wall paneling that the earlier investigation missed—possibly conveniently so. And after going through the pathologist reports again, it appears Burke might have tried to fight off her attacker. She has possible defensive bruising on her right arm. She could have tried to hit the weapon away with her arm, causing the first bullet to fly wild and lodge in the paneling. The second slug is what probably hit her in the face and killed her."

"So she looked right into the face of her attacker—she saw it coming," Mia said.

"Very possible." The chief stood, and Jagger and Mia followed suit. He held out his hand. "Your help has been invaluable Mr. McKnight, Ms. Sanders." He shook each of their hands in turn, a big forceful grip, a calm confidence about him.

"Justice will be done. For Cole. And I vow to do everything in my power to get to the bottom of these murders. Whoever planted that baby blanket on you knows what happened and is trying desperately to keep the past buried."

As they walked out into the sunshine Mia said, "I believe him, you know. I believe Peters will leave no stone unturned."

Jagger hooked his arm around Mia's shoulders, drew her close and kissed her cheek.

"What was that for?" she asked glancing up at him with a smile.

"Just because. And yes, I believe Peters, too."

The following afternoon, Jagger was feeling like a kid on Christmas morning as he turned off the road and drove through the ornate brass gates under the arch declaring he'd entered Dead River Ranch. Dust billowed behind him as he made his way down the quarter-mile avenue toward the big house.

He hit a number on his new cell phone as he neared the mansion. Mia answered on the second ring.

"You all packed?" he asked.

"I've been packed for nearly three weeks, McKnight, ever since the day you were shot! Where on earth are you?"

"Go outside." He hung up.

He'd gotten a ride into Laramie early that morning with one of the ranch hands. At a car dealership he'd found a good deal on a Ford truck, extended cab, along with a camper to go on top. The rig was in mint condition, and the camper came with everything from pots and pans to cutlery.

He drew the new rig to a halt outside the employee entrance and laid on the horn.

Mia came running out, then stalled in surprise, her hand going to her mouth and her eyes lighting up as blue as the sky behind her. She rushed up to the truck as Jagger opened the door and hopped out with a grin.

"So, what do you think?" he said, holding his right arm out with flourish. "Our new gypsy mobile."

She laughed, a sound of utter happiness and delight, and it warmed his chest.

She walked slowly around the rig.

"Are you *serious?* This is ours? When did you get this?" She was like a kid herself as she pranced around the truck and camper again. "Jagger, it's perfect! Tell me where you got it."

"Laramie, this morning. Comes fully equipped. The couple who owned it before hardly used it."

She stilled, something serious creeping into her eyes. "Are you okay to do this? I mean…with the big advance you had to repay and—"

He reached for her good arm, drew her toward him and he kissed her hard on the mouth. Then he stood back holding her at arm's length. "Mia, I've been saving my whole damn career. I never went on vacation. I never took sick days. I just went to the next job, the next story, and I kept going around the world for years." He looked deeply into her eyes.

"We're going to be good for a while, at least financially. A long while. We have everything we need right in there. We're going to hit the road and find our place. And when we do, we'll put down roots and build something. And there will always be stories to write, no matter where we end up."

"Jagger, I don't think I've been happier, or more excited about something in my entire life."

"Come, let's load up your stuff and get going while there's still plenty of light. We'll spend our first night on the road."

They said their goodbyes to the household staff, then went out to the stables where they found Dylan alone in the office.

Dylan seated himself on the on the edge of the desk, listening to Mia going on about their plans, his eyes intent on her.

"I feel bad, leaving you here like this, Dylan," she said, suddenly noticing the distance in his eyes.

He offered her a wistful grin. "Hey, I'm happy for you guys. My time will come. Still squirreling the savings away."

Mia glanced at Jagger. "Dylan, we wanted to ask you something, about your mother."

His eyes shuttered and his features turned guarded. "Like what?"

They told him about Faye Donner, the diner owner in Jackson who disappeared after Desiree's death. Jagger showed him the photo of Donner he'd taken from the internet.

Dylan took it and eyed it with suspicion.

"It could be her, Dylan," Mia said gently. "Faye Donner could be your mother. Yes, the hair color is different. And she's slimmer, younger—but look at her features."

He shook his head and handed the photo back to them. "I don't see it."

"Do you have any other photos of your mom when she was younger? Like from when you were born?"

Dylan frowned, almost a little hostile now. "What are you guys getting at? My mother is *not* Faye Donner from Jackson. We didn't come from Jackson."

"But you did arrive here when you were seven months old, after a baby had been seen with Desire Beale in Jackson."

"What? You're saying you think *I* could be Cole Colton—stolen by Desiree? You're nuts— That's ludicrous!"

"Do you have photos from before you came to the ranch? Any baby pictures of you younger than seven months?"

"No," he said, coolly. "My mother wasn't sentimental in that way. I have hardly any baby pictures at all." He paused. "Just a handful from when I was a teenager."

"You have the right coloring, Dylan," Mia said quietly. "And you're the right age."

"Look, you guys are just obsessed with this Cole Colton thing right now. I know my mother. I know my place in the world. I know where I come from." He pushed off the desk. "I should get back to work."

Jagger held a piece of paper out to Dylan.

"What's that?"

"Marnie Sayer's number in Jackson. She bought the diner from Faye Donner, and when I asked her about it I got the sense she was hiding something. I think the answers are there somewhere. If you want to talk to her—"

"I don't want to talk to anyone in Jackson." Dylan made for the office door.

Jagger put the piece of paper on the desk and he and Mia followed Dylan out.

A horse nickered in a stall nearby, and Mia gave a last look around the stables. She'd already said goodbye to Sunny.

"Look after my Sunny," she said, giving Dylan a hug.

"You know I will. Take care, Mia. It was good having you around."

"You, too."

He and Jagger shook hands, evenly matched in build and height, and yes, coloring, thought Mia as she watched them—they could pass for brothers.

Walking back to the house, Mia said to Jagger, "He looks like he could be a Colton, you know."

"He does."

"Even if it was possible that Faye took the baby from Desiree, why do you think she would come back here—what could there possibly be in it for her?"

"Lord knows." Jagger was quiet for a while as they approached the main entrance of the mansion. "In my experience, there are usually three reasons people do things, Mia. Fear. Love. And vengeance. Or a combination of the three."

Mia reached forward to open the great front door.

As they entered the hall, Catherine was hanging up the phone on a table at the base of the staircase, her face white with shock.

"What is it, Catherine?" Mia said, coming forward quickly.

"That was the police. It…it's Hank Drucker. His wife, Harriet, found him dead this morning. Hanged."

"Suicide?" Jagger asked.

"He left a note saying it was all a big misunderstanding and that he was sorry." Catherine ran a trembling hand over her hair. "But the police think it could be murder.

They're coming around later this afternoon to talk to the staff again." Her eyes filled with emotion. "When is this all going to stop?"

Mia and Jagger exchanged a glance. Drucker had taken his secrets with him to the grave, including the name of the woman he loved.

It was early evening by the time Jagger and Mia left the town of Riverton and began heading for Grand Teton National Park in their new gypsy mobile.

As they drove Mia leaned back and sighed.

"What's the matter?"

She angled her head and caught his eyes. "Happy sigh."

He grinned, and inside he felt light, free. And yes, happy. Just pure happy.

"I wonder what Drucker meant when he said he did it for love— Who do you think she is?"

"Maggie, maybe," Jagger said. "Someone from his past. Who knows?"

Mia leaned her head to the side, watching the scenery. "I'm glad we left it all behind."

He nodded.

Dead River Ranch was still a dangerous place, still teeming with dark secrets, and Jagger had plans to keep her safe. Forever.

As evening turned into a golden dusk and dry leaves blew in drifts across the road, Mia said, "My father used to say that all the other seasons existed solely to bring fall into being. It was his favorite time of year, when the salmon turned from the ocean to run upstream, their DNA wired to take them home, no matter how far they'd come down river or how far inland they had to go to return to that little mountain pool, or eddy or sandbank that spawned them."

Home. It was nebulous concept as much as it was a concrete one, Jagger thought as watched a sudden dervish of dust rising and swirling at the side of the road. A tumbleweed blew free of a fence. For a few minutes the ragged ball bounded down the road alongside them, and Jagger's mind returned once more to that tumbleweed rolling past the Dead River Diner.

The wind that had blown at his back as he made his way to Dead River Ranch that night was the same wind that blew at their backs now. He couldn't say why, but it felt right, good.

He sought her hand resting on the seat next to his and squeezed. "I love you, Mia."

She turned her palm up and laced her fingers softly through his. "It's going to be a good adventure," she said quietly. "I can feel it in my heart."

"Mrs. Jagger McKnight," he whispered with a smile.

"Wait until spring."

He grinned, and as the road curved away and up toward the mountains, the tumbleweed rolled off into a field, driven by the vagaries of wind.

* * * * *

A sneaky peek at next month...

INTRIGUE...

BREATHTAKING ROMANTIC SUSPENSE

My wish list for next month's titles...

In stores from 20th September 2013:

❏ Mountain Heiress — Cassie Miles

& Ready, Aim...I Do! — Debra Webb

❏ The Reunion — Jana DeLeon

& Trap, Secure — Carol Ericson

❏ Cowboy Resurrected — Elle James

& My Spy — Dana Marton

Romantic Suspense

❏ The Colton Bride — Carla Cassidy

Available at WHSmith, Tesco, Asda, Eason, Amazon and Apple

Wrap up warm this winter with Sarah Morgan...

Sleigh Bells in the Snow

Kayla Green loves business and hates Christmas.

So when Jackson O'Neil invites her to Snow Crystal Resort to discuss their business proposal... the last thing she's expecting is to stay for Christmas dinner. As the snowflakes continue to fall, will the woman who doesn't believe in the magic of Christmas finally fall under its spell...?

4th October

www.millsandboon.co.uk/sarahmorgan

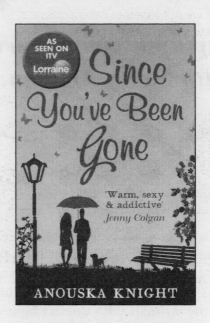

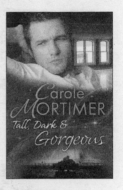

Join the Mills & Boon Book Club

Subscribe to **Intrigue** today for 3, 6 or 12 months and you could **save over £40!**

We'll also treat you to these fabulous extras:

- 🌹 **FREE L'Occitane gift set worth £10**
- 🌹 **FREE home delivery**
- 🌹 **Rewards scheme, exclusive offers…and much more!**

Subscribe now and save over £40
www.millsandboon.co.uk/subscribeme

SUBS/OFFER/11